"Don't go far," Addi[e]
today. I won't be able to
yipping and yapping up a[way] [ ] [ ] ...w she hadn't listened to a word she'd said and had raced toward her favorite playground, a stone crag that was about two hundred
and fifty yards from the cottage. Pippi loved to run and
jump among the boulders at the bottom of the overhanging stone cliff face, searching for the badger that lived
there.

Addie pulled the neck of her raincoat tighter. There
wasn't going to be any running and jumping on the
slippery rocks today if she had anything to say about it.
"Pippi, come back," she called, as Pippi's barks drifted
farther away.

"Pippi, come on. Come here, girl," she called again,
only to be answered by a succession of sharp, rapid
barks. "Oh, no." The last thing she needed was for Pippi
to dislocate a hip or something while scrambling over
the slippery stones. When Pippi's barks somewhere in
the fog in front of her became louder and more frenzied, tears streamed down Addie's cheeks as she stumbled blindly forward. Then, out of the fog, appeared her
little friend. Pippi danced in circles, barked, and then
raced back, only to disappear again in the heavy mist.

"Pippi, stop!" The barking turned to whining. "What
is it, girl?" Addie panted, catching up to her. "What's
wrong?" She scanned the ground, but all she could see
through the morning swirls of heavy mist was her furry
friend lying prone, whimpering alongside a blur of red
and white on the rocks in front of her.

Addie leaned forward and peered into the dense
rolling mist. "What the—" A piercing scream stopped her
mid-word, and she danced a step back. It was a woman's
body, but not just any woman. It was the same woman she
had spilled her drink on at the party the night before.

Books by Lauren Elliott

Beyond the Page Bookstore Mysteries
Murder by the Book
Prologue to Murder
Murder in the First Edition
Proof of Murder
A Page Marked for Murder
Under the Cover of Murder
To the Tome of Murder
A Margin for Murder
Dedication to Murder
A Limited Edition Murder

Crystals & CuriosiTEAS Mysteries
Steeped in Secrets
Murder in a Cup

Published by Kensington Publishing Corp.

A Limited Edition Murder

Lauren Elliott

Kensington Publishing Corp.
www.kensingtonbooks.com

Chapter 1

"Yikes! Slow down!" Addie Greyborne shrieked, wobbled, and white-knuckled the handlebars of her red, vintage bicycle as she swerved to the far left. "A little fast for this road, don't you think?" she grumbled, scowling over her right shoulder as a car whooshed past her on the narrow roadway.

She glanced down into the front wicker basket at her little passenger. "I know what you're thinking, and you're right," she scoffed, shaking her head. "After a year, I should be able to remember to ride on the left and not the right side of the street."

Pippi, her small tricolored Yorkipoo, perked her ears and sniffed the air as they sailed past the bakery.

"Pfft. Just like you to be thinking about filling your tummy again and acting so nonchalant about our near-death experience."

Pippi yipped.

"I know. I know it's because we've had too many near misses for it to faze you anymore, right?" Pippi let out another yip. Addie softly chuckled but inwardly thanked the powers that be she hadn't gotten them killed with her inability to adjust to the British driving system.

Addie tapped her feet slightly back on the brakes, slowing her speed as she continued to maneuver down Crooked Lane—named for good reason. It was Moorscrag, West Yorkshire's main shopping street and the location of her morning destination. She hopped off, balanced her bike on the kickstand, and secured it with a chain lock behind one of the wooden planter boxes out front. She grabbed her furry little friend from the basket and, once inside, set Pippi on the floor. Within seconds, Pippi scurried to her bed behind the sales counter and settled in with an *umph.*

"Good morning, Jasper," Addie called out to the young man teetering precariously on the top step of an old library ladder high overhead, and she shook her head in amazement.

While Jasper Henderson wasn't known for his brightness, he was a nice guy and didn't deserve the consequences of his "I'm invincible and can do everything" attitude, which fate sometimes toyed with.

"What did Mr. Pressman tell you about standing on the top of the ladder?" Addie exchanged her running shoes for a pair of flats from her backpack, then tossed her bag under the counter. "I seem to recall that he specifically mentioned the danger—"

"I know. I know," scoffed Jasper, descending to the wood-planked floor. "It's bad enough when the old man's here, but now yer talking like him and me mum too."

"And if your mom was here, what do you think she'd do, seeing you up there like that?"

"She'd give me a slap."

"Should I?"

"No." He hung his head sheepishly. "But there's times when it's the only way to get to the books Pressman wants me to sort through and insists on keeping in those dusty old piles on the top of the shelf." He gestured with a wild wave of his hand to the stacks of books Reginald Pressman, the owner of Second Chance Books and Bindery, insisted on keeping in the front area of the shop—and clearly had for the past thirty plus years—just in case a customer wanted to see one that was up there.

When Addie first started working for Mr. Pressman in the bookshop nearly a year ago—thanks to an introduction by way of her old high school boyfriend, now good friend and landlord, best-selling author Anthony Radcliff—her new employer told her he hadn't been through the books on the top of the shelves in a few years, which was an understatement. At the time, she'd offered to sort through them, but he'd hear none of it. He said he hired her to manage the front of the shop while he worked in the back on book restorations, but said not to worry. He'd be hiring an apprentice soon, and it would be a good way for them to have an introduction into the world of classics, so the books could stay where they were for now.

As it turned out, a few months later, he did hire

a bindery apprentice, but Jasper hadn't really proven himself to be the high-achieving student Mr. Pressman had in mind and required constant nudging to perform even the most basic tasks required of the craft, although it was a trade that Jasper professed was his lifetime calling. Given the young man's behavior, it was more like his mother had told him to get a job, and this was the only available one in the village. But Addie didn't have time to dwell on that. She was bursting with news and knew that Mr. Pressman would be as excited to hear it as she was to tell.

"Speaking of Mr. Pressman, isn't he in yet?" She asked, scanning the front room of the bookshop. "It's so unlike him to be late."

"He in't late," said Jasper, rolling the ladder over the track to the back corner of the room.

Addie waited for it and smiled at the click that told her he had remembered to secure the ladder in place this time, a safety feature she had initiated. It was a small but successful deterrent for some of the children in the village, who enjoyed zipping the ladder along the track from one end of the sidewall bookshelf to the other and back again.

"He just went to collect the post. He should be back soon, or so he said half an hour ago when he left."

"You were in early then?"

"Yeah. We . . . ah, I mean, *he* worked on that book for yer mate until late last night, and then the old man wanted me in early, so I could help him while he finished it up."

"He's finished restoring Tony's first edition of Emily Brontë's *Wuthering Heights*?"

Addie was glad Jasper corrected himself as to what his part in the restoration process had been. He might be able to convince the local girls down at the pub he had far more responsibilities here than he did, but until he proved himself to Mr. Pressman, he was not much more than the man's gofer.

"Uh-ha, that's what I said," muttered Jasper from the far corner.

"Did you hear that, Pippi?"

Pippi raised her head, stretched, shook herself, circled, and curled back down in her bed.

Addie let out a short laugh. "I know, you're probably already thinking about morning teatime and the treat Emily Green at the bakery will have waiting for you, but this is exciting news. It means the book will be ready for Tony to present to Hailey at their engagement party Saturday night."

"Did you say something?" asked Jasper, coming around the end of a bookcase with his face stuck in a book.

"Watch where you're going," she shrieked, as the young man bumped the sale-rack display on the end of the shelving unit.

He glanced up, looked blankly around, closed the book, and grinned. "What were you saying about Miss Granger?"

Addie couldn't stop the eye roll that overtook her and involuntarily groaned. "I said that's great news. Tony will have the book for their engagement party."

"Yeah . . ." Youthful hope disappeared from his eyes, and he dropped his gaze. "Their engagement party," he muttered, looked at the book in his hand, and held it up. "But don't ye think Hailey would like a newer copy of *Wuthering Heights* better? The one that guy wants to give her is older than Mr. Pressman and twice as wrinkled."

Addie squelched her second eye roll in less than a minute. There was no need to offend this lovestruck young man and make the remainder of her and Mr. Pressman's day worse for it. She knew Jasper had fallen head over heels for Tony's fiancée months ago, when Tony first brought Hailey into the bookshop to meet everyone. One look at the stunning, strawberry-blond-haired woman— who had a willowy physique that made her appear to be walking on air when she crossed the bookshop to take the young man's hand in greeting— had done its worst on the poor lad. He had fallen hopelessly in love.

When Jasper discovered she was a literary historian at the British Museum in London, he had confessed to Addie that he was thinking of changing trades and going back to school for his degree in literature. Since he was still here and, as far as Addie knew, hadn't registered at university, his mother must have talked him out of it by telling him he had the opportunity to learn a trade from one of the best bookbinders in the country and to appreciate that.

Since that first introduction, and as Hailey and Tony's relationship progressed, Second Chance Books had become a regular stop in the village for her whenever she came up from London. Jasper, of course, fantasized that she dropped by regularly to see him and continued to use the limited arsenal he had in his twenty-year-old bag of "how to woo a woman" tricks, completely ignoring or being oblivious to the fact that Hailey was over fourteen years his senior and planning to marry another man.

Addie drew in a deep breath, rounded the end of the sales counter, and tipped Jasper's face up from admiring the new book he held, making him look her straight in the eye. "You do remember that Hailey loves old books," Addie said softly. "So much so that she secured a job only a few miles up the road in Haworth and will begin work there early next year, after the current curator retires, and after she and Tony are married, don't you?"

"That's another reason to give her this new copy. She must get pretty tired of looking at old things all day and then to have to go home and look at another old book and that . . . that old man."

"I'll have you know that old man, as you called him, is the same age as I am."

"Cor blimey, I knew ya were old, but I had no idea how old." He stepped back and stared at Addie like she'd suddenly grown another head.

Addie hated to burst his love bubble, but enough was enough. *Be kind,* her inner voice shrieked, even though she wanted to scream in his face about his childishness. She bit her tongue and glowered at him when he turned away. Then she had an idea. Perhaps he needed to see the truth about Hailey for himself. She did drop in often without Tony, which might be why Jasper got the wrong impression about her visiting the shop as often as she did. No matter how many times Addie explained it, he couldn't understand that she was a true bibliophile, and the eclectic selection of classics found in Second Chance Books made any book lover drool. Her excitement when she came in had nothing to do with him.

She took a breath and smiled. "I hope you're planning to attend the party Saturday night. I understand it's going to be most entertaining, and there's going to be a very special guest in attendance."

"I knew it. Hailey told ya to invite me, right?" The young man's eyes lit up.

"Not if the woman's got half a brain in 'er head, she wouldn't," scoffed a gravelly, lilted voice from the far side of the bookcase. "Who'd want a gangly lovestruck boy hanging around 'er all night when she's set to marry a famous author? Give yer head a shake, lad." Mr. Pressman rounded the end of the bookshelf and pinned his faded brown eyes on Addie. "But who's this special guest who's coming?"

Addie bit her inner cheek to keep her smile in check. The fact that her boss, with his wrinkled skin and tousled gray hair, looked as old as the books he kept at the tippy top of his bookshelves never ceased to amuse her.

"That's what I've been bursting to tell you. Tony heard last night that his publisher, Lord Robert Bentley, and his wife, Lady Elizabeth, have also decided to attend the engagement party."

"Are ya daft, girl? It's been going on three years since his lordship set foot in Milton Manor, and that visit, after being gone near twenty years, only lasted one day."

"That's what Tony said. Interestingly enough, they also plan to stay on all next week to entertain their London friends who will be accompanying them."

"I wonder what's gotten into him," muttered the old man thoughtfully. "I thought that young woman . . . er . . . Lady Elizabeth, whom he eventually married after his first wife, bless her sweet soul"—he glanced up and crossed his heart—"couldn't abide country living? That's why they left and why they've not been back."

"I'm sure Tony will find out more as they firm up plans this week, but for now, that's all I know." She glanced over at Jasper, who'd clearly lost interest in the conversation and was perusing a nearby bookshelf, no doubt looking for another gift to bestow on Hailey this coming Saturday night. Her gaze settled back on Mr. Pressman. "I do know, though, that Tony has mixed feelings about it."

"I bet he has, especially if that little wisp of a girl has had a change of heart, and his lordship's finally decided to be lord of the manor again. It would mean Tony would have to move out, and that would be a loss. He's well liked here, and it's a boon to the village to have a famous author in residence. More so than that old windbag," he muttered.

"Um, I think, in Tony's mind, he's a bit more afraid that his lordship's arrival and continued stay will take the attention off the reason for the party and dim the light he hopes to shine on Hailey."

"Hailey's here?" Jasper thrust his head of brown, disheveled hair around the corner of the bookshelf, groomed it with his hand free of a book, and glanced expectantly at the door.

Addie shook her head. Her eyes fluttered painfully as she had to squelch her third eye roll in less than half an hour, and she focused on what Mr. Pressman held in his hand.

"Is that what I think it is by the 'Air Mail' sticker on the front?" She gestured to the brown envelope.

Mr. Pressman glanced down at his hand, as though seeing what he held for the first time. "Aye, sorry, lass. Yes. It looks like yer weekly update from that bakery lady." He held the envelope out to her, but his voice drifted as though his mind were still somewhere else. "Excuse me. I'll be in the back if ya need me." He slowly walked toward the back room.

His reaction to Lord Bentley's visit wasn't exactly what Addie thought it would be. Rather than being excited by the news, Mr. Pressman had seemed concerned and in no mood to talk about it. Addie shrugged, hoping he would open up over their morning tea about whatever had given him pause, and tore open the envelope.

Even though she regularly video-chatted with her best friend, Serena Ludlow, and her Beyond the Page Bookstore manager, Paige Stringer, she looked forward to Martha Stringer's weekly snail-mail updates, which were always filled with the latest gossip back in Greyborne Harbor, Massachusetts.

Not that she condoned gossip, but Martha was far more colorful and detailed about the goings-on in her hometown than her friends ever were.

She flipped open the three-page weekly report and hoped for something juicy today because Serena had been oddly vague about a number of things when they had video-chatted the day before. She excitedly scanned down the first page and let out a sharp gasp. "Marc's getting married?"

Chapter 2

"I have a bone to pick with you," snapped Addie, fixing her gaze on the small phone screen.

"Me?" Serena's brown eyes widened.

"Yes, you. I spoke with you yesterday and—"

"Mommy's here, Ollie. Okay, I'll be right there. Sorry, Addie, but—"

"Serena Ludlow! Don't you dare pull the mommy card on me. I know for a fact it's only seven in the morning there, and I can see little Ollie and Addie sitting at the table right behind you, happily munching on their breakfast. No, no, no, don't you dare look away from me to try to hide all those splotchy red freckles that match your hair and are no doubt popping up all over your face as we speak."

"Well, the kids have been feeling a bit off, maybe I caught—"

"Don't try to play me. I know you too well, and I know that's a sure, telltale sign that you're hiding something. I spoke to you not even a full day ago, and you never said a word about your brother getting married. I want you to look me directly in the eye and tell me, why the big secret?"

"Martha, right?"

"Don't go blaming her for you not being honest with me."

"I wasn't dishonest." The way she thrust it out, Serena's lower lip could have supported Addie's cup of morning tea.

"Guilty by omission then. But why the big secret, or did he tell you not to tell me for some reason?"

"No, and I was going to, honest." Then she added, mumbling, "You know, when you come home in two weeks."

"Why not now?"

Serena met Addie's gaze. "Because I was afraid you'd change your mind again about coming back. Like you have every other time this past year when something happened in Greyborne Harbor you didn't want to deal with."

"That's not true."

"Isn't it? Let's see, there was last year, when you were scheduled to return from your two-week holiday, but then found out that what's his name—oh yeah, the cad, Doctor Simon Emerson—"

"Simon is not a cad. He's a good man who was put in a very difficult situation."

"Have you forgotten how he blew you off for Laurel Hill? The same woman he told you didn't mean anything to him anymore?"

"I haven't forgotten, and I had a feeling that was eventually going to happen, which is why I broke it off with him, before I left, remember?"

"If that's true, then why didn't you come home after your two-week holiday, like you were scheduled to?"

"We've been through this so many times, Serena." Addie let out an exasperated breath. "You know well enough why. It's because then the wounds of what happened in the church, and everything else that transpired after, like discovering they also had a son together, were still too fresh. Plus, after finding out who I really was and not who I thought I was my whole life . . . well, I just needed a little more time before I went back and had to face the fallout from it all. You know all the 'poor Addie' looks I'd get around town. You should know. You talked to me every day. Did it seem like that news about them was something I could deal with back then? Not to mention having to explain to all the nosy types in town that my great-aunt wasn't really my aunt but my grandmother and that my whole life had been a lie."

"No. . . . I know it was a tough time for you, with so much going on," Serena said hesitantly, "but then later you didn't want to deal with the fact that Laurel sold her little house, and they bought a newer, bigger one for the three of them." She hung her head and sniffled. "It just felt like you never wanted to come home, and I miss you."

"I miss you too, and the kids, and my house and my shop and Paige and Catherine, but you know exactly why I couldn't come back after that bit of news. Their new house is right down the street from my house, which meant I'd have to drive by it every day." Addie shook her head. "I wasn't ready then to take a regular trip down memory lane about . . . about . . ." She dropped her voice, "what could have been between me and Simon had our wedding not imploded."

"See, every time something happened here, you stayed longer there—"

"I'm going to cut you off right there. It wasn't every time something happened in Greyborne Harbor. It was every time things changed between Simon and Laurel. You told me months ago that Marc was dating that woman . . . what's her name?"

"Whitney Wilder." Serena let out an annoyed sigh. "See, you can't even remember her name. Is that because you blocked it out?"

"No! But I do recall she is the new managing editor of the *Greyborne Harbor Daily News,* right? And I remember I told you I was happy that he'd finally found someone, and that someone sounded perfect for him, if she made him happy, didn't I?"

"Yeah, but since they decided to get married, I was afraid . . . well, I was afraid it might have stirred up old feelings you used to have for him, and you'd use it as another excuse not to come home," Serena said, her voice trailing off.

"Look," Addie shook her head in exasperation, "I know you always had a fantasy about us being related by marriage—real sisters, as you called it way back when Marc and I were together. Listen to me now, though: That isn't ever going to happen. I have no romantic feelings left for Marc. He was a good friend when I needed one before I left. No spark was rekindled. We're friends, that's all, and he must feel the same way too, because it wasn't long after that he and Whitney got together."

"You still had me then, didn't you? You didn't need Marc too."

"Yes, but he also helped me solve a murder that hit pretty close to home, remember?"

"Don't ever tell Police Chief Marc Chandler he helped you." Serena softly chuckled.

"Don't worry. I won't. So don't forget it was the outcome and what I learned about that seventy-year-old murder that also sent my world spinning out of control on top of everything that happened with Simon." Addie fought the tears that burned behind her eyes. "But forget about all that. Tell me everything. When's their wedding, where is it, and—"

"Addie!" Jasper called from the shop door. "The old man's looking for ya."

"Serena . . ." She glanced over at Jasper, who clearly was going to wait until he had accomplished the task Mr. Pressman had given him. Why he picked this task, of all the tasks he was asked to perform to see through to the end, she'd never know, but there he was. A look—of impatience, interest, or hope that he would overhear some juicy gossip to repeat later in the pub—crossed his face as he watched her intently. It was clear that he wasn't leaving until his mission was a success and he returned with her in tow. "Look, I gotta go. I'll call later, and you can fill me in, okay?"

"Okay, but you're sure you're alright with the news, and you're still coming home in two weeks?"

"Yes, and don't worry. I'm fine, love you, bye," Addie said with a quick finger wave before hanging up.

However, she was anything but fine. This news

hit her hard. Not for the reasons Serena assumed. It wasn't because she still harbored romantic feelings for Greyborne Harbor's chief of police, Marc Chandler. No, those were long gone. She had changed. He had changed. His relationship before Whitney with that horror of a woman Ryley Brookes was proof of that. But this news didn't settle well with Addie. It made her realize that her life back home would never be the same, and that the whole town was moving on. She didn't know how, or if, she'd ever fit in again.

She paused and smiled at the historic, twisted cobblestone lane with its herringbone sidewalks that ran in front of Second Chance Books and Bindery. She knew she'd never tire of seeing all the crooked little buildings on the narrow, winding street in the little West Yorkshire village of Moorscrag. It had been her refuge, and the perfect place for her to heal. As she shoved her phone into the pocket of her skirt and headed back into the bookshop, she hoped her decision to go back home in a couple of weeks wasn't made prematurely.

"Mr. Pressman," she called and waited for his reply. When none came, she looked questioningly at Jasper, who merely shrugged his indifference. She took a breath, counted one . . . two . . . three . . . until the feeling of wanting to throttle the young man passed, and she scurried around the end of the bookshelf that was a direct path to the back room. She crossed through the storage room and knocked on the side door that led to his small office and workshop. "Mr. Pressman, it's me, Addie. You wanted to see me?"

"Come in, come in," his strained voice warbled through the closed door.

She peered around the doorframe at his workbench but couldn't spot him when she stepped inside. "Mr. Pressman?"

His gray head popped up from behind a large wooden crate of books. "They're here!" He flashed her a toothy grin and gestured to the crate with a crowbar. "The books I bought on my buying trip to London last week that I told ya about." He leaned his free hand on the box and, with shaky legs, edged himself to a standing position and attempted to pry the top off. "I've just about got it," he puffed. "Then I can show you the surprise I told ya I found, purely by accident too, I might add," he said, heavily panting now.

"Let me. Why didn't you call Jasper for help with this?" Addie slid the crowbar from the man's fingers, inserted it between the box and the lid, and popped it off. "There." She passed him the crowbar and stepped back, allowing him to make the big reveal. It must be something pretty fantastic to have caused this state of excitement. Heaven knows, the news of Lord Bentley's return to the manor hadn't.

"Jasper couldn't even be bothered to tell me it had been delivered while I went to collect the post. Do ya really think I could trust him to take the lid off without damaging the precious cargo?" He pushed the lid off, and it crashed onto the wood-planked floorboard with a bang. "It's a book, and it's somewhere in here. I know I should have kept it separate, now where . . . where . . ." He continued to scour through the box. "Where is it?" He stood up. With a flushed face, he backed toward his workbench stool and sat down hard. "Give me a minute, will ya," he puffed.

"If you tell me the title, I could look for it."

"No, this book is so special. I want you to be, well, over the moon when I present it to you, lass."

"Now you've got me curious," she said, peeking into the box. "Is it a title I would recognize?" She skimmed the top book titles.

"Aye, but that's not what makes it so special." He gave her a sly wink.

"You're not going to give me any hints, are you?"

An impish gleam came to his eyes, and he shook his head.

It was clear he had overexerted himself and needed a long breather. "Okay, I guess I'll wait." She peered longingly into the box again, started for the door, but stopped, her mind struggling as to how to approach what was weighing on it. "I, um, I got the feeling, when I told you that Lord Bentley was coming this weekend, that you were less than impressed. Is there something I should know before he arrives?"

Mr. Pressman scoffed, muttered some Gaelic curse words he'd no doubt learned as a boy in Edinburgh, and looked up at Addie. "I can't bide the man, not now, not ever."

"Did something happen between the two of you?" Perhaps a woman was involved, given his wistful reaction to Lord Bentley's late wife.

"Aye," he said, his head hanging, "but it's not what ya think, lass. It's far worse, it 'tis." He shored himself up, his frail shoulders taking on the posture of a much younger man. "Jasper!" he shouted. "Jasper, I have work for ya back here!" He looked at Addie. "Ye can run the front of the shop today. I'll get his highness to catalog these books. I'm sure that won't be too difficult for the lad, but I have to go out for a while." He stared straight ahead and shouted again. "Jasper, where are ya, lad? Ye've got work to do."

Chapter 3

Addie paused in the doorway of the Crooked Lane Pub, secured Pippi tightly under her arm, and glanced in the direction of their usual table.

"Addie, over here." A familiar voice called her name. Since her eyes hadn't yet adjusted to the abrupt change in lighting, she grinned in the direction of the voice, then mentally crossed her fingers she wouldn't stumble into the lap of an unsuspecting patron while she cautiously made her way around tables to the booth by the entrance to the rear garden.

When Addie had first moved to Moorscrag and settled into her new job, it hadn't taken her very long to learn that, historically, in England, the pub was the social heart of a village, and Moorscrag was no different. Since going by herself to a pub or anywhere people socially gathered in groups was a situation she generally avoided, she had eased into it by attending Saturday trivia nights when she could inconspicuously sit alone at the bar. It didn't take long until she was befriended by Lexi Craven, daughter of Archie, the pub owner. Not only did Lexi work in the pub, she had also been born and raised in the village and seemed to know everyone. She went out of her way to make sure that everyone met Addie too.

Lexi had been wonderful those first few months when Addie was trying to make her way and find her legs again. A special bond was formed between them during that time and continued to this day. It was one that reminded Addie of the bond she and Serena also shared. Even though Addie, thanks to Lexi, had made other good friends too, Lexi was her main person here. Once Addie settled in comfortably and started to meet more people, she discovered she'd found her own *Cheers* situation. A place where everybody knew her name and would hail her the moment she stepped through the door to join her closest friends for a glass of wine or a pint after the shops closed. This was something that didn't happen back home in Greyborne Harbor, and it left her with a deep sense of belonging, which had contributed to her ability to heal after the personal trials she'd recently faced back in the States.

When Addie's English friends discovered that she'd had a hand in solving one or two murders back in Greyborne Harbor, they soon forgot their love of trivia and had made a new game out of testing her clue-gathering abilities. Over the past year, it had replaced trivia night and become their regular Saturday-night pub game. At first, they'd just given Addie a series of clues based on a real crime to see how fast she could come up with the answer. That became so popular they decided they all wanted to play, and a new game evolved.

Each week a pre-appointed detective chief inspector would pick a true-crime mystery. Then that person would draw names and form two teams of DIs, and then they'd race to put all the clues together to solve the true crime. The losing team would have to pick up the drink tab for the night. It was great fun and a tradition she hoped she could take back to the States with her and share with her friends there.

"It's about time." Her raven-haired friend Olivia Green, owner of Tea on the Green, a local teahouse, called out over the din in the room. "Did the old man have a dozen things for ya to do today before ya left?"

"No, actually he left this morning and didn't return, so I had to stay and lock up."

"There's room here beside me on the bench," said Emily Green, the owner of the bakery at the top of Crooked Lane. She looked more like Olivia's younger sister than a cousin, with her delicately sculpted Mediterranean ancestral features and coloring. "Just set our little friend down, and I'll scoot her over so ya can take a load off."

"Thanks." Addie set Pippi down and slid in beside her and noticed that it wasn't just the three of them meeting up today for their regular after-work tipple. "Hi, Nate, it's good to see you here." She smiled at the graying, brown-haired man across the table. "It's so rare you guys get to join us for an after-work drink. You know, with your shop staying open until eight most nights." Addie raised the glass of wine waiting for her on the table in a small toast of gratitude to her friend, Olivia.

"'Twasn't me. Ya can thank him for this round." She arched her thumb toward Nate, seated beside her.

"Then, thank you, Nate." Addie gestured with her wineglass and took a sip.

"What da ya mean, Pressman left this morning?" asked Emily. "Is he off to London again then?"

"No. Well, I don't think so," said Addie, toying with her wineglass. "To be honest, I have no idea where he went and why he didn't come back. It's so unusual for him."

"Is he ill?" asked Nate. "He is getting on, and things do happen."

"I don't think so. I gave him some news I thought he'd be excited to hear, but it only seemed to upset him, and then he just left." Addie shrugged and took a sip. "Is Ginny on her way, Nate?"

"Nah, all 'ell broke loose today, and her and that Charmaine Fernsby—Ya know, the lass who owns that little hairdressing shop over on Chapel Road?"

"I know who she is." Addie nodded. "I've never been in her shop myself, mind you. I see Eloisa at Tangled Mane." She glanced at the bar. "But Lexi went in there . . . once," Addie said, taking another sip in the hope it would ward off the laugh bubbling up in her chest when an image appeared in her mind of what her good friend looked like after she'd dropped in and seen Char last month.

Instead of getting purple highlights on the tips of her hair, as Lexi had requested, it ended up more like a peculiar shade of mud all over her head.

"I remember that," chuckled Olivia.

"Yeah, remember, and Char couldn't see the problem," Addie managed to squeak out before sputtering her mouthful of wine, which brought a raucous round of laughter from Olivia and Emily as they recalled their own memoires of that day.

The corners of Nate's lips crinkled upward. "Aye, Char can be a force all 'er own." He glanced at Lexi, still chuckling. "That's why Ginny ended up driving her. She's too much heart, me wife, she has. Char insisted and made her feel guilty. Ya know, the 'poor little me' act. That's her way, ya know." He leaned back on the bench. "Anyway, I guess the lass needed a ride to Haworth to pick up supplies for the shop. According to 'er, they've been slammed since the news broke today, and every woman and girlie in the village suddenly needs their hair done this week."

Addie's eyes widened, and she opened her mouth to speak.

"Don't believe it, though. The way she talked, ya'd think the King of England himself was coming and not Lord Bentley." He took a large swig of his beer and set the empty glass down. "Everyone ready for another pint then?"

"You mean you guys have already heard Lord Bentley is coming this weekend?" Addie looked from one face to the other. They all grinned and nodded.

"The whole village knows," said Olivia, draining her beer glass and gesturing to Nate.

"But how? Tony only found out last night."

"Mrs. Howard was at the market first thing today," said Emily, "and fit to be tied she was. She said"—Emily adopted a stiff-nasal accent—'I've been head housekeeper at Milton Manor for over forty-five years, and now that upstart of an author is bringing over his housekeeper and cook from America to give my staff a hand this next week. Can you imagine, my staff needing help from those colonists?' Then she harrumphed, ya know the way she does, and strode out."

"Oh no," Addie moaned. "That means Tony is bringing Mrs. Bannerman and Mrs. Ramsay, the cook, over from his Pen Hollow, Massachusetts, estate."

"You say that like it's a bad thing," said Olivia, with a short laugh. "I, for one, want to be there to see the fireworks when this other head housekeeper shows up and invades Mrs. Howard's domain."

"Ya might just get the chance," said Nate, his eyes sparkling over the rim of his tall beer glass.

"What do you mean?" asked Addie, afraid to hear what the answer might be, as images of her past experiences with Mrs. Bannerman, the reincarnation of Daphne du Maurier's fictional character Mrs. Danvers in *Rebecca*, flashed through her mind.

"According to what Char said, word is out that author friend of yers is hiring locals to help serve and clean guest rooms for the week. Only temporary work, but since us peasants weren't going to get an invite into the big shindig anyway, most see it as way to make a couple of extra quid and spend time hobnobbing with those posh Londoners too, in the classy digs of the manor house most have ever just seen from the lane. I expect there will be a queue in at the gates tomorrow, with folk clamoring for those jobs."

"I hope you're wrong about that. Tony can't stand people hanging around the gate. He's had too many overzealous fans in the past, and it makes him very nervous."

"I, for one, will be in that queue tomorrow first thing," said Olivia.

"Me too," added Emily.

"You're kidding, right?" said Addie, looking incredulously at her friends. "You've both been my guests at the house. What's to say I wasn't going to invite you?"

"Been no invite in my postbox. You got yours yet, Olivia?" Emily glanced at her cousin, who shook her head.

"That was the other thing Tony said last night." Addie avoided looking at her friends. "Since the guest list suddenly ballooned, as much as I want to, I don't know if I'll be able to invite all of you," she said, her voice dropping to a whisper.

"There ya go, Addie. Like Nate said, we can all use a few more quid these days, and who knows when else we'll have the chance to attend a party like that." Olivia shrugged and gulped down some beer.

"Even though we'd be working, not eating and dancing with you posh lot, we'd still have the bragging rights of being there, seeing the elusive Lord Bentley and his young wife, Lady Elizabeth," said Emily, with a short laugh. "No harm done. We knew from the start that it's Tony's engagement party to celebrate with his friends and family. Knowing you'd be going, we kinda kept our hopes alive that we could get an invite, but we're friends with you, not him, so . . ."

"I am really sorry, guys. I planned on inviting all of you. It would have made the whole evening more tolerable. I really don't like parties, especially formal ones with a whole room full of people I don't know." Addie ran her fingers through the fine hair on the back of Pippi's head as her little friend snored softly beside her on the wooden bench. "Wow, I had no idea that Lord Bentley coming would be seen as such a major event in the village. Exciting, yes, but I sure hope it doesn't cause a rift between us."

"Nah," Olivia waved her off, "that's why we'll all be in the queue tomorrow, though."

"Ya might put in a good word for us with the housekeepers, though?" added Emily, grinning. "Or are ya afraid of Mrs. Howard, like the rest of the village is?"

"She's not the one who scares me."

"Who then? His lordship? Because ya wouldn't be the first lass to say that about him," said Nate, pinning her with a concerned gaze.

"No, I've never met the man and don't know anything about him, except he owns that big publishing company that his son Lewis runs now. Why? What do people say about him?" Addie set her wineglass down and focused on Nate, who stared into his pint glass. "You were born and raised here in Moorscrag, right? If there are rumors about him, then maybe that's why Mr. Pressman acted so strange when I told him Lord Bentley was coming this weekend."

Nate continued to sit in silence.

"Come on, Nate. You said people were scared of him. Why?"

"Nah." He waved his hand dismissively. "Just rumors, dat's all."

"No, you know why Mr. Pressman got upset by the news. Did something happen three years ago when Lord Bentley brought his new wife here and then abruptly left the next day?"

"I don't know nothing about dat. No, it was twenty years ago, after his first wife died, that folk talked. Dat's all I got to say." He drained his glass and set it on the wood table with a plunk. "Another round?" He looked at each of them, got the nods, and headed for the bar to order.

"Do either of you know what happened back then?"

Olivia and Emily shook their heads.

Nate hadn't been wrong about the queue. The following day Addie's bike ride home after a long day in the shop, was anything but the enjoyable meander down a quiet English country lane she had grown accustomed to. The constant dodging of bicycles and cars and weaving her way around the throngs of villagers who stood, most for hours, waiting their turn for a much sought-after interview with the tag team of Mrs. Howard and Mrs. Bannerman, was never-ending.

After passing the gate to the main house, she sped down the lane, and as her cottage came into view, she breathed a sigh of relief. Since that day a year ago, when she was up from London visiting Tony for the weekend and received word from Greyborne Harbor that Simon and Laurel had officially announced their reunion as a married couple and that he was moving in with her and their son, Mason, the cottage had been hers.

Even though she had suspected Simon's reuniting with his ready-made family was on the horizon, the news still had her world careening sideways again and sent her crying on the shoulder of her old friend Tony, only to be consoled by the offer of a place to stay until she could face going home, no matter how long that took.

Tony had initially offered her a suite in the main house, but that heart-shattering day, after taking a long walk through the woods bordering the manor's property, she'd come across the old gamekeeper's cottage and knew immediately it was home. She moved her bag in that very same day and hadn't regretted her impulsive decision for a moment since. The close location to the small laneway that ran from the village of Moorscrag and along the stone wall bordering the moor made it the perfect choice.

Coming home had never felt so good. The cottage was a rustic retreat, with its stone fireplace and antique furniture. It was a place that today held so many happy memories for her on her path to healing. She couldn't imagine ever leaving it. The cottage had become her sanctuary, and she loved it more than anything. It was a place of refuge, with its thick stone walls and sturdy shutters protecting it from the elements. And despite the patchwork of different styles and eras—antique furnishings mixed with modern appliances and gadgets—it was a place of rest and rejuvenation with its comfortable furnishings and soothing colors.

She leaned her bike against the cottage wall and smiled as she ran her hand over the weathered, sandy-colored bricks, knowing that when need be, it could all be buttoned up to protect her from the ever-changing elements on the moors, and this past winter it certainly had been put though that test. For hundreds of years, these stone walls had kept the inhabitants of the cottage nice and cozy though the nastiest of West Yorkshire weather, and for that she was grateful.

As the week wore on, Addie had also been very grateful for her living situation for another reason. It had allowed her to keep her distance from Mrs. Bannerman, whom, she had heard through the staff grapevine, wasn't very keen on her new employment circumstances or the woman she was to share head housekeeper duties with.

Even though when she had moved in, Tony had extended Addie an open dinner invitation for any evening she cared to join him and Hailey for a meal, this past week she had declined. She would have loved to observe the two head housekeepers conducting interviews together and was left wondering if that's why the process to fill the positions was taking so long. It was said that, all week, the two women couldn't agree on anything.

However, the days of avoiding Mrs. Bannerman were over, and like it or not, tonight she was bound to meet up with the woman who had created a very haunting experience for Addie a few years back when she and Paige stayed at Tony's Pen Hollow estate. Addie shivered with the recollection of her past experiences with her as she relayed the latest news to Serena.

"I am just happy the party day is finally here because that means next weekend you'll be home!" Serena said excitedly through the small screen.

Addie reached over and out of camera view.

"Where are you? Are you hiding from me? Have you changed your mind again and are too afraid to tell me you're not coming back again?"

Addie turned her phone. "No, I was looking for lipstick that would work with this dress my cousin gave me when I was in London for the grand opening of her new store." She briefly scanned the camera over her off-the-shoulder, emerald, floor-length dress. "This is your color. What shade should I pick that would work with it?"

"What are the choices?"

Addie held up three different shades of lipstick tubes.

"Um, go with the golden rose or the nude. The brown is too dark for your skin."

"Thanks." Addie laid the phone down on the kitchen counter as she applied it. "Okay, done. How does it look?"

"You look beautiful, my friend." Serena beamed. "But I get dibs on that dress when you get back. Like you said, it's my color and would look so good with my red hair and skin coloring."

"Tell you what. Since I doubt I'll be going to any posh dinner parties—"

"Posh?"

"You know, those born with silver spoons in their mouths. The privileged and wealthy."

"I like that word," said Serena with a giggle. "One word says so much that takes us over here such a long-winded explanation to describe, doesn't it?"

"Yes, but I don't think I'll have much use for it in Greyborne Harbor, and I will happily give it to you as an anniversary gift so Zach can take you out for a night on the town in Salem or Boston or something."

"You mean it? I was only joking when I said I had dibs on it."

"I know, but hey, your anniversary is next month, right? And I want to make sure you have this to wear so you can shine like the star you are. Now, is that enough of an answer to your question about me really coming back next week?"

Tears streamed down Serena's bright-red, splotchy cheeks. "Thank you," Serena whispered. "But having you finally come home is the only gift I need."

"Now stop it, or you'll have me bawling too, and I don't have time to redo my makeup." She glanced at the antique clock on the fireplace mantel. "I gotta run. If I leave now, I can maybe still sneak in and avoid Mrs. Bannerman standing sentry at the front door."

"Go, if it means you can home faster. You're sure that coming home to Marc's wedding isn't going to give you another reason to stay?"

"No, it's not. I am surprised, though, that they just announced their engagement and are getting married in July. Seems awfully fast, doesn't it, or"—Addie's eyes lit up—"is she expecting?"

"Not as far as I've heard. I think it's more likely

that they're just both getting older. I guess they don't want to waste any more time dancing around the inevitable. Whitney wanted the wedding in June, but since Zach and I had a June wedding, they settled for July." Serena shrugged. "I guess when you know it's right, you don't wait. You just jump in with both feet, like they're doing."

"Yeah, I guess." Addie thought about her year-long engagement and wondered if that was a sign back then that she and Simon weren't right for each other. She shook it off and smiled. "Love ya. Chat soon." Addie blew her friend a kiss and clicked off.

Chapter 4

While Addie stumbled along the forest path toward the manicured lawns of Milton Manor's lavish gardens, she shook her head. She certainly hadn't thought this through—high heels to trek down a forest path? Really, what had she been thinking?

It also didn't help that her mind kept replaying her own engagement party nearly two years earlier. With the crushing sensation in her chest that often accompanied those memories, she mentally flipped off the switch. But with Tony and Hailey's wedding plans and happy-ever-afters burned into her brain lately, it didn't take long until her new thoughts took her straight to those of Marc and Whitney. She couldn't believe that, after only a few months of being engaged, they were ready to forgo the traditional engagement party and jump right into saying "I do."

Addie moaned when her shoe heel caught on a tree root, and she stopped, her chest heaving. She counted one . . . two . . . three . . . until the tears burning behind her eyes subsided. Twice in her life, she had thought she'd found that same kind of love as her friends had, with first David and then Simon, and twice it was snatched from her like the forbidden cookie from a child caught with their hand in a cookie jar. A moment of self-pity, maybe, but it just wasn't fair. She sniffed back the tears threatening to ruin her makeup and glanced back at the path behind her and then ahead at the obscured route to her destination.

One thing was clear, though. With the heaviness in her chest, her heart wasn't in the evening's festivities, as images of her own miserable past kept rushing back at her. Yes, it had been a year since her dreams had been dashed, but could she really face a party celebrating a couple's undying love for each other, where they would announce their intentions to say their own "I do's"? Right now, every fiber of her being screamed no, but . . .

She cared deeply for both Tony and Hailey. She really did, and truly wished them all the best. She glanced up the path again. "Big girl panties on. You hold on to that thought." She tensed her jaw, put her head down, and trudged onward. It was clear, though, from the ache still in her chest, that the evening was going to require an Oscar-worthy performance.

Near the main entrance to the manor house, Addie pulled her phone out of her small, beaded evening bag and glanced down. "7:05? Darn it!" She'd missed the short window of opportunity to avoid Mrs. Bannerman's sentry duties. Her only alternative was to slip in through the kitchen door and make her way upstairs to the grand ballroom. A room that, according to Tony, hadn't been used in over twenty years. But Lord Bentley had ordered it dusted off, and tonight it would be the venue for Tony and Hailey's celebration of love.

She cheerily greeted the kitchen staff, some she recognized as local villagers, no doubt the temporary hires that had kept the town buzzing all week. She paused long enough to have a quick catch-up with Mrs. Ramsay, Tony's cook at his Pen Hollow estate, and scooted up the back stairway to the main floor. Once at the top, she plastered a smile on her face, but when she caught a glimpse of her reflection in a mirror, she froze at the sight of the haunted eyes that gazed back at her.

"Be happy. You're celebrating love, remember?" she whispered and wearily made her way to the wing where the ballroom was located.

Addie scanned the sea of nameless faces in the ornately decorated ballroom for a familiar one. When she spotted Olivia, serving tray in hand, distributing flutes of champagne, Addie couldn't get to her side fast enough.

"Yes, please." Addie grinned, took a glass, downed it in a few gulps, and snatched up another.

"Better go slow. That's the real stuff, ya know. Not that cheap knock-off Archie serves at the pub."

"That's exactly what I'm counting on," said Addie. "The better quality, the less the headache, or, at least, that's what I'm told." She took another swig and heaved a sigh of blissful contentment.

Olivia eyed her thoughtfully. "Is everything okay?"

"Perfect," said Addie, flashing her a forced smile.

"Good." The tension left Olivia's face. "Hey, this is some bean feast, isn't it?" she whispered. "There's his lordship himself over there." She made a small gesture with her tray toward the group off to their left. "I haven't had a chance to get near them yet because people keep emptying me tray. Then I have to go back to the bar to refill, but it all disappears in the wink of an eye again. But I will say, I'm slowly getting closer to serving that tall, dark-haired fellow in the dark-gray suit." She glanced at Addie. "Do ya happen to know who he is?"

Addie scanned the group from London who'd accompanied the lord and lady for the week. "Yes, that's Colton Jamison, Tony's literary agent, and that brown-haired woman beside him is his wife."

"Of course, any man who looks like him is bound to have been snagged up already." Olivia focused on the group. "What about that darkish blond-haired bloke, there by his lordship's side?"

"That is Lewis, Lord Bentley's son. He runs the publishing house now since his father has semiretired, but Tony thinks he might be a bit of a gambler, so it's probably good to stay away from him."

"Yes, but is there a Mrs. Lewis Bentley?" Olivia asked coolly.

"Did you not just hear what I said?"

"Yes, but—"

"Olivia Green! Need the extra money, my foot!

You wanted this position to scope out eligible men, and don't deny it."

"Ya can't blame me, can ya? Ye've met the men in this village," she said with a laugh and started away, but not before Addie managed to grab the last champagne flute off her tray.

"Okay, now what?" Addie muttered and took another sip, searching the room for friendlies. Her friend Lexi, from the pub, was naturally working behind the bar, but it looked like she was swamped too. It seemed Addie wasn't the only guest enjoying the free-flowing champagne. Emily, like her cousin, was making the rounds of the room with her tray and appeared a little flustered by all the hands grabbing for glasses.

Addie swung around to check out the spread on the buffet table and say a quick hello to Nate and Ginny, who had been placed in charge of replenishing the offerings. Her timing couldn't have been worse. The only warning she had of an impending collision was a blur of red and white flowers as she slammed into a young, auburn-haired woman who flailed her arm around to block the collision, which caused Addie's drink to splash down the front of the woman's brightly colored floral dress.

"I'm so sorry," Addie cried and snatched a serviette from a nearby cocktail table. "Here, let me get that." She dabbed frantically at the woman's neckline, paying special attention to her ornate necklace. "I hope the champagne doesn't settle in the intricate gold filigree setting of that exquisite sapphire," Addie said, persisting in her dabbing.

The woman pushed her hand away. "I'm sure it's fine. Now, if you'll excuse me." She smiled weakly, plucked the serviette from Addie's fingers, and dabbed at her neckline as she disappeared into the crowd of Londoners congregated by the buffet table.

"And that's How to Make Friends 101," Addie mumbled, glanced at what little was left in her champagne flute, and set it on the cocktail table. She waved goodbye to Lexi as she passed the bar and headed out, only to encounter Tony and Hailey coming in.

"Addie, there you are. We've been looking all over for you," said Tony, his face flushed.

"I'm sorry I arrived a bit later than planned. Serena, you know how she is, had to catch up." She glanced from one somber face to the other. "Oh, no, was I supposed to be here earlier to help with preparations?"

"No, no, you've done so much to help out as it is. It's just that . . ." He gave Hailey a fleeting side glance.

"It's just that something has unexpectedly popped up," chimed in Hailey. "Victoria, or Vickie, my maid of honor—I've told you about her, right?"

Addie nodded.

"Well, she can't be here until tomorrow. It's her father, Sir Henry. He's feeling unwell tonight, and until they finish running tests at the hospital, she doesn't want to leave him. So . . ." She flashed Tony a "Help me!" side glance.

"Since you are my oldest and dearest friend,"

Tony jumped in, "we were hoping you could do the honors of introductions in Vickie's place so that we can formally make the engagement announcement? Pretty please?" implored Tony.

Addie looked longingly past them to the wide hallway, which led to her way out, and back at the eager anticipation in the couple's eyes. "Sure." Addie smiled, knowing this was also the moment Tony planned to present Hailey with the first edition copy of *Wuthering Heights*. She really wouldn't mind seeing the look on Hailey's face when he did, since Addie had witnessed every step of its restoration. She drew in a breath and smiled. "I'd be happy to."

Public speaking wasn't one of Addie's strong points, in spite of what Serena told her about loving the sound of her own voice sometimes. This was not one of those times. As she stood at the podium set up beside the buffet table, she glanced at the minstrel's galley above, wishing she were up there and far away from expectant eyes. She gulped in a breath and began introductions. Her mind sang out, *Brave face. This is a celebration of love.*

Her love of books was the only way Addie would make it through the remainder of the evening, and she plowed through her unrehearsed speech, while channeling her inner assistant to the curator of acquisitions, the position she'd held at the Boston Public Library some years back. The book Tony was about to give his bride-to-be was a gem, if she'd ever seen one.

Not only was it a first edition, but it was also a limited first edition, as only a handful of that print run was ever released. The story surrounding this particular edition was that a major typo was discovered after the first few copies were printed and printing was stopped. The error was corrected and the first run resumed, but not before those few copies with the error mysteriously disappeared from the print shop and were seemingly sold. Since no arrests were ever made in the suspected thefts, Addie had never been able to verify that exact story. She only knew this copy did contain the typo the first edition on display at the Boston Library did not have.

What was so magical about this book was the fact that Tony had stumbled across it in a second-hand bookshop in London's Southend and had paid only a few pounds sterling for it. He had no idea what he had until he had shown it to Addie.

After Tony and Hailey decided to get married and Hailey secured the position of curator at the Brontë Parsonage Museum in the Brontë's hometown of Haworth, only ten miles up the road, Tony thought the book would be an appropriate gift for her. He then hired Mr. Pressman to restore the book to its original condition, if possible. It was possible and turned out better than anyone ever thought, and now Addie would be able to witness the look on Hailey's face when Tony gave it to her as an expression of his devoted Heathcliff-type love for her, his very own Catherine Earnshaw.

Addie knew how much Hailey, a well-known literary historian, would appreciate it, and Addie was proud to be part of the celebration that would unveil the masterful restoration of this book to the world. As a matter of fact, Addie was far giddier about the book's presentation than she was about the actual reason for the party, the engagement. It seemed that events of a year ago really had taken a toll on the romantic in her, and she couldn't wait to get this event over with and retreat to the comfort of her cozy little cottage.

Introductions of the esteemed guests and the presentation of the loving couple complete, Addie stepped back and witnessed the shock, surprise, and love in Hailey's eyes as she opened her engagement gift from Tony. Wobbly spirit aside, Addie couldn't help but get out of her own head and feel genuine happiness for her dear friend and the woman he loved. In spite of her earlier misgivings, it had turned out to be a perfect evening, after all, for a seller of rare and used books. But it was time to leave.

Pippi, bless her heart, was good when left on her own at the cottage, but Addie needed a warm hug right now, and her furry little friend was the only one who could provide it. Besides, the band hired for the dance portion of the evening was warming up in the gallery, and that definitely was her cue to make her exit.

She looked around for Tony to say goodnight but only spotted Hailey, a book in hand, talking to Jasper. Addie focused on the cover and saw it wasn't the book Tony had given her. It was the newer edition of *Wuthering Heights* Jasper had discovered in Second Chance Books. She judged by Jasper's drooping head that the two were engaged in a serious chat, and Jasper didn't like what he was hearing. Perhaps the look on his face was an indication that he was finally understanding that Hailey Granger was going to be Mrs. Anthony Radcliff this time next year.

Addie's heart ached for the young man. First loves were always hard, but if anyone could get through to him without crushing his spirit, Hailey could. Addie crossed her fingers that his lost-love mourning period would be a short one so he'd stop his hopeless daydreaming about Hailey and the life he was never going to have with her. She did feel for him, and she did really like him, but it was time for him to get his head out of the clouds and back to work before Mr. Pressman fired him. If he'd only buckle down, he could have a great future. After all, he was being trained by one of the UK's—if not the world's—most gifted bookbinders and reclamation specialists still working in the craft.

She scanned the room, and it appeared as though Olivia and Emily were still swamped with distributing champagne, which meant Lexi was just as busy filling flutes at the bar. It appeared that Nate and Ginny were likewise being run off their feet in an attempt to replenish the quickly emptying buffet dishes. She took one last look around the room for an elusive Tony before quietly slipping out into the hallway.

"That's impossible, Robert," hollered Tony.

The raised voice echoing through the hallway came from over her left shoulder, and she turned and came to a full stop.

"I did not steal it from your personal library,"

Tony snarled. "And I have the sales receipt from the bookstore in London upstairs in my chambers to prove I purchased that book." His finger stabbed at Lord Bentley's chest.

"What in the world?" muttered Addie. It was clear this situation needed deescalating when Robert Bentley stepped back and made a grab for Tony's hand.

Chapter 5

Addie ran toward the two men, who appeared to have locked horns and were soon going to come to blows over a book.

"Your Lordship," Addie panted and nodded respectfully, and then looked questioningly at Tony. "Is there a problem with the copy of *Wuthering Heights*? Is it with the authentication I did and the fact that I allowed my appraiser's license to expire when I left Boston? If so, I can assure you that I still have the training and knowledge of years of experience—"

"Nothing like that, my dear," said Lord Bentley. "In fact, your appraisal was spot-on. I was only informing Tony that this particular book was stolen from my personal library here at the manor over twenty years ago."

"Then you know I didn't steal it," hissed Tony. "I

wasn't even in England then, let alone one of your authors twenty years ago."

"I am not accusing you of theft, Tony. I only wished to inform you that this"—Lord Bentley held the book up in his hand—"is mine, and I want it back."

"That's easy for you to say," snapped Tony. "Now that it has been authenticated and found to be worth a lot of money because of the typo."

"It's precisely that typo that initially made me suspect," Lord Bentley sputtered, and his nostrils flared.

"Why don't we go somewhere more private," Addie urgently whispered and glanced at a couple lingering by the ballroom doorway. "Then perhaps your lordship could explain how you are so certain this book is the same copy that was stolen from your library."

"It would be my pleasure," huffed Lord Bentley. "Might I suggest we reconvene in my library, since that is where the absolute proof can be found? This way."

Tony and Addie followed him down the hallway through to the east wing and into the large private library. Tony shifted from one foot to the other as they waited for his lordship to retrieve the key from a ring in his trouser pocket, unlock the door, and hold it open. He gestured for Addie and Tony to enter.

Once inside, Tony swung around and pinned Lord Bentley with a defiant glare. "Okay, where is your proof that the engagement gift I just presented to Hailey is your stolen property?"

Lord Bentley's chest puffed out, and he raised his hand and thrust his finger in front of Tony's flushed face.

As much as Addie wanted to take a moment and examine the depths of the room that had been off-limits to everyone, including Tony, when his lordship wasn't in residence, there wasn't time. Things were going from bad to worse now that they were out of view from guests' prying eyes.

"Lord Bentley, why don't you take a seat behind that beautiful carved walnut desk?" She placed her hands on his shoulders, urging him in the direction of his desk. "And, Tony, you come over here." She ushered her friend over to a vintage oxblood Chesterfield leather sofa and not so gently encouraged him to take a seat.

Addie drew in a shaky breath while keeping her eye on the two men and crossing her fingers they would remain where they were seated. "Now then, your Lordship, perhaps you could explain why and how you are so certain that this book, which Tony found in a secondhand bookshop in London, is one of yours."

Lord Bentley leaned back in his chair, lit his pipe, drew in a long, slow breath, and proceeded to relay the story of how, over twenty years ago, he was in London one week and stopped in at a rare-book shop, where he found a numbered edition of *Tamerlane and Other Poems* by Edgar Allan Poe. It was the first book Poe ever published and was under the pseudonym of "A Bostonian." It was very rare, and only about fifty copies were ever printed. Lord Bentley swore he had the same numbered copy, fifteen, in his library collection. When he returned to Milton Manor, he searched but discovered his copy, which was noted on his inventory list, was in fact missing.

After that discovery, he undertook a more thorough search and found that other books he'd recorded in his ledger had also vanished. It was then that he hired a young woman from the village to come and mark all the books remaining in his collection with an invisible ink that could only be detected with a black light—so as not to devalue the book—and then had her catalog every book she marked.

He pulled out his key ring again, unlocked a desk drawer, removed a large inkpad and a space-age-looking wand, and laid them on the desktop.

"Mind you, the thefts continued for a period of time," he said. "Because clearly the person stealing the books didn't realize they had been marked. But when one of the staff fell under suspicion and was dismissed, the thefts stopped. I had my London staff put out word to every bookseller throughout the UK and the Continent that my collection was marked in this way and to scan the title page for my seal. It appeared to work, as, over the years, a few of them have shown up, and I've managed to retrieve them." He set his gaze on Tony and then picked up the light wand. "Now, shall we see if I am, in fact, correct about this book?"

Tony sighed, nodded, and leaned forward, his eyes glued on Lord Bentley as he waved the light wand over the title page.

A smile of satisfaction crossed his lordship's pudgy face. "Just as I said." His smile broadened into a victorious grin.

"Let me see." Tony jumped to his feet, snatched the book, took the wand from Bentley's hand, and scanned the light over the page.

Addie didn't need to look. She could tell by the defeated hang of his head and slump in his shoulders that Lord Bentley had been correct. The book had, in fact, been stolen from this very library over twenty years ago.

Addie tried to clear her head of the events of the night before, but no amount of strong black coffee seemed to work. Lord Bentley's claim on the gift Tony had given Hailey had been an interesting turn of events, to say the least, and something no one saw coming. After the initial threat of the two men drawing blood seemed to have passed, they appeared to be working on an amicable solution to the problem. Addie finally felt it safe to leave them together in the library, and in the wee hours of the morning, she made her way back to the cottage.

Now, here she sat, only a few hours later, staring into her second cup of coffee, knowing no amount would work its usual magic on her brain fog this morning. The way Pippi was pacing by the door, perhaps she was right; a morning walk on the moors was just what was needed instead.

She took a quick peek out one of the front cottage windows to check the conditions outside, shivered, grabbed a sweater and her rain jacket, and glanced down at her friend sitting at her feet. "Okay, it's going to be a quick walk today. My brain isn't the only place the fog has settled in, so when

I say it's time to go, you'd better listen. Give me a minute to find my wellies, and then we'll be off."

"Wellies," she repeated, as she fished through the shoe cubby in the bottom of the bench by the door and couldn't stop the giggle that bubbled up from her chest as she pulled them on. She did love so many of the British expressions and was becoming more comfortable using them. *Wellies* was a perfect example, much like the use of *brilliant* to describe something wonderful and good, and *dodgy* for something not so much. Then there were *trainers* for runners or sneakers. She shook her head. "Yeah, like I'd be training for anything when I wear those," she chuckled. Or *kip* instead of sleep and *sloshed* for being drunk, which was far more civilized-sounding, in her mind anyway. Then, of course, there was *car park* instead of *parking lot*, but *wellies* was the best and far more fun to say than gumboots or rubber boots.

"Let's go," she said to Pippi, as she zipped her jacket and opened the door.

Pippi excitedly led the way down the path to the dry-stone wall, a sight that was common in many areas of England, but more so in Yorkshire, as Addie had come to learn. It was where she had fallen in love with the warm hug her own dry-stone wall gave to her cottage and the surrounding small garden.

Addie would be the first to admit that she had truly fallen in love with Brontë's wild countryside of Yorkshire and could see how nature had inspired books like *Wuthering Heights*. She inwardly chuckled. After her adventures in Yorkshire, she might even be inspired enough to write her own novel. She drew the cool, damp air into her lungs and relished the freshness of the morning. Life in Yorkshire was good, and the gnawing sensation in her chest told her leaving next week would be harder to do than she ever thought.

Addie couldn't believe how easily everything this past year had fallen into place, from the day Tony had helped her settle into her little cottage and introduced her to Reggie Pressman, who gladly gave her a temporary job she loved, to the day just a few weeks later when her old friend Catherine Lewis and her new husband, Felix Vanguard dropped off her sweet little Pippi at the start of their three-month honeymoon tour of the Continent, after having run off to London to be married. Especially after all she had recently endured back in Greyborne Harbor. It was like this was all meant to be, and she knew then that she had found a new home.

Yes, life has been good here. Moorscrag and her little cottage had been her refuge from a world gone mad and a life that had gone sideways, and she wasn't sure how she felt about leaving, or if she could. Was she really ready to go back and face all the demons she'd worked so hard to lay to rest over the past year?

At the wooden gate, Pippi yipped again, bringing Addie's mind back to the present, as her little friend was letting Addie know enough time had been wasted and she had things to do. "I don't think your friend, Mr. Badger, will be out today. Too much fog." Addie laughed and hurried to open the gate leading out onto a firmly packed riding trail used by both local bike and horse enthusiasts. What Addie loved most about the path that ran along the front of her cottage was it was closed to all petrol-powered engines except for emergency vehicles, which suited her just fine. She could live with the clap of horse's hooves much easier than with the roar of an engine any day.

Pippi gave her a short bark, scurried across the trail, and climbed up and over what the locals called a ladder stile. The gates in the dry-stone walls came in many different styles, but the ones that had been constructed along the length of the moor and the manor property line were simple, A-framed ladders, which allowed access over the stone walls from both sides.

"Don't go far," Addie hollered. "The fog's too heavy today. I won't be able to keep up." She could hear her friend yipping and yapping up ahead. Addie knew she hadn't listened to a word she'd said and had raced toward her favorite play-ground, a stone crag that was about two hundred and fifty yards from the cottage. Pippi loved to run and jump among the boulders at the bottom of the overhanging stone cliff face, searching for the badger that lived there.

Addie pulled the neck of her raincoat tighter. There wasn't going to be any running and jump-ing on the slippery rocks today if she had anything to say about it. "Pippi, come back," she called, as Pippi's barks drifted farther away.

Was it the dense fog muffling the sounds, or was Pippi already at the boulders? Addie picked up her pace, her heart racing as she walked as quickly as she could with her limited visibility over the un-even ground.

"Pippi, come on. Come here, girl," she called again, only to be answered by a succession of sharp, rapid barks. "Oh, no . . ." The last thing she needed was for Pippi to dislocate a hip or something while scrambling over the slippery stones. When Pippi's barks somewhere in the fog in front of her became louder and more frenzied, tears streamed down Addie's cheeks as she stumbled blindly forward. Then, out of the fog, appeared her little friend. Pippi danced in circles, barked, and then raced back, only to disappear again in the heavy mist.

"Pippi, stop!" The barking turned to whining. "What is it, girl?" Addie panted, catching up to her. "What's wrong?" She scanned the ground, but all she could see through the morning swirls of heavy mist was her furry friend lying prone, whimpering alongside a blur of red and white on the rocks in front of her.

Addie leaned forward and peered into the dense rolling mist. "What the—" A piercing scream stopped her mid-word, and she danced a step back. It was a woman's body, but not just any woman. It was the same woman she had spilled her drink on at the party the night before.

Chapter 6

Addie took deep, slow breaths while she sat on a boulder not far from the body. She tightened her arms around Pippi and cuddled her closer to her chest and slowly breathed in ... out ... in ... out. The British police service was—from what her UK friends had said—an entity unto its own and very dissimilar to the casualness she was used to with Chief Marc Chandler back in Greyborne Harbor. She wanted to make sure her head was clear when they started asking questions, especially the one about how she—she swallowed hard—had recognized the woman.

Through the dissipating early-morning fog, Addie could make out two figures heading from the lane by her cottage across the open moor in her direction. She heaved a sigh of relief when they drew closer. One was Meg Gimsby, a young police constable who often joined Addie and her friends after work for a pint at the Crooked Lane Pub. The other one, who appeared even younger, bopped along beside her like an excited puppy out for his first walk. This was going to prove interesting if Meg was the senior constable at the scene and perhaps not nearly as scary as Addie had conjured in her mind from streaming all those British murder-mystery television shows.

She rose to her feet to meet the constables, sidestepped around the body, took a cursory glance, and paused. Something was off. The fog might be lifting from the moor, but it clearly still blanketed her mind since the discovery of the body, and she couldn't quite place what seemed different now about the woman's appearance. She took out her phone, snapped an image to look at more closely later, hoping she'd be able to figure out why her spidey sense had gone into high alert, and gingerly made her way down the last of the rocks onto the grassy ground.

"Hi, Meg. You have no idea how glad I am they sent you," said Addie, relief evident in her voice.

Meg gave an awkward side glance at her partner and met Addie's gaze straight on. "If you don't mind, Miss Greyborne, it's Police Constable Gimsby, and this"—she gestured with a twitch of her head as she removed a notepad from her police jacket— "is my partner, Police Constable Poole, who will do a preliminary examination of the scene while I ask you a few questions, if that's okay?"

"Yes, yes, of course." Addie's gaze dropped. It seems her friends were right, and everything was by the book here. The fact that she'd had to help Meg get home after she'd over-indulged a time or two at the pub apparently didn't mean they were friends now that a body lay at Addie's feet.

"I understand, Miss Greyborne," said PC Gimsby, pen poised in hand over her notebook, "that you weren't the one to make the call to authorities after you discovered the body. Could you explain why that is?"

"I was shocked, and I didn't know where to call. I remembered that you and, well, Olivia—"

"Olivia?"

"Olivia Green." Annoyed by the line of questioning, Addie emphasized their friend's last name as Gimsby jotted something down. "She—and you—said that, a couple of years ago, the community police station here in Moorscrag was closed due to cuts in government funding." Addie shrugged. "I didn't know where the closest police station was now, that's all."

"You didn't think to call 999?"

"I, I didn't think it was an emergency, and in the States we dial 911, so my mind was—No, I didn't. The woman was already dead, and there was no crime in progress."

"And how can you be so certain she was dead? Did you touch the body to check for a pulse?"

Addie shook her head. "Just the top of her hand, but the skin was so cold, and by the coloring around her mouth and the empty look in her eyes . . ." Addie shook her head. "No, I didn't check further for a pulse."

"I see. So your close friend"—she flipped back a page in her notes and read—"Anthony Radcliff, called the discovery of the body in for you, is that right?"

This was ridiculous. Meg Gimsby knew exactly who Olivia and Tony were and that Tony was a good friend of hers and that she was living in his old gamekeeper's cottage. What was Meg playing at?

Addie looked over at the younger PC standing beside the body as he scratched his head. He then shrugged while he toyed with his pen and stared blankly off across the moor. Could it be that Meg was trying to establish her seniority over this young constable, who unmistakably was the same rank as her but was obviously new to the job and didn't have a clue how to conduct an assessment of a scene involving a dead body?

"Todmorden, Miss Greyborne," PC Gimsby sighed, as she continued to jot down notes. "I'm sure you have heard it mentioned a time or two as the nearest community police constabulary to Moorscrag now?"

"I guess I wasn't paying attention, or perhaps it was the fact that I just discovered the body of a woman who had evidently fallen to her death, and I couldn't think clearly in the moment."

Addie knew her tone was sharper than it should have been, but really? Meg was treating her like they had never met before. Something was up, and she needed to find out what was going on. Even if things were handled by the book in the UK, surely friendliness couldn't have been cut like police funding had been, could it?

Meg gave her a helpless shrug, then glanced over her shoulder at the young PC and whispered. "He's the Hamilton region DCS's son."

"The DCS?"

"Yeah, you know the DCS, the Detective Chief Superintendent of the Hamilton CID."

"Okay?" Addie looked dubiously at her. "What is the CID?"

"I thought you said you watched all those British police dramas on the telly?"

"I do watch them, but when they start using all those acronyms, my mind just kind of glazes over, and . . ." she shrugged her shoulders.

"The CID is the Criminal Investigation Department. Each locale or region has one."

"So he's a supervisor then?"

"Yes."

"Why didn't you just say so from the start?"

"I did."

"Okay then," Addie said, checking that he was still out of earshot. "Let's put on a good show for him so he tells daddy only great things about you and you get that promotion you want." Addie snapped her mouth closed as her peripheral vision picked up movement.

"Thank you," Meg quickly mouthed as he came up behind her. "Poole, what did you learn about the victim?" asked Meg, without removing her gaze from her notepad.

"Not much. It looks like the girl slipped, and now she's dead. Should I call it in, so we can get out of here?" He glanced around. "Moors give me the creeps, and I missed me breakfast, so an early lunch would suit me fine."

"Not so fast." Meg gripped her pen a little tighter. "Is she facing up or down?"

"Uh . . . up?"

"Any facial abrasions?"

"I don't think so."

"Did you touch the body?"

"No!" His chest heaved. "No, there's blood all around her head. You know, like she's lying in it."

"Any identification on or near the body?"

"I didn't see anything."

"No wallet, mobile phone?"

"I didn't see a handbag. Like I said, I didn't touch the body. Maybe she's lying on top of it?"

"Maybe?" Meg glanced over at the body and met Addie's skeptical look. "Did you see anything or notice anything peculiar when you found her?"

"I'm not sure." Addie's gaze traveled to the rocks where the body lay and scanned up to the top of the cliff face. "It's just that . . . Oh, never mind," Addie said, waving it off, and quickly glanced at PC Poole and gave him a weak smile. "I'm sure the constable's assessment is right. She slipped and fell."

"No." Meg pinned her with a determined look. "What were you going to say?"

"It's just"—Addie glanced at PC Poole and back at Meg—"if she fell, you'd think her face, arms, and hands would be banged up and some abrasions and bruising would be evident, right? And she wouldn't be lying flat on her back, but in a more, I don't know, crumpled heap because she'd fought to catch herself on her way down?"

"Yes, yes." Meg walked over to the body and bent down. "Well, she's dressed like she was going to a fancy dinner party."

"She was."

"Where?" She looked at Addie.

"She was at the manor last night for the engagement party."

"Do you know her?" Meg rose to her feet and stared questioningly at Addie. "You should have said so right from the start."

"No, no, honest, Meg. The only time I saw her was when I bumped into her and spilled some champagne down her front. Look, that crusty area around her neckline. If you test it, I'm sure you'll see what I'm telling you is true."

"So, you have no idea who she is?"

"No, I don't." Addie took a breath and looked down at the body. "Except—" It hit Addie what had been off about the woman's body. "She was wearing a necklace when I saw her last night. I guess I remember now that I'm getting over the shock of finding her."

"There's no necklace on her now."

"I know, but I recall it so clearly now. I turned around and bumped into her, splashing some of my champagne over her front. I was afraid the drink would get lodged in all the intricate gold filigree around the tiny diamonds and the raised stone in the center, making it look cloudy. I grabbed a napkin and tried to wipe it off, but she pushed my hand away, excused herself, and walked away from me."

Meg crouched down beside the body and looked up at Addie. "Was she drinking too?"

"I don't know. She didn't have a drink in her hand when I saw her, but the champagne was free-flowing all evening. Tony made sure his guests were enjoying themselves, that's for sure."

"All except this woman," chirped in PC Poole.

"See, I was right then. That free-flowing drink might have been the death of her when she stumbled out here, drunk, and then slipped and fell, right?" He grinned at them with satisfaction.

Meg's jaw tensed as she attempted to smile at the young constable. "Ahh, but there's no evidence that—never mind," she said, flashing Addie a look of pure exasperation before returning her attention back to Poole. "Constable, could you please do a search of the area around the body, and up on the cliff, and scan the rocks for any sign of a handbag, a mobile phone, or anything else that seems out of place or might have belonged to the deceased."

"What should I do with anything I find?"

Meg hung her head, muttered something incoherent, and then met Poole's inquiring gaze. "You place everything you find in an evidence bag for forensics, okay?"

"Got it," he said, setting off.

"Have strength, my friend." Addie gave Meg a reassuring squeeze of the shoulder and squatted down beside her. "You'll get through this, and hopefully you'll ace the detective's exams next month and be able to leave him behind."

"My luck, he'll be assigned as my PC since as a low-ranking detective constable, I won't have seniority for anything higher on the chain." Meg refocused on the woman's body. "What do you make of that odd marking around her neck?"

"It could be the abrasions made by the chain when it came off her neck."

"Meaning it would have had to have been removed by force."

"The question, I guess, is man or nature?"

"Yes, yes, it is." Meg stood up. "Poole," she hollered, "keep an eye out for a necklace too. Check to see if there are any branches the chain might have caught on."

"That'd be like finding a gnat in a hay bale," he yelled back.

"Just . . . just . . ." She clenched her fists and counted, "One . . . two . . . three." She pulled her mobile out of her jacket pocket. "Sir, I think there may be more to this death than a slip and fall on the crag." She stepped away from Addie and continued her conversation out of earshot.

When she returned a few minutes later, PC Poole was entertaining himself by playing a game of hand keep-away with Pippi.

"What did you find?" Meg asked him.

"Nothing."

"Nothing?"

"Nah, just a candy wrapper up top there. No sign of a handbag or anything."

"What about the necklace?"

"That could be in any of those rocks."

"Yeah, so did you look?"

He laughed when Pippi gently gripped his hand in her teeth. "Nah, too hard to get in there."

"Alright then," Meg said, her voice tight. "Put the evidence bag with the candy wrapper in the case for forensics."

"I didn't bag it. It was just one of those minty candy wrappers ya can buy anywhere."

"Constable Poole," her voice quivered, "everything, and I mean everything, you find at a crime scene is possible evidence." She paused, sucked in a deep breath, and quietly counted again.

"Okay," Meg said, glancing at Addie. "I'm okay now." She turned to Poole. "I've just spoken to the district office in Halifax for instructions on our next steps. They're sending out a detective sergeant, along with someone from the coroner's office and the forensic team, to further examine the scene and the body. The DS should be here any minute."

"I don't believe it," said Poole, ruffling Pippi's head.

"What is it you don't you believe, Constable?"

"That the DS will be here shortly," he said, meeting her exasperated gaze. "Ya see, if he takes the A646, it'll take about twenty-five minutes, and if the DS comes by way of A646 to the A6033, it's about thirty-six minutes. So yer wrong. The DS won't be here shortly, will he?" He flashed Meg a triumphant grin.

"And there he is now." Meg pointed to the figure striding across the moor toward them. "You see, Poole. I guess, as luck would have it, he just happened to be in Moorscrag for a break."

"Aye, got me there, Gimsby," PC Poole softly chuckled.

"So, while I get him up to speed, why don't you go back up to the cliff, bag that candy wrapper you left there, and take a better look for the necklace. Okay?"

He snatched the evidence bag she dangled from her fingers and stomped off toward the rocky path to the top.

"Don't forget to wear gloves," she called after him. "Give me strength." Meg looked up and crossed herself.

"That was lucky, the detective sergeant being in the village right now," said Addie.

"The DS is Ian Davis. Ring a bell?"

Addie's mind flipped through her mental files, and she let out a short laugh. "It's not that detective Emily's been seeing, is it?"

"One and the same." Meg grinned. "It's nearly eleven, so I was pretty sure he'd be at the bakery or on his way there for lunch when he got the call out."

"Good timing. I only met him once or twice, but he seemed like a great guy."

"He is, and that's why I stalled a bit calling in my scene report. I was waiting until I'd be fairly certain—well, along with a lot of praying—that he'd be in the village, and they'd have no choice but to send him out as the case detective sergeant."

"Meg Gimsby, how conniving of you," Addie laughed.

"Hey, after I got saddled with Bozo Poole there as a partner, I figured they owed me one."

"I've been meaning to ask. Who did you offend to get him assigned to you?"

"I think it was more like they had no other station to post him to. Nobody else would put up with him, so Superintendent Poole, trying to save face over the muck-ups of his son over at the Hamilton station, had him shipped off to Todmorden, a small station where he could keep an eye on him better and hopefully lessen the damage he could do. Ya see, we don't get many murders around here." She looked past Addie and smiled. "Good afternoon, Detective Sergeant."

"Gimsby," he nodded. "Miss Greyborne, nice to see you again." He gazed up at the overhanging rock outcrop and squinted. "Who's that up there?"

"That would be PC Poole, sir."

"Not Superintendent Poole's son?"

"The same, sir."

"Bloody 'ell. How did you draw the short straw, Gimsby?"

"Just lucky, I guess, sir."

"Yeah, well, your luck won't be getting much better because I've been reassigned to the new guy."

"Not DI Parker, sir?"

"One and the same, Detective Inspector Noah Parker, freshly demoted and cast off from the Met in London."

"The Met?" asked Addie.

"The Metropolitan Police in London," whispered Meg.

"And the rest of the country, should they so wish, it seems." DS Davis scowled. "Give me the facts as you see them, so I can report to the DI."

"Yes, sir." Meg read her notes to DS Davis.

He made notes of his own, glancing frequently in the direction of the body before he approached it and began his own examination of the site. Addie hovered nearby, telling him her observations when she had come across the body.

"Would that be DI Parker now, sir?" Meg pointed in the direction of Addie's cottage.

"If it walks like a duck . . ." Davis squinted off into the distance.

"What's he doing here now?" asked Meg. "I mean, sir, the forensics team hasn't even arrived yet, and no reports have been submitted. We still don't know if it was an accidental death or something else."

"I heard he had trust issues with a few of his fellow officers back at the Met, but I never thought his distrust would extend to me here." DS Davis rose to his feet. "I guess you'd better straighten your cap, Gimsby. Update your notes and see if you can keep that"—he waved his hand toward Poole at the top of the cliff—"out of his way. I think we're both in for a good grilling here."

"Ooh-ooh, he is easy on the eyes, though, isn't he, sir?" said Meg from behind her binoculars.

"Constable Gimsby!" bellowed DS Davis. "May I remind you that is a senior officer you're talking about?"

"Yes, sir. Sorry, sir." She lowered the binoculars, thrust them into Addie's hand, and, with a slight head jerk and a grin, urged her to have a look.

Chapter 7

"Tell me something, Detective Inspector Parker." Addie squeezed her arms around her middle, hoping it would quiet the grumbling in her stomach, which seemed to just now match the snarky tone of her voice as it rang back at her in her own ears.

When she'd left home this morning for a short walk with Pippi, she had no idea she would be having a midday rendezvous on the moor with a police inspector. Who also just happened to look a lot like that actor who played Sherlock Holmes in those *Enola Holmes* movies, Henry Cavill or whatever his name was, but she did know that if her low-bloodsugar, hangry monster was going to be kept at bay, she was going to need something other than his good looks to feed on, and soon.

"What would you like to know, Miss Greyborne?"

DI Parker asked distractedly as he continued to read the paper he held in his hand.

"Is badgering a witness and asking them the same question twenty different times in twenty different ways by four different people generally a tactic that works well for you?"

When he raised his head and met her gaze, Addie had to divert hers. For the first time, she worried that Serena's nervous facial mottle-monster condition might actually be contagious. Addie stared at the toes of her wellies, wondering how fast they'd be able to take her across the moor and far away from this man, whose deep fog-gray eyes unexpectedly blurred her vision and muddled her senses, just like the actual fog on the moor had done earlier.

"Now," he said, closing a file folder, "the crime-scene investigator has confirmed that there is a clear marking of a chain having been around the victim's neck, and the chain isn't there now. So, may we get back to the little issue of the missing necklace, perhaps?"

Her head snapped up, and she looked at him in disbelief. "Wait. Is that what this game of twenty questions has been about? You're treating me as a suspect for stealing the necklace?"

"At this point, that's all we have to go on, isn't it?"

"I don't believe it. You think she just happened to slip from up there and fall to her death, and then I just happened to come across the body, see the necklace, and pocket it, or are you suspecting me of murdering her so I could get my hands on it?"

"The thought had crossed my mind."

"Except you have no evidence to prove any of that, and, besides, I have an alibi for last night."

"Which is yet to be confirmed, but what makes you so certain she died last night and not early this morning while you were, say, walking your dog?"

"Because I overheard the crime-scene investigator tell you that he can't pinpoint the time of death until the postmortem is complete, but he estimates that death occurred between eleven p.m. and one a.m., and I told you all repeatedly where I was and with whom, and it most certainly did not involve a late-night walk on the moor." Addie's voice quivered with rage. "I've also repeatedly told you, PC Gimsby, PC Poole, and DS Davis, that when I saw the victim, once in the early evening at the party last night, she was wearing a necklace, and when I came across . . ." Addie glanced over at the rocks where the CSI was working. "When I came across her this morning while walking my dog, she wasn't, and that's all I know about it." She crossed her arms over her chest and steadied her defiant gaze on him. "Besides, if I did push her, why would I call it in and then hang around until the police showed up, knowing I'd have to answer questions about it?"

"Suspects in murder cases have been known to do all sorts of odd things, for kicks, or to try and establish their innocence."

"So, you are investigating this as a murder and not an accident, then?"

Addie could almost hear an eye roll from him as he glanced up from his notebook. "Tell me, do you generally walk the moors in a heavy blanket of fog, especially in such a treacherous area, or just today?"

"And do you generally avoid direct questions yourself, by diverting the subject of your inquiry by asking another meaningless question?"

He quirked a brow.

"Fine, don't tell me if it's a murder or not. I can wait for the autopsy report that will be a matter of public record."

"Eventually," he said, a half-smile tugging at the corner of his mouth. "Now, if you don't mind answering my, as you called it, meaningless question."

"We've been through all this ten times over." Addie boldly met his gaze. "Plus you had PC Gimsby search me. DS Davis took my rain jacket, and you made a point of telling me he would pick up my boots later for evidence. Thank you, by the way, for letting me keep them on for now." She squirmed at the sight of the damp soil in the shaded area under the stone outcrop. "And you had PC Poole retrace my steps to make sure I didn't remove the necklace from the body and hide it someplace. What's next? Are you going to arrest me and what? Force me to have an X-ray so you can see if I swallowed it to hide it until later?"

"Hmm, I hadn't thought of that." His gaze never wavered while he methodically tapped his pen on the notepad. "Don't tempt me, Miss Greyborne. I'm pretty certain I could get a court order for that X-ray within the hour."

"What? You can't be serious?"

"This brings us back to you, Miss Greyborne. You said yourself that the victim was wearing an ornate necklace last night, and now she's not, correct? And you think, with strong conviction, based on the bruising around the marks on her neck, that the chain was torn off her before she died and not after? Tell me"—he pinned his unwavering gaze on her—"do you have medical training, or did you slip up during the twenty questions, as you called them, and are speaking from personal experience?"

Addie stood, wide-eyed and mouth agape, not capable of putting the answer to his question into words.

His gaze remained fixed, but without a word, he abruptly turned and strode over to the CSI beside the body.

He was joking, right? She'd found out the hard way that the English would often say one thing when they really meant something completely different. When she'd first started working at Second Chance Books, it had caused her a lot of confusion with customers and attempts to figure out if they were literal in what they said, only to discover later she had been the brunt of a joke, delivered with a straight face, of course. It seemed the British used irony for everything, from mocking enemies to play-fighting with friends. She hoped DI Parker's words were meant with a sense of that famous British, tongue-in-cheek humor.

Addie cuddled Pippi to her chest and shuffled from one foot to the other, not sure what she should do now. DI Parker had not told her to stay put, leave, or even have a seat on a boulder. All she knew was that she needed coffee and food. Her quick morning walk with Pippi had turned into anything but, and based on her recent outburst, she was starting to come unraveled due to dehydration and starvation.

"DI Parker! A word," she yelled.

Meg Gimsby paused her search around the base of the cliff and gave Addie a horrified look.

DS Davis, who was labeling evidence bags, coughed and stifled a laugh. "You're a brave woman, Miss Greyborne."

"What?" Addie looked from one to the other and shrugged.

DI Parker, slowly—as in stop-motion cinematography slowly, at least in Addie's dehydrated fuddled mind—turned toward her. She held her breath at the sight. All he needed, with that strong Romanesque profile, was for his silvery-streaked dark hair to be a tad longer and sprayed with water droplets so he could do a head flip worthy of a men's cologne television commercial. She gasped and blinked, bringing her thoughts back to the present . . . and reality. Lack of food and water was getting to her, making her hallucinate.

"May I return to my cottage now? I'm feeling a bit . . . a bit off. It's been a long morning and—"

"Don't leave town. We'll be in touch soon, Miss Greyborne."

"Thank you." Addie shook off the last remnants of what had clearly been a delirium-induced daydream. "Ah, and I'm sorry about—never mind. I'm just tired and hungry, I guess."

Parker didn't say a word with his mouth, but the amused flicker in his eyes told her he found her current hangry state most comical, and she struggled to give him something that resembled a smile when she turned and left.

The rational side of her brain told her it was his pompous attitude and the steeliness of his cold heart shining through his gray eyes, which apparently made his eyes sparkle when he spoke to her—that's what had unnerved her. Yes, that was it. After all, she'd read once that gray eyes were even more striking when they were illuminated in the natural sunlight, and given the position of the noonday sun, it was no wonder she had detected a glimmering effect, right? The irrational emotional side of her brain, however, couldn't agree more with Meg Gimsby: *He was easy on the eyes.*

It was funny that, with all the people she'd met this past year, not one of them had stirred her core the way this man had. Was it because there were memories of Marc, her, and murder, and that's what she found exhilarating, not the man himself? As she set off across the moor to her lane, she tightly secured Pippi under her arm, just in case her little companion felt the need to return to her new friends. There was no way she could look DI Parker in the eye again today, maybe not ever if her imagination wasn't going to behave.

By the time she reached the cottage and deposited Pippi beside her water bowl, Addie knew, by her frazzled state of mind and nerves, that she couldn't let anything come between her, a large mug of steaming coffee, and whatever food she could scrounge in her pantry. She jumped at a loud pounding on the door.

"Please don't be DI Parker," she whispered,

opening it. She sighed with relief. "Tony, I was going to call you after—"

"Thank goodness you're here. I tried to get to the moor after your call," he said, sliding past her in the small entry way. "But the police have the lane closed so I had to come the back way through the forest. What on earth is going on? Whose body did you find?"

"I was just going to make coffee. Do you want some?"

"I want to know why Hailey just called me and told me that the police are now crawling all over the manor and flower gardens and questioning all the staff."

"Has anyone spoken to you yet?"

"No, and why would they?" He took a seat on the overstuffed sofa. "Whose body did they find? Is it someone from the party last night?"

Addie relayed her morning adventures as she made coffee and took a seat beside him on the sofa. "I snapped a photo of her before the police showed up." She scrolled through the images on her phone and held it out to Tony. "Look here. Do you know her?"

Tony briefly peered at the photo, then looked away. "No, I don't know her, and I don't remember seeing her last night."

"I do, and I bumped into her, spilling a drink all over the front of her dress." Addie stared at the picture. "There must be other pictures of her." She looked at Tony. "You hired a photographer last night, didn't you?"

"Yes, he was everywhere and got to be a little annoying, actually. I was starting to think he might really be paparazzi and the photos would end up in every rag publication in London."

"Did he send you the picture files yet?"

Tony checked his emails and shook his head. "He did say it could take a day or two until he had them sorted."

"Maybe you could rush him along. There must be more pictures of this mystery woman wearing the necklace she had on when I saw her earlier. In my photo, she isn't wearing it anymore. If we can find other pictures of her, we might be able to figure out when she lost it or who she was with, which might tell us who she is and maybe who would have wanted her dead."

"You don't think she just slipped and fell, but that she was murdered so someone could steal her necklace?"

"It kind of looks that way, and from what I recall of the necklace, it was old, and if the center sapphire was genuine, it was worth a lot of money."

"A guest from my party murdered?" He shook his head. "No, that can't be. Except for a few of Robert and Elizabeth's friends from London, I know everyone who was there. It had to have been an accident. That is a very dangerous part of the moor, and there's been more than one tragedy in that area over the years."

"I know, but it looks like the necklace might have been ripped off her neck before she died."

"Really, so you think someone pushed her?"

"It's hard to say with certainty until the pathologist's report comes back, but, yes, it kind of looks that way."

Tony looked thoughtfully at Addie. "Which means

she might have argued with someone on top of the cliff? Whoever tore the necklace off her—"

"She either stumbled back in the struggle, or once the thief got what they wanted, they pushed her to keep her quiet."

Tony's phone pinged. He grabbed it and grinned. "He just sent the unedited photo files. Let's see what we have." His eyes scanned over the screen. "This isn't going to work. There are hundreds of pictures here, and going through them all on this little screen is going to make us both go cross-eyed, not to mention take the rest of the day."

"Then email them to me. We can browse through them on my laptop."

"Good plan. There, you should have the files now."

Addie began scanning the rows of images. "There are lots of photos of guests as they arrived and always the ever-vigilant Mrs. Bannerman standing in the background. He got some good shots of that reception line you and Hailey arranged to introduce Lord and Lady Bentley to guests as they arrived."

"The one you missed out joining us in."

"Yeah, well, I got Serena delayed, remember?" Addie squinted. "But I don't see her in any of these early images. I wonder who she came with?" Addie scrolled farther down the rows of images. "Oh, wait. Here she is, look." Addie pointed to an image. "She's hard to make out as she's in the background."

Tony peered at the screen. "Are you sure it's her?"

"Yes, I'd know that dress anywhere because I sloshed champagne all over it."

"It seems strange she's only in that one picture, though." Tony took the mouse and began scrolling down the page of images. "Wait, here she is again."

Addie studied the image. "Yes, but she's still in the background. It's almost like she knew the photographer was there and didn't want to be in any pictures."

Tony scrolled farther and let out a sharp gasp.

Addie peered at a very clear image of the woman she'd spilled champagne on. "What is it? Do you know her?"

Tony shook his head. "I've never seen her before in my life, but"—his face paled—"the necklace she's wearing . . ."

"Yes, that's the one she was missing when I came across the body this morning."

He zoomed in on the image. "I'm fairly certain that's the necklace I bought Hailey from an antiques shop in Leeds a few months ago to give to her for our one-year dating anniversary." He clicked the magnifying-glass icon and continued to study the picture. "It sure looks like the same one I gave to Hailey at a restaurant in London."

"Doesn't she still have it?"

"No, she wore it all through our meal, but when we got back to her flat later, she discovered the necklace was gone."

"What do you mean gone?"

"When she took her coat off, it wasn't around her neck anymore."

"And you think the necklace this mystery woman is wearing is the one Hailey lost?"

"It sure looks like it, at least in this picture. Are there any more of this woman?"

Addie scrolled through the images, but any others of the woman wearing the red-and-white-flowered dress were too far away to get a good look at the necklace.

"Go back to the close-up," Tony said, peering over her shoulder. "Hailey was devastated at the loss of the necklace. We called the restaurant, but no one had turned it in at that point. They promised someone would call if it showed up. We even went back that night to retrace our steps from the restaurant to the car park. I reported it to the police and gave a photo of it, along with the appraisal from the antiques store, to the insurance company. They said it might turn up if an upstanding citizen found it and turned it in. Otherwise, it was probably long gone. We kept hoping we'd get it back, but . . ." He sighed. "I put it down to a faulty clasp. Of course, Hailey was sick with regret that she didn't check the clasp before she slipped it on. Antique jewelry and all. I told her it was just as much my fault. I should have had it cleaned and checked out by a local jeweler before giving to her."

"It looks like someone did find it and never bothered to turn it in."

"Yeah, when I purchased it, the fellow at the antiques shop said it was handcrafted and one of a kind. He'd had it appraised and"—Tony whistled—"it was worth a few pounds." He stared at the image on the screen. "Maybe the faulty clasp was how this girl lost it too?"

Addie looked at the image. She couldn't make out any marks around her neck in this photo. However, she was positive there were none when she tried to wipe the champagne from the woman's neck, which meant that whatever force had caused them had happened later. "Maybe, but she did have the marks on her neck when I found the body." She started to click through more images and paused. "Tony, look at this one. There isn't a close-up of our mystery woman, but see where she's standing."

He squinted. "She's kind of behind me and Hailey. This is a picture taken early in the evening, when we were chatting with Lord Bentley, Lewis, and Colton. Before Lord Bentley and I got into it about the stolen copy of *Wuthering Heights*."

"Yeah." Addie involuntarily shivered with the memory. "How did that end up after I left and once you both finally got back to being civil to each other? Did you remain that way, or did you have to be put back in your corners?"

"No, we came to an agreement about letting our respective lawyers work it out since I did have a sales receipt. In the meantime, the book will remain locked up in his library safe."

"That's too bad. You know that Hailey will be sad that she can't have her engagement gift."

"Yes, but the word from his solicitor was the court would probably rule in favor of Hailey's claim."

"That's wonderful but speaking of Hailey . . ." Addie clicked the magnifying glass icon. "Do you think Hailey saw the mystery woman last night and recognized the necklace she was wearing?"

"If she did, she didn't say anything to me. Why?"

Addie pointed to an image on the screen where Hailey appeared to be focused on the woman in the red-and-white-flowered dress standing by the buffet table.

"No, she would have told me if she saw someone wearing her necklace. You didn't see how upset she was by losing it that night. She'd have been thrilled for it to reappear."

Thrilled enough to kill to get it back? Addie swallowed hard and uneasily glanced at Tony.

Chapter 8

"You're going to have to tell the police about the necklace, Tony," Addie whispered hoarsely.

"Why?" he replied, closing the laptop with a thump. "You can't possibly think Hailey would have killed this woman over it, can you?"

"Of course not, but there is a dead woman on the moor. I saw it around her neck last night, and these pictures verify she was wearing the same necklace you just identified as the one you gave Hailey. If you withhold that information from them now, and they find out about your ownership of the necklace, they will start thinking Hailey or you did have something to do with her death."

He stood up, and his knuckles whitened as he gripped the table edge. "I only said it looked like the same one. There's no proof, now it's gone missing, that it was the same necklace."

"Except the pictures, along with the claim you said you filed with the police and insurance company, which the police here can easily trace." Addie shifted uncomfortably in her chair and met Tony's pointed glare. "Besides, you said the antiques dealer told you it was a one-of-a-kind handcrafted piece of jewelry, so it's not mass-produced."

"He must have been wrong then, right?"

"Or it's like the police told you when you reported it. All you can do is hope someone finds it and is honest enough to turn it in. This woman or someone she knows must have kept it instead of taking it to the lost and found, as everyone hoped would happen."

Tony paused his frantic pacing, and his voice dropped. "Maybe so, but there's no way Hailey would have killed anyone for a necklace. I know her. It's all a coincidence. It's been months since she lost it. I'm sure she's forgotten all about it."

Addie drew in a deep breath and went to Tony's side. "I agree with you. The Hailey I know wouldn't have done anything like that, but—"

"Besides, if she did see someone wearing her necklace, she would have said something to me."

"Yes, but we did get tied up with Lord Bentley for a long time over the *Wuthering Heights* book."

"And you think that because Hailey couldn't find me she traipsed across the moor with this stranger in the dark, took the necklace off her, and pushed her over the edge of the bluff to keep her quiet?"

"No, I'm not saying that, but I do know how the police look at these sort of things, and I'm only asking the same questions they will be asking when they talk to you. After all, there are a few hours when you weren't at the party, and they will have my statement and Lord Bentley's to prove that, so they're going to assume that if Hailey did see this mystery woman wearing it, she wouldn't have been able to tell you, would she?"

"Yes, but she told me this morning that when she couldn't find me and was told I was seen leaving with Robert Bentley, she got upset. She thought I had abandoned her at our engagement party to talk business, so she went up to bed. So, you see, she couldn't have followed the mystery woman outside. She was in bed."

"Okay. For a minute, pretend I'm that inspector fellow. After you tell me what she told you this morning, I am going to say something like"—Addie straightened her back, puffed out her chest—"So, she was there when you went up later last night?"

"Of course, she was. Do you think she lied to me about where she was for those few hours?"

"It must have been really late when you went up because Addie Greyborne told us she didn't get back to her cottage until one-thirty, and when she left the library, you and Lord Bentley were still there together."

"See, you really do think she killed the woman, don't you, Addie?"

"No, I don't. Just be prepared, though, because the police will be asking you plenty of questions like that, hoping to push a button that might make you slip up and tell them something incriminating about yourself or Hailey." She laid her hand on her dejected-looking friend's arm. "Come on, I'll make some tea, and we can look through more photos to see if we can find any that help us figure who she was or, at least, who she came with, okay? Then when you tell the police about it, we can hopefully point them in another direction."

"You're right. There must be—"

His words were drowned out by a knocking on the door.

"Sit," she said, steering him to a chair. "I'll get rid of whoever it is."

"Unless it's Hailey," he called. "We can ask her straight out if she knows anything about this mystery woman wearing her necklace."

Addie swung the door open. "Meg, er, PC Gimsby, I mean."

Meg drew in a staggered breath. "PC Gimsby is best since I'm here on official business and was wondering if you know the whereabouts of—" She awkwardly glanced past Addie. "Is that Tony I see in the kitchen?"

"Yeah, we were just going to have tea. Would you like to join us?"

Meg removed her police cap and stepped into the small kitchen. "Anthony Radcliff?"

"Yes." Tony looked up from the computer screen. "Hi, Meg, are you joining us for tea?"

"I'm afraid not. I'm here on police business."

"What's that?" Tony sheepishly closed the lid of the laptop and pushed it away.

"I just have a few questions about the party held up at the manor house last night. We've been interviewing the staff and other guests, but it's taken until now to track you down."

"I hadn't realized you were looking for me," he said, rising. "Sorry, I just checked in with Addie as

I was the one to call in the incident this morning, and we"—he glanced uneasily at the laptop—"we got talking and . . ." He fished his phone out of his trousers pocket. "Yeah, sorry, I see I missed some calls. I must have put it on silent. What can I do for you?"

"Addie, can you give us a moment, please?" said Meg, keeping her gaze pinned on Tony.

"Sure, um, will you need to talk to me too?"

"Not at this time. I think we have everything we need from you for now."

"Okay then. I guess I'll just take Pippi outside for a bit."

"Thank you," said Meg, still focused on Tony. "Is everything okay, Tony? You appear nervous about something."

"No, not at all. I've just never been interviewed in a murder case, that's all."

Meg removed a notebook from her jacket pocket and took a seat. "Since it hasn't officially been classified as a murder and if you didn't have anything to do with the young woman's death, you have nothing to worry about, right? I just have some questions about the guest list and everyone's whereabouts last night during the time in question, to try to get a better idea of the young woman's movements."

"Right," said Tony, following her gesture to have a seat across the table from her. "But I don't remember her or even recall ever having met her before."

"But you do know what she looked like? How can that be?"

"Addie has a picture of her."

"She does, does she?" Meg turned to Addie, who was still hovering in the doorway. "You took a photo at the crime scene?"

"Um, yes."

"Thank you. I'll let you know when we're done in here, and then you and I can have a little chat."

Addie smiled weakly and nodded.

"Anthony Radcliff, can you tell me . . ." Meg Gimsby's voice faded as Addie shut the door.

This wasn't going to be good, but certainly there was no law against her taking the photo if it helped identify the woman, was there? Or was there? Addie stood at the bottom of the ladder stile, letting Pippi know, in no uncertain terms, there would be no afternoon walk on the moor. With a most displeased yip, Pippi perked her ears forward and proceeded to explore freshly made horse tracks along the path when a car horn gave a short beep behind her.

"DS Davis, I was just about to give you an earful for driving on the bridle path." She laughed as she approached the detective sergeant as he got out of his car.

"Afternoon, Miss Greyborne. I understand PC Gimsby is inside with Tony Radcliff?"

"Yes, she just got here."

"How long has he been here?"

"A while, why?"

"Because constables have been trying to find him for hours."

"I assure you he wasn't in hiding, if that's what you're suggesting. We were busy looking at photos

the photographer took at the party last night to
see if he knew the woman I found, and I guess he
didn't hear—"

"You have photos from the party?"

"Yeah, Tony and Hailey hired a photographer to
take pictures throughout the evening. We were
hoping Tony knew who she was or, at least, who
she came with to try to figure out—"

"I'll need those pictures right now." He started
for the cottage gate but stopped. "You two didn't
delete any, because our crime team can retrieve
them, you know?"

"Of course not, why would we?"

"Because they are now evidence in a murder inquest."

"So, she was pushed."

"And you were right. The coroner said the
chain was ripped off her neck before she died. He
says her fall might have occurred during a struggle
over it as there are . . . there is evidence suggesting
that." He started for the cottage again but turned
and faced Addie. "This means that Detective Inspector Parker is now officially in charge of the
case. You'd better make sure you have your facts
straight when he talks to you next."

"But I've already given my statement to him,
you, and Meg. It's not going to change now that
we know her death wasn't accidental."

"Just be prepared to answer all the same questions you've already answered. Parker doesn't believe anyone outside of London—I should say
him—knows how to run a proper murder inquiry."

"He does know you're a detective too, doesn't he?"

"Tell him that. Us country folk are all incompetent, according to him, I suppose, or that's how he makes us feel."

"If he believes that, then why would he transfer here from London?"

"He didn't request the new assignment. He was told he had two options: Take the relocation, along with the demotion from a detective chief inspector to an inspector, or resign."

"Demoted and relocated. That sounds like something big must have happened back at the Met."

"Yeah, and everyone in the Hamilton, West Yorkshire Police Department, including me, is too afraid to ask him about it. I did hear it was something to do with his wife, though. Speak of the devil." Davis gestured toward a car driving toward the cottage. "Be prepared is all I'll say." Davis chuckled as he closed the cottage door behind him.

"Inspector." Addie nodded in greeting as he came through her front gate.

"I take it my team is inside?"

"Yes." Addie studied the toes of her wellies to avoid any contact with those glimmering gray eyes that seemed to unnerve her every time he set them on her. "DS Davis said it seems it wasn't an accident, but that she was—" She looked up when she heard the click of her cottage door closing.

"Can you believe that? He just dismissed me without even so much as a 'May I go into your home?'" She looked to Pippi for agreement about the DI's rude behavior, but Pippi ignored her and rolled on her back on a patch of grass. "I have

never met such a pompous, arrogant . . ." She
growled again, at a loss for words. Pippi hadn't
seemed to notice, though, since she was doing her
best impression of a corpse while she exposed her
belly to the sunshine.

Addie had to forget about the inspector. He
wasn't worth it. How a wife would put up with a
man like that she'd never know, but she did know
that once Tony told him about the necklace and
where he was at the time of the woman's death,
then everything would be okay. Her heart sank
when she recalled Tony's hesitancy to tell them
about having bought the necklace for Hailey.

"Oh no!" She needed to make sure Tony was
forthright about his connection to the necklace
and shared the photos of the woman wearing it.
Adrenaline pumped through her as the consequences of him not telling them coursed through
her, and she considered her options. She could
make an excuse and go in, but judging by her earlier experiences with Parker, she'd be repri-
manded for interfering in their investigation or,
just as bad, have the door slammed in her face.

She studied the door and quickly disregarded
the possibility of eavesdropping. The door was
heavy oak, which made that impossible. She hadn't
left a window open, it seemed, as she scanned the
two ground-floor front windows. She looked up. The
bedroom window curtains fluttered in the warm
afternoon breeze coming off the moor, and she
momentarily contemplated climbing the ancient
trellis that ran up the side of the cottage and . . .
and what? Do her best impression of Spiderman

when . . . if . . . she managed to make it up the rickety old ivy trellis?

She braced her shoulders and took a deep breath. After all, it wouldn't be the first time she'd had a door slammed in her face. "Come on, Pippi. We need to get you an afternoon treat before you starve to death, right?" Addie took a step forward, but stopped when the door opened. PC Gimsby stepped out, followed by Tony. DS Davis and DI Parker flanked him as they escorted him toward the front gate.

"What's going on?" Addie looked at Meg. "Where are you taking him?"

"It's a police matter," said Parker.

"I can see that." Addie swung around to face him. "The question is why?"

"Further questioning is all I can say at this time."

"Okay?" She frowned and swallowed. "I'll let Hailey, his fiancée, know what's going on."

"I wouldn't worry about it." He gestured to her mobile phone. "Constables are taking her in as we speak."

Chapter 9

Addie kept one eye on the bookshop door and the other on the phone screen. Jasper hadn't come in yet, and if Mr. Pressman arrived before him, it would make a most unpleasant start to the day. She refocused on Serena's image on her phone, trying to remember what she'd last said. "I know I'm babbling and distracted, sorry. I don't think I got more than two hours of sleep last night, and this morning is shaping up to be one of those days."

"It's understandable, given what happened."

"I know, right? I just can't believe the police are convinced Tony and Hailey are connected to the murder of the mystery woman, though."

"Well, they are connected by way of the necklace, aren't they?"

"Yes and no. Tony said it was lost months ago."

"What does Hailey have to say about it and the woman?"

"I haven't been able to talk to her. All I know is they were both taken into custody yesterday afternoon, and they're still being held."

"Have they been charged?"

"Not yet, as far as I'm aware, so they're going to have to be released soon. At least I think the laws around that are similar in England to the ones in the States."

"I'm sure it'll all be sorted out soon, and if there are still loose ends to be tied up, Tony can afford a team of lawyers to look after that, and you'll be able to fly home next Sunday knowing everything is okay."

"I know it will all work out. There's no way either of them could be responsible. Besides, Lord Bentley and I were with Tony during the window of time the coroner says she died."

"See, there you go. You can fly home with peace of mind."

"Yes, but . . ." Addie bit the inside of her lip. "It's just that Hailey doesn't seem to have any witness for her whereabouts during that time. It's only her word that she went to bed."

"Someone must have seen her. Just let the police do what they do best, and that's investigate."

"Apparently, they are of the mind that Hailey saw the woman with the necklace on. To make it worse, there were pictures from the party of her hanging around Tony and Hailey. Their thought is Hailey saw the necklace and thought Tony had given it to the woman because he was having an affair with her, and during Hailey's confrontation about it, they argued, and the woman ended up at the bottom of the cliff."

"That doesn't even make sense," said Serena. "If it was one of a kind and not a mass-produced item, and Tony gave it to Hailey, and she lost it, he had to have been the one who stole it back, only to give it to another woman? How silly is that line of thought?"

"You haven't met the inspector in charge of the case. To be honest, that explanation doesn't surprise me."

"But it's not even logical without proof Tony knew this mystery woman."

"I guess pursuing that theory is part of their current investigation."

"To me, it makes more sense that Hailey saw the woman wearing the necklace and wanted to get a better look at it to see if it was hers, and they struggled over it and—"

"I'll stop you right there. Hailey doesn't have a violent bone in her body. If she had seen the necklace, she would have asked the woman about it, yes. Maybe some small talk to find out how she came into possession of it and all that. Then she would have tracked Tony down and talked to him about it."

"But you said earlier that she didn't know where Tony was, and she got upset and went to bed. No alibi, remember?"

"Yes, but I'm pretty sure she wouldn't have dragged the woman out onto the moor in the dead of night and thrown her off the top of the crag. She's afraid of heights anyway."

"Do the police know that?"

"I really don't know, I assume Hailey will—"

The bell over the door jangled, and Mr. Pressman, arms full of books, scooted around the doorframe as the door swung closed and dropped his armload on the counter. "Where's Jasper? I have more of these for him to go and collect."

"I'll have to call you back," Addie said and clicked off the video call. "Ahh, he's not in yet. Is it something I can help you with?"

"Not in yet? But it's going on teatime."

"I know, but . . ." Addie glanced toward the door and shrugged. She had no idea what to say. She couldn't even cover for Jasper since he hadn't called to say he slept in, been abducted by aliens, or arrested for murder. She recalled the image she and Tony had discovered of him eyeing the mystery woman wearing the necklace.

Her heart did a flip at the thought, and her mind raced with the possibility. Had Hailey told him about the necklace at some time during the evening? Maybe when she was talking to Jasper about his gift to her, the woman passed by. Hailey recognized the sapphire pendant and said something casually like, "I had a necklace exactly like that one, but I lost it. What I wouldn't give to have it back."

That would be all it would take for a lovestruck young man to swing into full knight-in-shining-armor mode and do whatever it took to retrieve the lost gemstone for his lady love. Oh my. This did open up a whole new line of thinking. She looked at Mr. Pressman and realized he was staring at her.

"Well?"

"Well?" She helplessly winced.

"Don't try to cover. I'll be having a word or two with our young apprentice when he does decide to grace us with his presence."

Deflect, deflect, Addie mentally chanted. The day was difficult enough without a world war breaking out in the bookshop too. "What do we have here?" Addie asked as she scanned the spines of the cloth-bound books he'd deposited in front of her.

"Mrs. Landry, over at the flower market, came across these at a charity shop in Leeds and is convinced these are actually worth the king's weight in gold."

Addie picked up *Around the World in Eighty Days* by Jules Verne and glanced at the title page. "This is a publisher's classics reproduction. It's not worth more than the cover price."

"I tried to tell her, but she thinks she's sitting on a gold mine. Anyway, I told her you would take a look, and I'd get back to her."

"Okay, but I can tell, just by looking at the covers, that she's going to be disappointed."

"Ever since that article in the London *Times* about that woman that came across an early edition of Chaucer's *The Canterbury Tales*, everyone thinks the books they find at a charity shop or at a book sale will make them rich."

"Yeah, then Tony finding that limited edition copy of *Wuthering Heights* in a used bookshop doesn't help either. It's been like that antiques television show around here lately, with everyone bringing in all the old books they can find to have them appraised."

Addie chuckled as Mr. Pressman came around the counter and gave Pippi a scratch behind the ear.

"What cha' looking at there?" He gestured to the images of Saturday night's party open on Addie's laptop.

"These are photos of Tony and Hailey's engagement party. I'm going through them, hoping to find a close-up of the woman who was found dead on the moor by the crag."

"Hmm, I heard about that. Nasty business, 'tis."

"Yes, and so far, no one seems to know who she was or who she came to the party with. I've been searching through the hundreds of images, hoping I can find something that will give us some answers."

"Ya could print off a picture of her and ask some of the High Street merchants if they know her or if she went into their shop?"

"I'm sure the police will do a door-to-door, don't you think?"

"Aye, but many won't talk to the likes of them, especially since our local station closed and constables have descended on us from all over Yorkshire."

"Yes, I've heard it used to be very neighborly dealing with the local PCs."

"Now ya never know who's going to show up. Gone are the days when we knew our lads and lasses and counted them as friends and could have a pint with them in the pub." He shook his head and continued making notations about Mrs. Landry's books in a ledger.

"You're right. Maybe if locals are asked by some-

one they know, they'll be more forthcoming."
Addie clicked on a photo of the woman. "Do you
recall her ever coming in here?" Addie gestured to
the screen.

Mr. Pressman removed his wire-framed glasses
and squinted at the photo. Addie waited for a response from him, but none came. He did have a
habit of zoning out and often needed a nudge to
stay on task.

"Do you ever recall her coming into the bookshop?" She glanced up and leapt to her feet.
"What is it? What's the matter?" She steadied his
wobble and gently guided him onto her stool. "Do
you know her?"

He didn't say a word, only shook his head, but it
was the graying of his skin that concerned Addie.
"Are you okay? Should I call the doctor?"

"No!" His voice strained to get that one word
out.

"Would a cup of tea help? I know you British—"

"This is the young woman that died Saturday
evening?"

"Yes, yes, it is. You do recognize her, then? I'm
sorry. If I'd known that you knew her, I wouldn't
have been so casual about—"

"Not her . . ." His voice cracked as he unsteadily
forced out the words. "The, the necklace."

"You've seen this necklace before?" Addie's
mind raced as she tried to figure out when and
where that could have happened. "Did Tony show
it to you before he went to London and gave it to
Hailey at their anniversary dinner?"

"Tony? When did he have it?" Mr. Pressman
looked up at Addie, tears blurring his faded brown

eyes. He sniffled and, with a trembling hand, tugged a wrinkled white hankie out of his trousers pocket.

"It's a necklace he bought for Hailey in Leeds a few months ago as a gift to celebrate their one-year dating anniversary. That was the same night he asked her to marry him."

"Leeds? He found it in Leeds? Where? On the street, in a field?" The tone and pitch of his voice rose as did the level of his agitation.

"No, in an antiques shop, but I think you'd better start from the beginning and tell me about this necklace. Can you do that?" Addie asked the question tentatively, as she wasn't quite certain Mr. Pressman was as well physically as he claimed to be. "Are you sure you don't want me to call the doctor or at least make us a nice cup of tea?"

"I can't." His cheerless gaze returned to the image still open on the screen, and his voice dropped to barely a whisper. "That is an heirloom necklace that had belonged to my stepdaughter."

"You have a stepdaughter?" Addie double-blinked with her confusion. "I'm sorry, I don't recall you every mentioning her."

"No, I never have. I don't talk about Mollie." His voice drifted to an inaudible whimper, and he sniffled without taking his focus from the image on the screen.

"Umm, you said it was an heirloom. Was it a necklace you'd given your late wife?"

"No," Mr. Pressman dabbed his damp eyes with his hankie. "It had been given to Mollie's mother, Julianna, by Mollie's natural father many years ago. Then, after my wife, her mother, passed when

Mollie was fifteen, I kept it and gave it to Mollie on her eighteenth birthday. It was her family heirloom, and I had nothing but this wee shop to give her, so I thought . . . that was over twenty years ago."

"What happened to Mollie's natural father? Did he die when Mollie was a baby?"

"He never was in Mollie's life. I met Julianna when I went to Leeds on business one time. She was originally from here, Moorscrag. I had seen her around the village a time or two, but I was a few years older, and we never mixed. But when I saw her sitting in a café, crying, I couldn't help myself. She was so beautiful and looked so vulnerable and alone."

Tears leaked from the corners of his eyes and rolled down his sallow cheeks. He dabbed his hankie again and sniffled. "It turned out she was pregnant. She never told me in all our years together who her baby's father was, but since she had been working at Milton Manor for a year before she suddenly left, I always suspected it was someone associated with the manor house. She never confirmed it, and I accepted her reasons for not wanting to talk about it and raised her child, Mollie, as me own."

"Where is Mollie now?"

"She's . . . she's dead, like her ma."

Chapter 10

Addie set a large cup of Mr. Pressman's favorite Earl Grey in front of him and slid onto a wooden crate of books he'd had shipped from London. "There, I put the CLOSED sign on the door and left a note on the counter for Jasper when he comes in. You drink some of that and catch your breath for a few minutes, okay?"

He nodded and brought the cup to his lips, but set it down on his desk and stared curiously at Addie. "Did you say when Jasper comes in?"

"I did," she said, playing her fingers over the handle on her mug. "But forget about him. I'll deal with him later if you want to have your tea and then go home for a bit of a lie-down."

He shook his head. "I'll be alright. It was all a long time ago. I was just surprised to see that necklace again after all these years. I thought it was lost forever." He took a sip and gazed around his workshop over the rim of his cup. "You know, this was all going to be Mollie's one day."

"I'm sure she would have loved that." Addie softly smiled through the aching pangs in her chest.

"When Mollie was little, her dream, when she grew up, was to become an expert bookbinder just like me, her old dad." A smile tugged at the corners of his age-creased lips. "Aye, I was the only father she ever knew, and she wanted to be just like me." He puffed his chest out. "Her whole life, I taught her everything I knew, and she took to it like a duck to water, she did. A real natural gift she had, that one." His smile grew as the distant look in his eyes did too. "So, when Lord Bentley offered her a position through the spring and summer at Milton Manor to assist him in marking all the books in his private library with that invisible ink and then had her catalog them for insurance purposes—"

"She was the one who stamped all his books?" Addie set her cup down.

"Aye. The job was only temporary, but she said it would pay her enough money to move to London for a few years so she could get the wanderlust out of her soul before she settled down here in Moorscrag and helped me run the shop. That was always the plan anyway." Mr. Pressman's eyes grew dark. "His lordship"—he practically spat out the word—"even promised he would give her a reference for a position at Spink & Thackray—"

"Spink & Thackray? That's one of the most established and trusted bookbinders in the UK."

"Aye, it is that. I was pleased for her, of course.

Besides me," he softly chucked, "that was the best place to learn the trade, but deep down, I was afraid that, once she started there, she'd never want to come back to this." He waved his hand around his small but functional workshop.

Addie could tell, by the darkening of his eyes, that the memories he was reliving had a lot to do with his current feelings toward Lord Bentley.

"But that Bentley, the high and mighty publisher he is, made her see it was the best place for her to go and work and learn what he said I couldn't teach her."

"He actually told your daughter that?"

"Aye, to hear him say those words, like I was an apprentice meself, broke her heart just as much as it did mine, but for another reason." He swiped his tear-filled eyes with his hankie. "But she was so excited when, on his word, they hired her, and she started counting down the days until she could leave here, leave me." He sniffled.

Addie gently took hold of his cool, frail hand, giving it an understanding squeeze. "That must have been hard on her and you."

"It was. I was afraid he was right, and she'd never want to come home." He brought his cup to his lips but set it back down. "Her work at the manor took a bit longer than they had planned, though, which made me happy. Ya see, soon after she began marking and recording his lordship's books, she discovered that some of his first editions were missing. Of course, she took her concerns to him."

"He did mention something about that Saturday

at the party. Apparently, they thought they found out who was behind it and dismissed that person, and the thefts stopped soon after."

"Aye, as I recall her saying, some of the main-floor staff had noticed a young housekeeper named Fern something." He shook his head. "No matter, the girl had been seen entering and exiting the library on several occasions, but when asked about it, according to Mollie, she always had an excuse as to why she had been in there, even though straightening the library was not among her duties. She was dismissed shortly after." He gazed into his teacup. "I wonder whatever happened to that lass. She was well liked here in the village, but she just sort of vanished after that."

"Didn't the police investigate the matter any further?"

"Nah, there was no solid proof against her—or anyone, for that matter. Only the missing books, so that was the end of it, from what I could tell."

"Is that when Mollie moved to London?"

"Aye. The day I dropped her off at the Haworth station to make her connection into Leeds, then onto the Big Smoke, was the last I ever saw of her." His slender shoulders shuddered.

"Did, did . . ." Addie placed her warm hand softly on top of his cool one. "Did she die while she was in London?" Addie's voice cracked. The idea that Mollie had met her end so far from home and those she loved tore at her chest.

He wiped his hankie across his damp cheeks and shook his head. "The Christmas following her move, she planned on a trip home for the holi-days." A smile replaced his downturned lips with what clearly was a fond memory. "We were so excited. She had so much to tell me about her new life and work and a new young lad she'd met that she said was . . ." His voice drifted, and he sniffled. "I think we were both just plain giddy as we planned it all over the telephone."

"I imagine you were. It sounds like it was a lovely Christmas."

"Aye, it would have been," he said in a strangled whisper.

Would have been? Addie's breath burned in the back of her throat.

"Just days before Christmas, my Mollie took the train from London to Leeds. There was even a record of her purchasing a ticket onto the Haworth station, where I was to meet her." His jaw tightened. "But she never got off the train. A few days later, her body was found on the moor, outside of Haworth at the base of a crag, and the necklace she'd worn every day since her eighteenth birthday was gone. That same necklace the woman in yer photo is wearing."

He blew his nose noisily, sniffled, and shoved his hankie into his trousers pocket. "Twenty years later, her murder remains unsolved." He stood and, on shaky legs, made his way to the door. "I think I will go have that lie-down." He opened the door but turned back. "I only hope this recent moors murder can be solved, and the family of that young lass can know justice was done, or twenty years from now it will sit in their craw, cold and empty, as it does in mine."

Chapter 11

Throughout the remainder of the morning and into the early afternoon, Addie couldn't help but compare the tale of Mr. Pressman's daughter's murder to the one that had occurred twenty years later: Two young women, both last seen wearing the same necklace found at the bottom of a stony crag. Those thoughts didn't help her mindset as she fought the what-ifs of Jasper having disappeared without a word too. When death hung in the air, it was easy to see it lingering everywhere, and Addie's mind kept taking her down that dark path. So, when the single bell over the door clanged, Addie's chest constricted. She expected the worst— constables bringing news no one should have to hear.

She stared steadily at the figure looming in the doorway, and then quite unexpectedly, she knew exactly how her father had felt when she was late coming home. She wobbled between being relieved to see Jasper was alright and angry that he had worried her about his whereabouts. She decided a hug first, then the lecture, just like her father used to do with her.

"Whoa, wait a minute there." Jasper's hazel-brown eyes widened as he pulled away from her grasp. "I like ya fine, Addie, but I think ya got the wrong idea."

"Don't be silly, you big oaf. I'm just glad to see you're not lying in a gutter somewhere. Do you have any idea how worried we've been?"

"Oh, right." He ran his hand through his unruly hair. "Well, I didn't have me mobile, so—"

"Wait a minute. You really expect me to believe that you, Jasper Henderson, were without your mobile phone? I thought there was some law about it having to be taped to your generation's hands or something."

His face contorted, as he thought about what she said, and he grinned. "I see what ya did there. That was an American joke, weren't it?"

"No joke, but why didn't you call and let us know you were going to be late, at least, to tell us you were okay?"

"I told ya, I didn't have me mobile."

"Again, why would you be out without your mobile phone?"

"Because the coppers showed up at me mum's door at seven, dragged me out of bed, and drove me to some old barn at the end of Chapel Road to question me."

Addie stared at him, waiting for the punch line to his joke.

"I mean it. They've set up a whole copper station out there. A Mobile Incident Station, or at least that's what I heard that Davis bloke call it when he led me into the barn. I tell ya, there's desks with telephones and computers and them white boards ya see on the telly, and there's coppers crawling over the place."

It was Addie's turn to stare at him. "You're kidding?"

"Nah, it was pretty exciting, until they started asking me questions. Then guilt set in."

"What do you mean by guilt?"

"Ya know how 'tis talking to coppers. Ya always feel guilty even if ya've got nothing to feel guilty about. Like when they asked about the woman in the red-and-white-flowered dress and wanted to know—"

"Wait, so you did see the woman in the red-and-white-flowered dress?"

"Ya, well I didn't notice her until Hailey pointed her out and asked me if I knew her."

"Did you?"

"Nah, never seen her before, but I wasn't thinking much about her. Hailey had just returned the book I gave her, so I was pretty gutted and wanted to leave and have a few pints with me mates."

Addie glanced down the aisle, making sure there were no prying eyes or ears. "What exactly did they ask you?" she whispered, leaning toward him.

"There was a photo on that Davis's computer,

and it showed me and Hailey having a bit of a chin-wag." His face lit up. "They wanted to know what we were talking about, that's all."

"And what about the woman in the red-and-white-flowered dress?" She waited for him to elaborate, but he just stood there with a goofy grin on his face. "Jasper, what were you talking about?"

"It was a picture of when I gave her that book I showed ya. The *Wuthering Heights* book. Ya said she was going to work at that museum, so—"

"Yes, I remember all that, but what were you talking about?"

"I'm a gentleman." He looped his thumbs under his armpits and stood taller. "I'm not about to kiss and tell the likes of you, especially after ya gave me that hug 'n' all."

Addie took a breath and silently counted to three. "Jasper, this isn't kissing and telling." She struggled to keep her voice even. "This is important. Tony and Hailey were taken into custody yesterday as suspects in that young woman's murder."

"My sweet, sweet Hailey is in the nick?" His face paled, and he staggered a step back.

"Yes, she is in jail. So, whatever you told the police might be the difference in her staying there or being released. It's important."

Jasper's fingers whitened as he gripped the edge of the sales counter. "What if what I said was the reason they tossed her in the nick?"

"I doubt it." Addie clasped his heaving shoulders and steered him around the counter to the stool behind it. "They were taken into custody yesterday, and you weren't questioned until today. So

I'm sure it's something she told the police, which is why they wanted to talk to you today and not the other way around."

"Then if I confirmed what she said, they'll have to let her go, right?" He looked up at Addie, his eyes filled with optimism.

"Let's hope, but that's why it's important to know what they asked you about and what you said."

He pointed to the classics section, where he'd found the book he'd given Hailey. "I told them about the book and how happy she was with it." His hand went to his cheek, and he smiled softly. "She even gave me a little kiss." His bright eyes darkened. "But then she told me she couldn't accept it because she was going to marry Tony." His upper body tightened, and he shuddered.

"Did that make you angry?"

He dropped his gaze. "Nah, it stung, but it's not like everyone hasn't been saying she could never love a bloke like me anyway."

She tipped his head up and fixed her gaze on his empty one. "I hope you know it's not you she couldn't love. It's just that she met Tony first and fell in love with him. It's not because there's something wrong with you."

"That's what me mum said."

"Your mom is a smart woman, so listen to her and know there is someone even better for you than Hailey, just waiting until the time is right for you to fall in love with her as much as she loves you, okay?"

He nodded.

"Good." She patted his arm and gave him a reassuring smile. "Now what did you tell them about the woman Hailey pointed out to you?"

"I told them I've never seen 'er before in me life, but she sure got under Hailey's skin. She even asked me to follow the woman to see if I could find out who she was or who she was with."

Addie sat down hard on the counter edge.

"Then she said she had to go find Tony. I looked where the woman was going, and when I turned back to tell Hailey I didn't feel much like doing it and that I only wanted to leave—since she shattered me heart and all—she was gone." His eyes moistened. "I just wanted to get as far away from her as I could, but when I searched the room for a few minutes to tell her I was leaving—even though she probably wouldn't have cared if I stayed or left—I quit looking and met me mates at the pub."

Addie's mind raced from one thought to another. One thing she knew from her father, who had been a NYC detective, and from Marc Chandler was that the police didn't ask too many questions they didn't know the answers to. They simply wanted people to confirm what they already knew. This meant they were aware that Hailey saw the woman wearing the necklace Tony had given her, and this fact opened up so many other questions for them.

"Did you come straight here after being released?" She glanced at the wall clock, which showed the time was going on four. "It doesn't sound like that should have taken up most of the day?"

"Nah, they made me sit in a little room for hours. Then that Detective Sergeant feller—Davis, yeah, that's his name—well, he came in and said I was free to leave. I went home, showered, and came here. I just left there an hour ago; ya can ask me mum. She had to drive out to the barn to collect me and bring me home."

"They must have been checking your alibi and talking to your friends to see what time you joined them at the pub Saturday night."

"My alibi? Does that mean I was a suspect?"

Her text alert pinged, and she grabbed her mobile. "It's Tony. He's been released."

"And Hailey?"

"He doesn't say," Addie said, getting off the counter. "But I'm going to need you to stay and lock up today." She slipped off her apron. "I have to get to the manor house to find out what's going on."

"But I gotta meet me mates at the pub. I guess if the coppers went round to talk to 'em like ya said, I might owe 'em a pint or two for their trouble."

Addie leveled her gaze on him. "I'm sure your mates will still be there when you close up here, won't they, since it seems to be their second home."

"Aye, but it's not every day the coppers call ya in to help solve a murder, is it? Me lads will want to hear all about it."

"You mean, you didn't stop and tell any of them on your way here?"

His mouth opened, but no words came out, but she could tell by the flicking in his eyes that he was trying to think of what he should say so as not to wind her up.

"That's what I thought." Addie shook her head,

picked up a dancing Pippi, and tucked her under her arm. "We'll see you at nine tomorrow morning, won't we?"

Jasper reluctantly nodded and jerked his head toward the back. "Is the old man going to raise bloody 'ell about me not coming in now too?"

"No," she said from the doorway. "No, he's not here, but"—she made a V with her fingers and pointed from her eyes to his—"you'd better not let him down and close early, though."

Chapter 12

The bike ride down the country road to the manor was more like it had been when Addie first arrived in West Yorkshire. Miles and miles of dry-stone walls bordering narrow twisty roads, and gnarled trees and little barns dotting hilly fields as far as the eye could see. She drew in a deep breath and relished the scents of sweet grasses mingled with wildflowers that lingered in the air. It was truly a bike ride that invoked her idyllic image of the quiet rural life in England she'd always dreamed of.

The fact that she didn't have to weave her way around villagers vying for the manor's temporary jobs allowed her to recapture that dreamy state of gentle country living. That was, until she approached the main gates of Milton Manor and her little daydream bubble burst.

She certainly hadn't expected the throngs of

lookie-loos congregated at the closed gates, no doubt hoping to catch sight of the elusive lord and his young bride, whose visitation was clearly still causing a stir among the locals. Addie pushed hard on the pedals and went past the locked gate, gave a cursory wave to someone who called her name, and zipped along the road until she reached the end of the high stone-and-iron fence that surrounded the manor's front gardens. She hung a sharp left and headed up the bridle path that ran by the moor and along the front of her cottage.

In tune with the optimism of her current mood over Tony's release, Addie decided that, since she had to take the long way around, the trek from her cottage through the woodlands to the manor would be just what Pippi needed in order to stretch her legs after a long day cooped up in the bookshop. She, on the other hand, decided that she'd stretched hers enough on the ride home and let Pippi know that in no uncertain terms, and she struggled to keep up with her exuberant little friend on the footpath leading to the manor's kitchen door at the rear.

"Miss Greyborne! How good it is for these old eyes to see you again," cried Mrs. Ramsay, Tony's cook from back in Pen Hollow, Massachusetts.

"I told you Saturday night that you hadn't seen the last of me." Addie chuckled and pinned an excited Pippi under her arm as the little dog tried to get to Mrs. Ramsay for the treat waiting in the woman's pudgy hand.

Mrs. Ramsay grinned and held out her hand, and Pippi snatched up the morsels of bacon.

"Hi, Amy." Addie gave a little finger wave from her hand under Pippi's belly. "I didn't know you were coming from the States with Mrs. Ramsay and Mrs. Bannerman."

"I'm glad I did come; someone has to keep an eye on this one." She grinned and jerked her head in Mrs. Ramsay's direction. "The way Cook there's been hoarding them bacon slices left over from breakfast service, you'd have thought she was expecting you." Amy laughed and dumped the vegetables she'd been chopping into a bubbling pot on the stove.

"You just never know who might come through that door and be hungry for a bite," said Mrs. Ramsay, wiping her hands on a kitchen towel.

"Like this morning," chirped in Amy. "Mr. Radcliff came in that way, but he didn't stop to eat, did he?" She looked at Mrs. Ramsay, who shook her head.

"No, he didn't." Mrs. Ramsay's eyes filled with concern. "But can you imagine the master himself coming in through the kitchen like a scullery worker and then telling me and Amy here to pretend we didn't see him as he snuck upstairs?"

"Did he say anything else?"

"No, but I knew wherever he'd been couldn't have been good. He did look like the dog's breakfast, didn't he?" She glanced over at Amy, who confirmed her words with a nod.

"Maybe he just wanted to shower and change before he spoke with anyone else?" suggested Addie.

"Could be. He was looking quite a bit better when he came back down, wasn't he, Mrs. Ramsay?" Amy stirred the bubbling pot and turned the heat down.

"He was, but you know as well as me, Amy, that back home he would sit a spell and have a coffee with us instead of just passing through, barking out orders, like he did when he left again."

"He went out again?" Addie paused at the end of the large central cook's table which also served as an island.

"He did," Mrs. Ramsay scoffed and muttered a few words Addie couldn't make out as she sprinkled flour over the island top. "You know, here, everything's so darn topsy-turvy. I never know if I should be bowing to him or curtsying, like that Mrs. Howard woman told me I should with his lordship." She banged a lump of dough on the counter. "All I know is I'll be glad when that whole lot leaves for London, and me and Amy can get back to Windgate House."

"Yes, things are done very differently back at the Radcliff family estate, aren't they?" Addie gave a supportive smile, even though a queasy uneasiness settled in her stomach. "Did Tony, er . . . Mr. Radcliff say where he was going when he left again?"

"No, I assumed to pick up Miss Granger, though, since she wasn't with him when he came in."

"But he didn't say anything specific?"

"No." Mrs. Ramsay pinned her gaze on Addie. "What's happened that you're not telling me?"

Was it possible in a village where news spread like wildfire that Mrs. Ramsay didn't know? "Has Mrs. Bannerman said anything to you or have any of the other staff mentioned what happened to Tony and Hailey yesterday?"

Mrs. Ramsay placed a hand on her hip and curiously stared at Addie. "No, nothing. After the weekend, Mrs. Howard let all the extra staff go and assigned me and Amy the breakfast and lunch shift, and—"

"And also dumped all the dinner prep on us," Amy added from the stove. "We're exhausted, with no breaks." She waved a large serving spoon in the air. "Then she has her cook, Mrs. Stewart, along with her three kitchen helpers, come in to finish off the dinner *we* started." Amy slammed the spoon on the counter.

"We've hardly been out of this kitchen long enough to take a breath, let alone keep up with the goings-on." Mrs. Ramsay snorted.

"Well." Addie glanced from one disheveled woman to the other. "Maybe you're looking at it all wrong," she said, with a hint of optimism in her voice.

"What do you mean?"

"Perhaps it's a compliment and not a punishment. Maybe Mrs. Howard has overheard that his lordship and his guests prefer your cooking over Mrs. Stewart's?"

"I never thought of that." A soft smile clung to the corners of Mrs. Ramsay's lips. "Do you think so?"

"I know that I, for one, have appreciated the taste of American food since you've been here, but it's what I'm used to. Maybe the Londoners, who are used to having a wide selection of ethnic foods at their disposal, are enjoying the not-so-typical British food too?"

"Yes, yes," said Mrs. Ramsay, punching the dough ball on the table. "Maybe you're right." Her round face lit up with a widening grin, but then she scowled. "But I suppose that's why neither of us has heard anything about what happened. Are you saying my boy is in some kind of trouble?"

"It certainly looks that way," said a clipped, crisp voice from the shadows.

Addie's heart plummeted at the sight of the dour-faced woman, dressed head to toe in a uniform of black dress, stockings, and shoes, standing in the kitchen doorway. "Mrs. Bannerman, I didn't know you were there." Who was Addie kidding? She never knew where the housekeeper was or when she'd show up. Addie had convinced herself when she first met Mrs. Bannerman, back in Massachusetts, that the way the housekeeper could silently appear and then disappear proved she was an ethereal spirit or something.

The woman's disdain-filled gaze flitted from Pippi and locked on Addie. "Miss Greyborne, live animals are not permitted in the kitchen."

"Which is why I am keeping a tight hold on her." Addie gestured to Pippi, locked in the crook of her arm, and forced a smile though her tightening jaw. This was exactly the confrontation she had managed to avoid since the woman's arrival last week, and she cursed the fact that today she had been caught and cornered.

"What's happened to our Mr. Radcliff?" Mrs. Ramsay crossed her herself.

"I was just coming to inform you that Mr. Radcliff will be in attendance for dinner. However, after the trying past twenty-four hours, he will be taking his meal in his private suite. Please inform the evening staff to make up a tray and take it up to him." She started to turn to leave, and Mrs. Ramsay slammed her hand on the dough ball.

Mrs. Bannerman eyed her over her shoulder. "Was there something else, Mrs. Ramsay?"

"There most certainly is." She moved toward the housekeeper, her ample chest heaving. "I raised that boy too, just like you did, and I want to know what kind of trouble he's gotten himself in, because the way everyone's acting, it must be pretty serious."

Mrs. Bannerman's face softened with Mrs. Ramsay's heartfelt words. "Yes, yes, you have, and you deserve to know." She proceeded to explain what had occurred on Saturday night, as indicated by Addie's discovery of the body on Sunday morning. She repeated the questions the police had asked all the guests and had started asking staff, which, ultimately, had led to Tony's release from custody.

"They haven't talked to me or Amy yet."

"I'm sure they will, after they've finished questioning those who were upstairs throughout the evening."

"I was," piped in Amy.

"You were?" asked Mrs. Bannerman, in disbelief.

"Yeah, I had to take buffet pans up throughout the evening. They were emptying as fast it took me to replace them. I spent the whole night between here, the back stairs, and the ballroom. I think I used that old dumbwaiter more than it's been used in a hundred years."

Addie tucked a restless, growling Pippi tighter under her arm. "Did you happen to see a woman wearing a red-and-white-flowered cocktail dress on any of your trips to the ballroom?"

Amy's eyes widened. "I did—why? Did she steal something? I wondered about her, the way she was skulking around."

"No," said Addie, "she—"

"She's dead," said Mrs. Bannerman abruptly. "She's the woman Miss Greyborne found out on the moor."

"You're kidding?" Amy tottered a step backward and leaned against the sink. "Ten to one it was that Mrs. Howard who killed her."

"What do you mean?" asked Addie.

"I saw Mrs. Howard that evening. She looked like she was taking a keen interest in the young woman."

"How do you mean?" Mrs. Bannerman pinned her beady, birdlike eyes on Amy.

"I saw her. The first time I went to refill the trays. The young woman walked by the buffet table, and Mrs. Howard was watching me, to make sure I did everything to her standards, but then the young woman walked past her. Mrs. Howard turned pure white. After that, every time I went upstairs, she was within about ten feet or so of that dead woman, just watching, staring at her and popping those little mint candies she always eats in her mouth, ya know, like she was nervous about something."

Mrs. Bannerman raised a displeased brow. "Why did I not notice this?"

"It was when you were at the door, checking invitations and taking coats. Mrs. Howard was monitoring the staff in the ballroom then."

Mrs. Bannerman nodded. "Yes, it would have had to have been then."

"Then you must have seen her when she arrived?" said Addie.

"No." Mrs. Bannerman shook her head. "I don't recall anyone wearing a red-and-white-flowered dress. Although there were a few guests that arrived in larger groups—friends of Tony's, they said—and had been to the house before, so they took their own coats to the parlor. She might have been with one of those groups."

Addie looked at Amy. "Do you have any idea why Mrs. Howard took such a keen interest in this woman? You did say she skulked around. Did you get the impression she was there for another reason than celebrating the engagement?"

"Like to rob Mr. Radcliff or his lordship?" piped in Mrs. Ramsay.

"No, it was more like she was there to watch someone herself."

"Anyone in particular that you could see?" asked Addie.

"She seemed to keep pretty close to that group from London who came up with his lordship."

"When you say watching them, could it have been because they were her friends and she just wanted to keep them in sight, so she didn't feel . . . I don't know, alone, or—"

"No, it wasn't that kind of watching. It was more like spying, you know, all secretive. Like the way Mrs. Howard was keeping an eye on her. I'll tell you, Mrs. Howard sure didn't like something about the woman. No siree, I could see it in her eyes."

"Amy," said Addie, "you do know that you will have to tell the police about this, right?"

"I will when they ask. I learned a long time ago not to go borrowing trouble from the likes of the police, and me coming forward about Mrs. Howard can only lead to trouble, if you know what I mean," said Amy, going back to her pot on the stove.

"You can't wait for them to come to you," snapped Mrs. Bannerman. "This is too important. Did you not see Mr. Radcliff when he came in this morning? The poor man is beside himself with all this. He was released, but the woman he loves was left sitting in a jail cell because she doesn't have an alibi."

"She's right, Amy. This might not be an alibi for Hailey, but any information the police have that show there are other suspects to consider can only help her case, right?" Addie crossed her fingers behind her back and gave an uncharacteristic conspiratorial glance to Mrs. Bannerman.

Amy looked up from the pot she'd been stirring, set the spoon on the counter, and met Mrs. Ramsay's encouraging nod. "Okay," Amy said, her voice growing stronger. "To heck with what Mrs. Howard thinks or does to me. I work for Cook here. So I'll do it, for our Mr. Radcliff."

Chapter 13

After their shift was done, Mrs. Ramsay and Amy kindly offered to take Pippi for a walk so Addie could talk to Tony. She slipped the tray, painstakingly arranged by Mrs. Stewart, into the dumbwaiter and raced up the two steep flights of stairs to meet it. Addie crossed her fingers that the antique elevator wouldn't pick that moment to break down.

While she waited for the dumbwaiter to make its journey to the second floor, Addie couldn't help but ruminate over how Mrs. Stewart and her staff took over and presented Mrs. Ramsay and Amy's cooking as if it was their own. Perhaps she'd been wrong when she told Mrs. Ramsay that the lord and lady preferred her cooking to Mrs. Stewart's. Maybe it was as she'd feared: Mrs. Howard was punishing Tony's American staff for him inserting them into Mrs. Howard's household.

The dumbwaiter clunked into position, and when Addie opened the door and slid the covered plates out, she decided that even if she had to force-feed Tony, he was going to eat this meal prepared with Mrs. Ramsay's love. She took another whiff as she headed for his suite, and her growling stomach approved of the smells wafting up from the tray.

"Dinner is served!" she called out, as she swept into his suite and set the tray down on a table by the window.

Addie's fears about Tony not having an appetite were set aside a short while later when he pushed a cleaned plate away and asked if there was dessert. She retrieved a side plate of fresh fruit and a small container of sweetened whipped cream from the tray. "There," she smiled down at him as he perched on his chair at the writing desk. "This will help keep your energy up as we figure out who we can ask about Hailey's whereabouts for the two hours in question." Addie poured their tea. "Is there anyone you can think of whom she might have told where she was going or who would have seen her upstairs in her room? A chambermaid perhaps? Someone must be able to vouch for the fact that she had a headache and went to bed early, like she told you she did."

"I don't know who we can ask," he said, taking a cup and saucer from her hand. "It's like I told the police. I can't vouch for her whereabouts since I was in the library with you and Robert." He took a sip from his cup and stared helplessly over the rim at Addie.

She pulled a chair over from the sitting-room area in his suite. "And I certainly can't since I was upholding your alibi."

"Which is why I'm sitting here now and Hailey's not."

Addie took a sip of her tea. "We have to think, Tony. If she was mad enough at you, for, as she believed, deserting her, that she stomped off and went up to bed, she must have said something to someone, right? After all, she's spent enough time in Moorscrag over the past year to have made friends in the village. Someone she would have confided her frustration with you to."

"I can't think who. She has her university friends and some friends through her work back in London, and they've been up the odd weekend. Although, when we got back the RSVPs, none could make it for the party, other commitments and all. We told you about her maid of honor, Vickie, and her ill father, the count." He took another sip and shook his head. "Aside from you, I can't think of anyone in the village that she feels particularly close to."

His words tugged at Addie's heart. How sad that such a lovely person as Hailey Granger had not one friend at her own engagement party. She wished she'd known that others beside Vickie hadn't been able to attend. She would have taken more care to spend time with Hailey throughout the evening. As much as Addie had felt like a stranger in a strange land Saturday night, it must have been worse for Hailey. Then to have been deserted by her one constant, Tony; it was no wonder she'd feigned a headache and left. She must have felt alone and isolated when it was supposed to be her party.

Addie took a deep breath and then shuddered. Friends? Oh dear. How in the world was Addie going to tell *her* friends that she couldn't go back home? Not until she was sure Hailey was out of danger. No, that was not a conversation she wanted to have. She and Tony had to get to the bottom of this, and quickly. Addie had a flight to catch that weekend or she'd be facing something far worse than Mrs. Bannerman's condemnation. She'd be facing the wrath of Serena Ludlow.

"Okay, so," said Addie, pacing the large room, "according to what you told me, the police spoke to the chambermaid assigned to Hailey's wing, but she didn't see Hailey enter her suite that night, correct?"

"That's what I overheard." His gaze followed Addie as she continued her pacing. "It seems Mrs. Howard went upstairs and told all the maids they could go down and enjoy the music in the ball-room from the servants' door, with strict orders, of course, to make certain they didn't interfere with the serving staff's comings and goings or she'd put them to work doing jobs she knew they weren't trained for."

"Mrs. Howard." Addie snapped her fingers and paused. "I completely forgot what Amy said today," she cried excitedly and retook her seat. "It seems that Mrs. Howard took a keen interest in our mystery woman."

"What do you mean?"

Addie recapped what Amy had told them in the kitchen earlier and then sat back, grinning. "So, you see, we have another suspect to give the police. Hailey wasn't the only one at the party who was disturbed by her presence."

"What are you talking about? Why would Hailey be disturbed by this woman?"

Addie opened her mouth and snapped it shut. She had forgotten to tell Tony what Jasper had said. "I guess I didn't fill you in on a few details I've learned while you . . . well, while you were indisposed."

"Clearly you haven't. As I said, why would Hailey have been disturbed by this woman?"

Addie told Tony what Jasper had shared. She repeated the part about the new copy of *Wuthering Heights* he'd given Hailey and how she graciously thanked him, but returned it, and how when the woman passed by them, she became upset. "Don't you see? She must have recognized the necklace the woman was wearing, the one we spotted in the picture as being the same one she'd lost."

Tony's face turned from its usual country-air robust coloring to a sallow gray before Addie even finished getting the words out. "Do you know what that means?"

Addie swallowed hard, afraid of what he was going to say.

"It means the police do believe Hailey had a strong motive for wanting to see the woman dead."

"Which is why we have to tell them about Mrs. Howard," Addie said. "According to Amy, she followed the woman around the room all evening. That is something they need to know, and soon."

"Except Mrs. Howard never saw the necklace I gave Hailey for our anniversary, so she was following her for another reason. Perhaps she didn't think she fitted with the crowd and thought she had crashed the party or something." Tony set his saucer down with a clatter. "Was it Jasper who told the police about Hailey becoming upset by the sight of this woman?"

"Yes, but that's not information you can expect someone to keep to themselves, is it?"

"No, I suppose not. It's just that it really makes it look worse for Hailey . . ."

Addie lowered her head. "And here I thought, when I heard what Amy had to say, that we had another suspect to offer up to the police. I guess I never thought about Mrs. Howard not being able to recognize the necklace and just assumed that's why she was following the woman."

Tony stood up and replicated the path Addie had taken around his suite. "Now we have to find out if anyone saw Hailey go to her suite and then did not see her leave again. It seems to be the only way to get her off a murder charge, because, if nothing else comes up, that's exactly what will happen tomorrow."

"There is also the fact that the necklace originally belonged to Mollie Pressman. I think if we can find out—"

Tony stopped pacing and stared at Addie. "Who in the world is Mollie Pressman?"

"Oops, forgive me." Addie slid down into her chair and looked sheepishly at him. "I learned some really important things while you were in custody, and they're all just swirling around in my brain right now. I guess I need a crime board to help keep everything straight."

"Forget about the crime board. Just tell me from the beginning what you know about Hailey's necklace."

Addie took a deep breath and repeated what Mr. Pressman had shared about his daughter, Mollie, and how the necklace was a family heirloom. "So, you see, she'd worn it every day since he gave it to her on her eighteenth birthday, but when they discovered her body on the moor by Haworth, it was gone. Just like it was with the woman I found."

He shook his head. "It can't be the same necklace. How would it have ended up in an antiques shop in Leeds twenty years later?"

"Perhaps whoever killed Millie sold it and eventually it turned up in the antiques shop, where the owner was unaware of the necklace's history. Or maybe the necklace was stolen from the thief at some point. But that really isn't the point here. What's important is that the necklace is linked to two women's murders, so we have to find out why and what makes it so special to someone that they would kill twice for it."

Tony raised his head and leveled his gaze on Addie. "I'm going with your second theory. If whoever killed Mollie twenty years ago was in possession of it all those years and it was stolen from them, that person must have been quite surprised to see this mystery woman wearing it and was willing to kill again to get it back."

"This means that Mollie's killer of twenty years ago may have been at the engagement party."

"Yes, I suppose that's what it does mean."

Chapter 14

Addie propped her chin on her hand and tried to focus on the scribbles she and Tony had spent the night jotting down on the makeshift crime board they'd created on the backs of pieces of engagement gift-wrapping paper.

As midnight had drawn closer and after hours of spinning their wheels reviewing everything they each knew about the murder, it had become clear they were going to have to set up a crime board. After tiptoeing through the manor, searching for sheets of paper to write on, and settling on the discarded gift wrapping, they had set up their board. Secretly, of course. They had decided that until they had a better idea of what and who they were dealing with, their side investigation would remain between them, especially as there was a high possibility that the murderer was a guest at the manor.

The growing light outside the window cast a soft

golden glow over the distant moor, and Addie realized it was no use. She was done. A pang of jealousy gripped her when she glanced over at her furry little friend snoring softly from her improvised bed bedside the fireplace—a soft warm bed of blankets Amy had arranged for Pippi last night after she'd walked, fed, and given her a dish of fresh water. A bed, food, and water, preferably water filtered with coffee and a touch of steaming cream, was exactly what Addie needed right now. How in the world was she ever going to make it through her shift at the bookstore today?

"Tony, are you asleep?" she quietly called to the backside of the figure stretched out on his sitting room sofa.

"No, I wish I was, but . . ." He flipped onto his side and stared at her with haunted eyes. "My mind won't turn off. I can't believe Hailey has spent another night in jail for a crime I know she couldn't have committed."

"Then we have to prove it."

"Isn't that exactly what we've been trying to do with all that?" He waved his hand erratically toward the wall beside the fireplace, where they'd taped up the bits and pieces of paper.

"Yes, but so far, we've only focused on Hailey, who could give her an alibi, who else might have a motive for killing the mystery woman, and who else knew about the necklace."

"What else is there?"

"I still think we need to go back to the beginning, even before Mollie Pressman died, and find out more about how Mollie's mother came into possession of the necklace."

"That's got to be over forty-five years ago."

"I know." Addie rose and tapped her finger on a line they had written about the history of the necklace. "But as we've determined, there are two young women, twenty years apart, who were both in possession of the same necklace. Both murdered and both found dead on the same moor only ten miles from each other. And in both cases, the necklace may have vanished with the killer."

"Right, and we know in our hearts that Hailey didn't kill this latest woman."

"Or the one before her, given it happened over twenty years ago."

"Yes, given the age, it would have been impossible," said Tony. "So, unless Hailey read about the first murder and set about copycatting it, she couldn't have murdered this current woman, could she have?"

"No, but someone did. My guess is that someone was the same murderer in both cases and not a copycat."

"How can you be sure of that?"

"A copycat killer would have had to do some planning and research, be familiar with the first case, and plan the second one, right down to the woman wearing the same necklace that night. Since no one at the party seemed to know who she was, it seems more of a spur-of-the-moment killing. There was clearly no planning involved, because no one knew ahead of time that she was going to be there. She wasn't on the guest list, and who would know that she would be wearing the necklace?"

"Unless it was like a blind date."

"What do you mean?"

"Say she met this copycat killer online, and they arranged to meet at the party. They needed a way in which to recognize each other. She said she would be wearing a sapphire-and-diamond necklace, and he said . . . well . . . then he said that he would be wearing . . . whatever. A few guests and staff the police interviewed did mention that this mystery woman appeared to have been looking for someone in the crowd."

"You're right. I can see why you're a gothic mystery writer, because that's an angle I had never considered." She faced Tony, who was now sitting up and staring at the makeshift crime board. "And perhaps one that requires some exploration."

"By the police, right? We can't go hacking into someone's computer or online dating sites."

"No, of course not. They have the resources to check her phone and computer history and to follow up on anything suspicious. I really don't want a hacking charge on my record. I'll run this theory past Meg to see what she thinks, and then she can take it to DS Davis."

"Okay, so now we're back to what we can do legally in our investigation, and I agree with you. Since we've exhausted all the what-ifs around the murder, our obvious next step is to go even further back and find out more about Mollie's mother and the history of the necklace."

"Yeah, because there must be something about it that can explain why there are"—she tapped the board under where she had written *Mollie* and *mys-*

tery woman—"two women who both met their end on the moors of West Yorkshire."

"As it stands, it all sounds like something right out of one of my novels."

"At least someone's novel. Remember, where Mollie's body was discovered wasn't far from the area on the moor by Haworth, which served as the inspiration to Emily Brontë's *Wuthering Heights*." Addie reread the notes they had made. "Creepy, isn't it? Almost like someone picked that location because of the book." She looked over her shoulder at Tony. "Or am I seeing something there because of what we went through with Lord Bentley regarding your limited edition copy of the book."

"Probably, but all that aside, the moor makes a perfect place to murder a person or, at least, dump a body, and these two women weren't the first ones to be found on one in Yorkshire. The entire area is quite desolate, and the chances of anyone stumbling across a body are slim. When they do, it's generally years later, and the case has turned cold, making it harder for the police to solve. Most likely what Mollie's and the mystery woman's killer thought, but they hadn't counted on Brontë fans searching for Thrushcross Grange or a dog walker coming across a woman in a red-and-white-flowered dress so soon after."

After the all-nighter Addie had with Tony and the crime board, she had been so sleep-deprived that she wasn't certain how she even made it through her shift. Thank goodness, the murder had caused such a stir throughout the region that locals and tourists alike were swarming into Second Chance Books and Bindery, looking for every gothic novel and Golden Age whodunit written. Stock disappeared off the shelves faster than Addie could ring up sales and Jasper could restock. The frenzy of the day had certainly made time fly by, so much so that Addie hadn't even had time to call Mr. Pressman to make sure he was okay after he'd left a message on the answering machine saying he wouldn't be coming into the shop.

When Jasper finally turned the door sign to CLOSED and switched off the main overhead lights to reinforce the fact that they were indeed closed, the sudden crash of adrenaline made Addie's knees wobble, and she knew she'd have to muster the last of her willpower to pedal her bike home to her bed.

Success in her journey led to another crash of adrenaline as she grabbed Pippi from the carrier basket and stumbled through the door, her mind set on one thing and one thing only: sleep.

Her thoughts were jolted by incessant text-notification pings coming from the phone in her backpack. She fished it out and noted ten missed texts and a phone call from Serena. "Ah, not now, my friend, I can't. I simply can't deal with people right now." She dropped her phone on the kitchen's butcher-block island and filled Pippi's dishes with kibble and water. For a fleeting moment, she debated filling the kettle, but let it sit empty. Sleep was what she needed. Sweet, sweet sleep.

Her phone rang out another call and noisily vibrated on the countertop. She glanced at the screen, stared at the contact image she'd saved of Serena, and groaned. Then she plastered a smile on her face and pressed Accept Call.

"Hi there, how—"

"Hi there? That's all you have to say after ignoring my texts and calls all day. I was starting to think you went and got yourself arrested, right alongside Hailey."

"No, as you can see"—Addie scanned the phone around the cottage kitchen—"I'm home, all safe and sound, but why in the world would you think I was in jail?"

"I assumed that inspector you seemed to tick off the other day decided he'd had enough of your interfering ways and locked you up. You know, you're not in Greyborne Harbor, and not everyone is as tolerant of amateur investigators as Marc was."

Addie fought the eye roll that caused her left eye to twitch.

"What's wrong with your eye?"

"Nothing, so what's up that you had to call and text me all day? I was working, if I can remind you."

"I just wanted to check in and make sure you're leaving this murder investigation to the professionals, and you'll be on that plane home on Sunday."

Silence filled the air.

"Addie, you still are coming home on Sunday, aren't you?"

"Welllll . . ."

"Addie?"

"It's just that since I was the one to find the body, and Hailey is still the prime suspect, and Tony, who is a dear, dear friend, is completely beside himself, and—"

"I'll take that as a no, you're not."

"Yeah." Addie winced. "I guess I'm not, now that I hear it out loud like that."

Chapter 15

Despite having aroused the wrath of Serena Ludlow, Addie had slept like a baby. She had never been more secure in her decision to postpone her trip back to Greyborne Harbor.

She showered, brushed her teeth, and dressed, repeating over and over in her mind that this postponement was different. It was about making a wrong right. While people—and her conscience—could have argued that this was just like the multitude of other excuses that had cropped up during the past year, she knew that wasn't the same. She could not leave with a dear friend under the suspicion of murder, and she definitely couldn't leave Tony to pick up the broken pieces of his heart if it all went south and the very worst ultimately happened and Hailey was found guilty by the courts.

As her coffee brewed, she leaned her elbows on the windowsill facing the moors. No, this had nothing to do with her not wanting to go home to face a past that could never exist again. She had come to terms months ago with the fact that she wasn't who she thought she was, and that someone else back home wasn't who she thought he was either. She might never achieve her own happy ending, but by staying to see this situation through, she could bring about a happy ending for two people she cared for deeply.

By the time she placed Pippi in her basket carrier and set off for the bookshop, everything about her recent decision had settled into an inner peace she hadn't felt in a long while. "You know, Pippi, I'm starting to think that, deep down, I don't want to go back to Greyborne Harbor."

Pippi let out a woof.

"I know it seems crazy. That's where my life is . . . was, I guess. My house is still there, my bookshop, my friends, but so is a past that can't be changed, and I'm kind of liking this new present I've created based on the new me. What to do, what to do?" She drummed her fingers on her bike handles as she sailed around the corner from Moorshead Road onto Crooked Lane.

"Mornin', Addie," a cheery voice called out.

Addie gave a quick wave back to Mrs. Hawthorn, who was setting the sandwich-board sign in front of her antiques shop.

"Good morning." Addie waved and yelled as she flew past Ginny sweeping the sidewalk in front of the post office. Still smiling, Addie hopped off her bike, secured it to the planter box in front of Second Chance Books and Bindery, paused in the doorway, and surveyed Crooked Lane. Yes, she could take comfort in the decision to postpone her return yet again to Greyborne Harbor. "Sorry, Serena," she whispered, entering to the jangle of the overhead bell.

"Mornin', Addie," Jasper's voice drifted down to her from the top of the rolling ladder.

She opened her mouth to give him her usual rebuke in this situation, but quickly snapped it closed again when she spied Mr. Pressman standing at the bottom, taking a book from the boy's hand. "Good morning," she called and dashed behind the sales counter, set Pippi down, and proceeded to quickly exchange her running shoes for flats.

"Here, let me get these out of your way," she said, joining them and picking up the pile of books that lay at Mr. Pressman's feet. As she secured them under her arm, she read the cover titles. "*The Canterbury Tales, Grimm's Fairy Tales, Mary Poppins, The Tale of Peter Rabbit?*" She gasped. "All these are first or early editions. Is this what's been sitting up there collecting dust all this time?"

"As you can see, me dear, we're finally getting to them."

"Yes, but I never saw them on any of the inventory sheets, and they are worth a fortune to the right buyer. They need to be front and center in a window display."

"Exactly why they are seeing the light of day now, me dear," Mr. Pressman said, steadying his gaze on her. "Ye see, we're running low on inventory, and there's not enough in the coffers to order what we need to restock in the general and popular-fiction areas. Those are the big money-

makers with the tourists." He took another cloth-
bound book from Jasper's hand and glanced at
the title. "These, as you said, are worth a lot to the
right buyer when they come long, not the daily
shopper."

Addie's heart plummeted. "We're broke?"

"Not actually broke," Mr. Pressman said, "just
short a wee bit on disposable dosh to keep our dis-
tributor happy." He reached up to take another
book from Jasper's hand. "Nothing to worry
about, though. It's a temporary situation that we
can make right as rain with these."

Jasper shrugged his shoulders and passed Mr.
Pressman a copy of *Black Beauty.*

Addie recalled that Mr. Pressman had said he
would clear out his thirty-year stockpile of classic
books one day, but the fact that he now said it because there were money problems didn't sit well.
Business had been good this past year. He seemed
to get enough requests for book restoration and
rebinding to keep him happy, but then again, she
had no idea what the numbers actually were. Perhaps it was something she should have been managing for him. He did have a habit of taking up
and setting off to London on buying trips whenever the urge struck him. Had this last trip and the
crate of classic books he'd returned with put them
in the red with the bank and their creditors?

"Are there any books you recently purchased in
London that we could add to this classics collection for the window display?"

"Aye." He snapped his craggy fingers. "The
books from London. I forgot." He headed off toward the back room without another word.

Jasper climbed down and eyed Addie. "Da ye think he's okay?"

"I'm sure he's fine." Addie laid her hand reassuringly on his arm and smiled. "I know the news about the young woman found on the moor last weekend brought back some bad memories for him, but the fact that he came in today, and early at that, is a good sign, I think."

"Except," Jasper leaned closer to her and whispered, "he called me Mum at seven this mornin' wanting to know why I was late into the shop today."

"Oh dear." Addie eyed the doorway Mr. Pressman had disappeared through. "Perhaps I'd better go and check on him."

"Ye do that. I'm going to the bakery to get a coffee and something ta eat. Me Mum rushed me out the door, saying how much Mr. Pressman must depend on me since he made a point of calling for me to come in early. I didn't have the heart to tell her that he's been acting odd all week, taking off, not saying where he was goin' or not showing up at all. Now he says the shop's broke, and we have to sell these dusty old books to pay the bills. I hope there's enough dosh fer me wages." Jasper was mumbling as he headed out the door.

"Here it is," Mr. Pressman called from the back. "I told ye I had something special for ye, and I finally found it in the crate—buried on the bottom, of course—but take a look at this." He grinned mischievously, holding out a book covered in brown and beige.

Addie finished locking the rolling ladder in place and looked at the image on the dust jacket, which depicted an Egyptian scene. Her heart skipped a beat, and she shuddered, trying to catch her breath. "Oh my goodness, this looks like the dust jacket on the first edition of Agatha Christie's *Death on the Nile.*"

She flipped to the copyright page. "It is. Look, it was printed in 1937 by Collins Crime Club in the UK."

"That's not the best part. Go back to the title page."

Addie flipped back a page, her eyes narrowing as she read. She snapped her head up and stared at Mr. Pressman. "This Anita mentioned here can't be my grandmother, can it?" She looked at the cover again and back at the inscription. "You said you found this in a shop in London, so how can that be?"

"How many Lord and Lady Bentleys are there?"

Addie steadied herself against the bookshelf behind her and reread the inscription.

> *Our dearest Anita, here is a simple reminder of our first shared adventures, save the murder, thankfully. Her Ladyship, my young son, and I shall always cherish the time we spent together under the Egyptian skies. We are forever hopeful this was only the beginning of a lifelong friendship and the first of many adventures we four rapscallions might share.*
>   *Fondly, Lord and Lady Bentley and Robert*

"It has to be for Anita Greyborne," said Mr. Pressman. "I've told you she was a regular visitor to Moorscrag over the years she lived in England. I al-

ways assumed she came to speak with my father because of their shared love of books; she was con-
stantly bringing him ones she'd come across in her
travels for him to restore or repair. Now I see that
she came across our wee shop when she was a guest
at Milton Manor under Robert's father and mother,
and that's how her and my father's friendship
grew."

"Were she and Robert's father, you know . . ."

"Oh no, me dear. Anita made it very clear, not
only to me dad but to all the lads in the village,
that she wasn't interested in anything other than
travel and books."

Addie thought about what she knew about her
grandfather David's death, and she understood
how easy it would have been for Anita to wall up
her emotions. It was something Addie very nearly
did herself after she lost her David. If it hadn't
been for her move to Greyborne Harbor and the
friendships she had developed with Serena and
Marc and then Simon, she might well have ended
up like her grandmother. Who was she kidding?
She was thirty-six and still single. Maybe her and
Anita's paths and futures weren't entirely different, were they? After all, she had gone to England
to heal a broken heart and try to put the pieces of
her shattered life back together, just like her
grandmother Anita had. She looked at the book,
and a faint smile formed on her lips. She was more
like Anita than she ever knew.

"Can I take this? I'd like to ask his lordship
about it to see if it was for my grandmother."

"Of course, I bought it for ya. Do with it as you

please, but 'tis funny Bentley's never asked ye about yer grandmother, isn't it?"

"What do you mean?"

"Greyborne can't be that common of a name. Wouldn't he have wondered if you knew Anita Greyborne?"

"Well, it is a fairly common name in Massachusetts, and it was over sixty years ago, so perhaps he forgot about having met her. He would only have been a young boy traveling with his parents then, wouldn't he?"

"Aye, he is a few years younger than me, so he would at that. Probably forgot, he did."

"That must be it. Thank you for this, though." She gestured to the book in her hand. "It means a lot to me."

"Don't thank me yet. Let's see if your grandmother was the recipient of that book; then we can celebrate it finding its way back to you." He started for the back room but turned to Addie. "Ye know how our young Jasper is all moon-eyed for that Hailey Granger?"

Addie nodded.

"It was that way for me with yer grandmother." He gave her a wink and chuckled, then toddled off to the back room.

Addie couldn't stop the laugh that bubbled up inside her and was still chuckling when Mr. Pressman returned.

"There was one other thing I meant to tell ya."

"What's that?" Addie struggled to compose herself, but couldn't get the image of a lovestruck young Mr. Pressman following her grandmother around like a puppy dog the way Jasper did when Hailey had come into the shop.

"There was a couple of other things I'd forgotten that Mollie mentioned the last time we talked before she was supposed to come home that Christmas."

"What was that?" Addie hesitated to hear the answer. It was clear that his sudden switch to talking about Mollie meant that their conversation had opened up some deeply buried memories, and she hated to think the questions she'd asked were causing him despair.

"She asked me if his lordship was here at the manor for the holidays yet. I told her I wasn't sure, but I could check. She said no, and that she'd drop by his London offices herself and see. I asked why, and she said because she'd found something she knew he'd want to get back."

"Get back," said Addie thoughtfully. "That means it was something of his to begin with. Did she say what it was?"

"Said she'd found a book that belonged to his lordship."

"Did she say what book?"

"Not really. Only that her arriving at Haworth station was serendipitous and that I'd understand when I picked her up."

"Haworth! Does that mean she found the copy of *Wuthering Heights*? The same one Tony also came across in a bookshop in London years later?"

"She only said that she'd found it in a bookshop, and she knew Bentley wanted it back, especially since the bookshop owner gave her a description of the man who'd sold it to him a couple of months before."

"Really? She knew what the thief looked like, which means the poor maid who was accused and dismissed wasn't the thief, and Mollie had proof. Did she say what the bookshop owner told her so you could let Lord Bentley know?"

"Sadly, no, she didn't. She said she wanted to see me face when she told me who it was, and, well, we were downright giddy about her coming home. All she said after that was we had lots to talk about when she got here."

"That means no one learned what she knew before she died."

He shook his head.

"Then she said"—his eyes filled with tears— "she'd found me the perfect Christmas gift, and she knew I was going to love it. I never got that gift, though." He sniffled. "I don't know what happened to it either, because when the police gave me her suitcase she'd had with her on the train, there was no book and no gifts."

"Did they think she'd been robbed and murdered?"

"That was the thinking, I suppose, as there didn't seem to be another motive, especially since her necklace was missing too."

After Addie saw Jasper and Mr. Pressman off for the evening, she busied herself with locking up. She couldn't help but replay what Mr. Pressman had said about Mollie possibly being able to identify the book thief. If that was the real motive for her murder, then the necklace might have just been a theft of opportunity. She was dead, so why not increase the spoils by taking a necklace too. Or was the necklace the targeted theft and the book a theft of opportunity?

Either way, that meant the killer was on the train with Mollie twenty years ago and might well have been at the engagement party, as she and Tony suspected. But who, twenty years later, would have been taking that same train, who knew about the necklace being Mollie's, and who would want to kill again to keep their secret?

Chapter 16

Mr. Pressman's words rattled around in Addie's head as she walked her bike three shops down to the corner and went into the Crooked Lane Pub. Twenty years ago, Hailey would have been about fifteen. If her theory about Mollie's killer and the mystery woman's killer being the same person was right, Hailey shouldn't even be considered a suspect by the police. But first, she had to convince the insufferable Inspector Noah Parker that her theory was sound and the two murders, even though they were two decades apart, were connected.

However, it did open up another new angle. The two big questions now were who at Milton Manor and in Lord Bentley's circle today would have been around back then, and what could the motive be to kill two young women?

"Did ya hear?" cried Emily excitedly, as Addie

set Pippi on the booth bench and scooted in beside her.

"Hear what?" she asked, gesturing to Nate for a pint when he got up to get a round from the bar.

"Grab some packs of crisps too," Ginny called out to him as he disappeared into the crowd around the bar.

"Addie, didn't ya hear what I asked ya?"

"Sorry, Emily, I just had a really long day and wanted to make sure Nate was going to get me a pint too. What is it I was supposed to have heard?"

"They've identified the woman you found on the moor."

"What? Really? Who was she?"

"Ivee Hargrave," Ginny blurted out.

From the look of dejection on Emily's face, she clearly wanted to be the one to announce the news, but not one to be bested, she quickly followed up. "The maid's daughter, the one they said stole his lordship's books all them years ago."

"I bet," piped in Olivia, "she was at the manor Saturday night, casing it for more of his lordship's property to steal. Her mum probably burned through the dosh she got for all those books, and they needed to make another score."

"That might be a good theory." Addie scratched Pippi's ears as the little dog dozed on the bench. "It would explain why she was an uninvited guest at the party and no one knew her."

"I heard her mum lives in Leeds. Pretty sure that's a question that inspector fellow will be asking her."

"She's still alive?"

"Oh yeah," added Olivia. "Been there since she was sent packing from Milton Manor, as best I can recall. I wasn't that old, but I remember me Mum and Dad talking about it."

"Mmm." Addie sighed, after taking a long-awaited sip of the beer Nate set down in front of her. "Thanks, I needed this."

"What did I miss?" He took a seat beside Ginny, handed her a packet of crisps, and tossed two more in the center of the table.

"We were just talking about Fern Hargrave's daughter, Ivee."

"Ow, that's sad. I knew Fern well back in the day. The news about Ivee is going to kill her."

"Were you friends when she lived here and worked at the manor?" Addie leaned forward to hear him over the after-work din around them.

"Aye, back then, I worked as one of the gardeners on the estate." He took a gulp from his glass. "She was a good lass, hard worker, had the little 'un to support after her tosser of a husband up and left her and the bairn. I never thought she got a fair shake from Bentley neither when he up and sacked her with no proof."

"There was no proof?"

"Not that I ever heard. She was devastated. It crushed her. No one else in the village would hire her, and she up and left for Leeds. Last I heard, she got a job cleaning trains. Had to make a living with the wee one to support, didn't she?" He toyed with his pint glass. "Poor lass."

"Ya be careful there, mister," said Ginny, her blue eyes mischievously sparkling when she gave him a good-natured poke in the ribs. "I'm going to start thinking ya were sweet on her."

Nate's face pinked up, and he let out a half-hearted laugh, and from the wistful look in his eyes, Addie figured he just might have been.

Ginny didn't miss his reaction either, it seemed, and she squirmed uneasily on the bench. "I'm sure that good-lookin' copper, Noah Parker, will go around and talk to her. Maybe I should go with 'im?" She coyly flipped her head of bobbed, silver-streaked, dark hair and gave Nate an impish side glance. "Ya know, to introduce him to her, him being new in these parts and all. I'm sure he'd love the company of—"

"Ya think the bloke's a looker, do ya?" Nate returned the playful poke to the ribs, and with lips puckered, he leaned into her cheek. Ginny turned her head and kissed him smack on the lips and joined him in a hearty laugh.

Addie was about to join in the laughter when what Nate had said reared up and smacked her in the face. She forgot all about the loving couple. *Fern worked on the trains as a cleaner!*

"I have to go!" Addie gulped down the last of her pint, grabbed a startled Pippi, and breathlessly bolted out of the pub.

"Did you hear that, my friend?" She set Pippi in her basket. "The mystery woman, who isn't a mystery anymore . . . well, her mother worked on the trains about twenty years ago! She could have seen something the day Mollie was killed. Like whom she sat with or talked to. It's a lead we've been looking for. Wait until that Inspector Stick-Up-His-

Back-End and Tony hear this." She unfastened the lock on her bike.

"There she is!"

The echo of the familiar voice, a voice that should not be hailing her across the street in Yorkshire but over the phone, sent shivers through Addie, and she spun around. "Serena? Paige? What the—?" She squealed as her two old friends darted across the road toward her. "I can't believe you're really here." She grabbed them and held them in a three-way hug.

"Someone had to come to make sure you eventually got on a flight to come home, didn't they?" Serena said through tears, not letting go of the hug they shared.

"I just . . . I can't believe . . . how . . . when did you guys decide this? This is crazy." Addie seized her two old friends again and wept. "This is just the best surprise ever!"

"I know, right?" Paige laughed, her grin as big and wide as her sparkling blue eyes. "It was such fun knowing we were going to surprise you like this." Then her eyes darkened. "It is okay that we came, isn't it? Nikki and Catherine are covering the bookstore, and Mom said she'd watch Emma, so I thought," she shrugged, "why not tag along?"

"I didn't argue with her," said Serena. "Or my mom when she offered to babysit for a few days to give me a break. We—"

"Just thought, it's been a while since we three have had an adventure, and maybe we could help?" Paige timidly added.

"Yeah," said Serena. "The faster this is solved, the faster you can get home, where you belong."

"Ooh, you guys." Addie seized them both again and cried into the tangled mass of red and blond hair. "You're just the best friends ever!"

"That was good," said Serena, pushing her plate away, "and I definitely needed it after that two-mile hike from the village, but I'm afraid our arrival has spoiled your plans for the evening, hasn't it?"

"What are you talking about?" Addie asked, rising to clear the small cottage table and set the dishes in the sink.

"Weren't you going to run your latest theory past that detective inspector?"

"I was, and the timing of your visit is perfect because when I talk to him, I have to make sure I've dotted all my i's and crossed my t's. Don't get me wrong, Tony's been wonderful to work through all my far-fetched theories with, but he can't take the place of Greyborne Harbor's number-one crime-solving team when it comes to figuring out a real-life whodunit." She turned to face Serena and Paige from where she stood by the sink. "I needed you guys here for this because you keep me grounded."

"And we need you to come back home," said Serena, pouring a cup of tea from the pot on the table. "The sooner we can get this murder solved, the sooner you can be on a flight to Massachusetts."

"Speaking of home . . ."

By the time they had caught up on the day-to-day of life back in Greyborne Harbor and started to review the information Addie and Tony had collected about the murder, the evening had slipped into the dead of night. As Addie gently laid a throw blanket over each of her friends, asleep on opposite ends of her sofa, she smiled, appreciating that not much had really changed between them in spite of their yearlong separation.

The next morning, Addie called Mr. Pressman and explained she had two friends unexpectedly arrive from America and requested a couple of days off from the shop. He agreed with the promise she would bring them by sometime for tea.

With that settled, the next step was approaching Tony for a favor. Once Addie had explained the plan to head to Leeds to speak with Fern about the necklace, he was more than happy to ask Lord Bentley about releasing to Addie the use of his car and chauffeur for the day. It was a half-hour drive, compared to a one-and-half-hour train trip, which would have left Addie and friends without transportation once they arrived in Leeds.

Besides, if riding a bike on the opposite side of the road had proven to be a challenge for Addie, then a car most certainly would, and neither Serena nor Paige volunteered, much to her relief. She needed the quickest route possible too, so she could take her information to Inspector Parker and hopefully have Hailey released from jail.

Serena eyed the long street of sandstone, terraced homes, or town houses, as she was used to calling them back home. "So, we're just going to march up to the door and ask a woman we've never met about the necklace her dead daughter was wearing?"

"I would expect we'd use more tact than that, but, yes, basically," said Addie. "We need to find out as much as we can about her daughter, Ivee, so we can figure out why she was at the manor and who there might have wanted her dead."

When the chauffeur came around the curve of the narrow road, Addie's stomach lurched. "Darn it!"

"What's wrong?" asked Paige. "Are you having second thoughts? Because it's not too late to change our minds. We could go for lunch instead of harassing a poor woman who just received notice her daughter was murdered." Paige looked hopefully at her.

"Slow down," Addie said to the driver as they approached number 22, the last known residence of Fern Hargrave, according to Nate. "I hope I'm wrong, but that looks suspiciously like Inspector Parker's car out front."

"There, you see, it's just as Paige suggested. Lunch it is. I have never been to Leeds, and I want to visit at least one tea shop while we're here." Serena's voice carried an undertone of relief.

"Pull over," said Addie, eyeing the two-up, two-down attached cottage. "You guys can stay here if you want, but I'm going to offer my condolences and see if I can pick up on anything Fern says that might explain what happened Saturday night and what she knows about a necklace that seems to have something to do with two murders."

Addie hesitantly got out of the back of Lord Bentley's limousine, took a deep breath, then another, steadied her shoulders, walked up the short path to the front door, and raised her hand to ring the bell, but jumped back when the door flew open.

"Miss Greyborne, how nice to see you. And what, may I ask, brings you here today?"

"Inspector Parker, DS Davis, how nice to see you again," she said, motioning to the car, where Paige and Serena had rolled down the side window just enough to make eavesdropping a tad bit easier. "I—we—just stopped by to offer our condolences to Fern."

"You did, did you?"

"Yes." Addie shuffled uncomfortably.

"Thank you, Mr. Tinker," said Inspector Parker over his shoulder before shutting the door. He looked over at Addie, shook his head, and motioned for her to go the street.

"Did you just call the man in number 22 Mr. Tinker?"

"I did."

"But isn't that where Fern Hargrave lives?"

A mischievous glimmer lit up his eyes as Addie struggled to think of ways of defending her actions.

"New tenant," Parker said, keeping his gaze focused on Addie.

"Does he know where Fern is now?"

"He said she was long gone before he moved in."

"That's too bad." Addie glanced at the neighbor's cottage on the left side of number 22 and spotted a face peering out from an upstairs window. "What did the neighbor on the other side say?"

"No one home. We'll come back later."

"I see." Addie glanced up. The face was gone, but the curtain was still fluttering. "Well, I guess we'll have to come back another day to get her new address so we can offer our condolences about her daughter."

"Condolences to Fern Hargrave?"

"Naturally, who else?" Addie didn't miss the snicker DS Davis tried to cover with a cough, and there was no mistaking the mischievous glimmer in DI Parker's eyes. "What's going on here? What aren't you telling me?"

"If your detective skills are what you think they are, you would know that Fern Hargrave died some months ago."

"She did?"

"She did," said Inspector Parker matter-of-factly.

"Then what brings you by?" she asked. "Or did you only discover she died when you talked to the new tenant?"

"We are hoping to get some contact information from the previous owner Fern rented from, as I have a few questions for him."

"About the necklace you thought I took off her daughter's body, right?"

"Yes, Miss Greyborne, about the necklace, for one thing."

"And did you get the information?"

"I don't think discussing an active inquest is in West Yorkshire Police Department's best interest at this time, especially since you were once considered a person of interest."

Addie's mouth dropped, but she was at a loss for words.

"How about you just leave the inquiries to the police, and then you don't have to worry about it." He shook his head as he passed her on the sidewalk to his car. "Sergeant, please see that Miss Greyborne doesn't bother Mr. Tinker or any of Fern Hargrave's old neighbors either," he said, got in his car, flashed a doubtful smile, and drove away.

"Well, I never!" Addie fumed as his gray Vauxhall Corsa disappeared down the road.

"Sorry, Addie," DS Davis said, "but you heard the inspector. You're going to have to leave now, and I'll be watching to make sure you do. My job could well be on the line here."

"Yeah, I get it. I think we're all starving anyway, so we'll go get some lunch before we head back." Addie settled in between Serena and Paige in the back seat.

"Lunch sounds great because this so-called lead sure turned out to be a dead end," Serena said.

"Not exactly," said Addie, turning to look out the limo's back window. Just as suspected, Davis was following along in his car. They reached a crossroads. One direction led to the city center and the other to the motorway. "City center please, Willis," Addie called out to the driver.

"Yes, ma'am."

The limo headed into the shopping district of Leeds, while Davis's car turned and headed off to the motorway, either going back to Moorscrag or to Hamilton and his police station.

"Okay, Willis, can you turn around and go back to number 22 again, please?"

"Yes, ma'am."

"Sorry, girls, lunch is going to have to wait."

"What's going on, Addie?" Serena squirmed and looked out the back window. "Who have you been watching, and why are we going back to the cottage where Fern Hargrave doesn't live anymore because she's, well, dead?"

"I just want to make sure that sergeant wasn't going to follow us for the rest of the day. Now we can go back to Fern's place and maybe get some answers."

"But she's dead," repeated Serena.

"I know, but when you were eavesdropping, did you hear Parker say there was no answer at the neighbors' on the other side of her flat?"

They both nodded.

"Well, I spotted someone watching us from the upstairs window. My guess is that person just didn't want to talk to the police."

"What makes you think they're going to want to talk to us?"

"Who could resist that sweet face of yours?" Addie laughed and pinched Paige's cheek as they pulled up in front of number 22 again.

Chapter 17

Addie kept her eyes on the two upstairs windows, searching for any sign of movement, looked at Serena, and crossed her fingers when they reached the door. "Ready?"

"I don't know. I'm not sure what to say?"

"Well, we are all American," whispered Addie. "We could pretend to be lost."

"Good plan," said Paige, reaching around Serena for the door buzzer, but before she could press it, the door opened.

"What da ya want?" asked a robust woman with brown, silver-streaked hair. Her gaze darted past Paige to the street and then focused on the three standing on the step. "Are ya with them coppers that I saw ya talking to earlier?"

"No. No, we're not," Addie said quickly.

"As a matter of fact," added Serena, "they told

us to leave the area, so they wouldn't be happy to find out we're back."

"Then why are ya?"

"I understand that Fern Hargrave was a neighbor of yours?" Paige asked shyly.

"Aye, she was that."

"Did you also know her daughter, Ivee?" said Addie hopefully.

"I knew Ivee. Why? What's she to you?"

"I was . . . I was the one." Addie hesitated, looked at Serena, and back at the woman and whispered, "I found her body out on the moor."

"I see." The woman's face paled, and she lowered her gaze and stepped back. "I think ye best be coming in, then."

Addie glanced around Mrs. Fenton's small sitting room and smiled at the photos of a girl who appeared to be about the same age as Ivee had been. Another one, offset behind it, caught her eye. She picked up a silver heart frame and studied the photograph. There was the same girl, and beside her stood a younger Ivee. They were laughing and had their arms draped over each other's shoulder, making them appear to be close friends.

Mrs. Fenton came in then with the tea tray, set it down on the coffee table, and glanced at Addie still holding the photo. "That would be Ivee with me Alice. They were the best of friends. Knew each other most of their lives, they did."

"It's a beautiful picture," Addie said, setting the frame back on a side table. "Your daughter is lovely."

"She is that, and if ye play ya cards right, you'll be able to meet her when she gets here from London."

"We wouldn't want to impose," said Paige, helping herself to a cookie from the tray in front of her and taking a bite. "This is delicious. What kind of cookie is it?"

"It's a biscuit," whispered Serena. "In England they're called biscuits, and if I'm not mistaken, that looks like shortbread."

"Ya would be right," Mrs. Fenton said. "Paige, sugar, lemon, or milk with your tea?"

"Milk, please."

"Serena?"

"Lemon for me, thanks."

"And Addie?"

Addie paused her visual inspection of a potted violet and shook her head. "No, thank you. It looks like Ivee was more like a family member than a neighbor." Addie gestured to a roughly depicted daisy with *Happy Mum's Day, Love Ivee* painted on the plant pot. "Did she make this for you?"

"She did, when she was just a little 'un. She and Alice liked to pretend they were real sisters, and I was their mum. This was like her second home, with Fern having to work all them shifts on the trains. She was like a second daughter to me. She and Alice even shared a flat in London after they finished college. That's how we found out that she, well"—Mrs. Fenton wrung her hands—"that our dear sweet Ivee was gone. The Met police went to her flat, and my Alice was there, and . . ." The woman sobbed into her tissue.

"I'm so, so sorry. I had no idea Alice and Ivee were roommates," said Addie.

"Aye, that's why Alice is coming back. She's bringing Ivee's belongings with her. We didn't know what else to do with them since her mum passed some months ago and she has—had—no one else."

"Wouldn't the police in London have wanted to keep her belongings since her death is under an ongoing investigation?"

"Aye, they did take her laptop, looked at the rest, said there didn't appear to be anything else that could help them, and told Alice she should keep everything, in case."

Addie didn't miss the "I can't believe our luck" look on Serena's face, and then she looked at the anguish on Mrs. Fenton's. "This must be very hard for you, for both you and Alice, having been so close and all." Addie took the teapot from Mrs. Fenton's shaking hand and guided her to a wing-back chair. "Here, let me get your tea. Lemon or milk?"

"Hey, Mum! It's just me." A voice, punctuated by the sound of a door banging in the front hallway, echoed through the house. "If ya want to give me a hand, I got some more boxes out in the car." A young woman with spiky, rose-blond hair stopped short at the sitting-room door. "Sorry, Mum, didn't know ya had company."

"Hello, me darling," Mrs. Fenton bounced to her feet and crossed the room and quickly kissed the perky blonde. "This is me daughter, Alice. Alice, these are the women who found poor Ivee out on the moor."

"We didn't." Serena motioned to her and Paige. "She did." She pointed to Addie. "We're just visitors from America, but she lives here, or did, and now she's coming home, and . . ."

"I think she got the idea," said Addie, with a short laugh. "I'm Addie Greyborne, and yes, I was the one who found your friend. I—my friends and I—are so sorry for your loss, and we came to give our condolences to you and your mom." Addie eyed the box Alice held in her arms. "Do you want some help with that?"

"Sure," said Alice, balancing the bin on her hip. "Where do ya want these, Mum? There's three more in the car, and all her clothes are still back at the flat in London."

"I'll just the pull the chair away from the corner, and ya can put them there for now. We'll have to figure out what to do with it all later."

Alice handed Addie the bin. "How did you say you knew Ivee?"

"I didn't. It's just that I live in the same village she was from when she was little and where she, well, people there still remember her and her mother, Fern, and that's where I found . . . so I thought . . ." Addie spied an ornately carved jewelry box on the top of the pile in the bin. "It looks like Ivee was a jewelry fan, like her mother, or so I've been told by some of her old friends in Moorscrag." Addie knew her about-face in the conversation had been abrupt, but with Alice eyeing her like she was expecting Addie to grow a third head or something—which, if she kept up the charade much longer, she just might—she had to think fast.

"We are very sorry to hear about Ivee, especially since she was like a member of your family, but"— Addie bit her tongue so as not to blurt out the question most on her mind—"we were—"

"We were wondering if you've ever seen this necklace before?" Serena shoved her mobile phone under Alice's and then Mrs. Fenton's noses.

And so much for subtlety. Addie flashed Serena a "What are you doing?" look.

"What?" Serena shrugged. "It is what we came to find out about, isn't it?"

"Yes," said Alice. "That's the necklace her mother left for her or, at least, told her she was leaving for her, a kind of nest egg."

"How so?" asked Addie.

Mrs. Fenton sat on the sofa. "Ya see, it's a necklace Fern told me she found years ago while cleaning the train from London. It had fallen down a crack between the seats or something. Anyway, no one came forward to collect it, so she kept it. When she had it appraised, it turned out it was worth a few bob."

"A few?" cried Alice. "It was worth hundreds of thousands. One of a kind, she was told, and it was supposed to go to Ivee when she passed."

"She's right." Mrs. Fenton glanced back at the girls and continued. "It was an inheritance like. Fern never had much, at least not worth leaving Ivee, but when she found this, it was something, right? Something to make up for all them long hours she had to work, something so the girl would know her mum really did love her."

"Ya," said Alice, "except when her mum got sick

and that landlord of ours seized everything she had in the flat and sold the necklace to pay Fern's back rent."

"It's true," said Mrs. Fenton. "Ivee tried to fight it, but the court sided with him. He didn't say nothing about the necklace, and Ivee had no proof her mum owned it since she'd only found it. Everything else the courts decided he could confiscate and sell because she owed him money. She was sick, ya see, and couldn't work. I helped her the best I could. Me husband didn't leave much when he passed, but we get by, and I tried . . ."

"I'm sure you did. It sounds like you gave Fern more than enough help with babysitting and looking out for Ivee all those years."

"Aye, but I couldn't stop her from . . ."

"From what?"

"From what she did next."

"What do you mean?" asked Addie.

"After all the money that was owed in rent was paid back, the landlord returned what was left of Fern's belongings. Since the necklace hadn't been mentioned in the court proceedings, Ivee hoped it was still there, but she searched through everything and realized the dolt had found it and sold it."

"Ya," said Alice, "she lost hope she'd ever see the necklace again. But there she was at work one night, and some woman was wearing the necklace her mother gave her."

Addie gasped. "Was Ivee a server at that restaurant on Park Lane in London?"

"Ya, we both are—were."

"So, did she offer to buy the necklace from this woman?" Addie hoped her face didn't telegraph the fear about what she thought she was going to hear next.

"Na, she wasn't going to pay for what was right-fully hers, was she? No, when the woman was leaving, she helped her put her coat on and remembered her mother always saying she should get the clasp fixed. It was easy enough to have it slip open and into Ivee's hand."

"So, the clasp really was broken," she whispered thoughtfully as she took in what Alice was saying.

It was no wonder Hailey thought that's why she lost it, at least until the night of the party. Then, she must have recognized Ivee as the waitress who helped her with her coat, and put two and two to-gether. No wonder no one came forward to say they'd found it because it had never been lost. It had been stolen by the very same woman crashing her engagement party.

"Was Ivee planning on selling the necklace?" asked Addie.

"Ya, but not right away. There was someone she said who needed to see her wearing it."

"Did she say who?"

"No, just someone from her mum's past, and she said that person would be very shocked to see the necklace again."

"But she never said who."

"Nah, and that's why I guess she went to that party out there at the manor—to rub whosever nose in the fact that she had the necklace."

"I wish there was some way we could find out who that person is."

"Why is it so important to you?"

Addie gave Alice and her mother a brief recap

of Hailey and the necklace and Hailey being arrested for the murder.

"And ya don't think this friend of yours is guilty?"

"No, she is the kindest person on the face of the earth."

"But if she saw Ivee wearing what she believed to be her necklace, then would she be kind?"

"Yes, she would have gone to her fiancé, my friend Tony, for him to take care of it."

"Maybe he did."

"No, he was with me and Lord Bentley."

"I know that name," said Mrs. Fenton. "Fern mentioned it a lot over the years."

"She did?" Addie asked.

"Yes, she used to work for him until there was something about stolen books. I'll tell you, Fern never stole anything in her life. She was set up on that one, she was."

"It's just too bad she's not here anymore for us to ask."

"If she was," said Mrs. Fenton, "we wouldn't be having this conversation. She would have still had her necklace to pass on to Ivee. Ivee wouldn't have gotten it into her head to go to the party to show off, and she wouldn't be . . ."

"You're right," said Addie. "But sadly, that's not how things played out. So now, we are trying to find the real killer because I can't believe my friend Hailey killed anyone for a necklace that Tony had just given to her the same night it disappeared. It wasn't like she'd had it for ages and it had sentimental value for her or anything."

"Yeah, it's not like it was her family heirloom," said Paige, taking another biscuit.

"No," said Addie. "There had to have been some-one at that party who the necklace meant more to, the person she mentioned to you. I just don't know how we're going to find out who that was."

"It's too bad dead folk can't talk, isn't it?" Alice said.

"Here's a business card for the bookstore in Moorscrag where I work." Addie handed Alice a card. "Because dead people can talk, so if you—"

"You mean like a séance or something?" Alice's eyes widened.

"No, no. I meant they talk to us in different ways. Like through old journals, diaries, or let-ters." Addie recalled the treasure trove of informa-tion she had learned through her Grandmother Anita's old journals as she eyed the bins of Ivee's belongings in the corner. Her fingers itched to sort through them, looking for anything that might tell them whom Ivee expected to see at the party.

Alice followed Addie's line of sight to the bins. "If there's anything in her papers, I'll let you know."

"Thanks, or if you remember something she said, which at the time didn't seem important but in retrospect might be a clue to helping us figure out who this person was at the party, please call. Here's my mobile number." Addie dug a pen out of her handbag and scrawled it on the back of the card. "Anytime, day or night, I mean it." She smiled and folded Alice's hand over the card as they said their goodbyes to her and her mother.

Chapter 18

Addie sat at one of the outdoor patio tables at her friend Olivia Green's teahouse, Tea on the Green. "You know, now that we're safely back in Moorscrag and not flying down the motorway—"

"On the wrong side of the road, I might add," blurted out Paige.

"It's not considered the wrong side of the road over here," Serena said with a short laugh.

"I just don't know if I could ever get used to it." Paige shook her head and shivered.

"Which is exactly why I ride a bike and don't drive a car. It makes it easier to swerve out of the way in one of my American moments." Addie smiled her acknowledgment at the server as she set down three cups and the pot of tea. "But, as I was saying, I've been thinking about what Alice and her mom told us."

"I've been thinking we should have gone to the

pub after that drive back on the evening rush of the motorway traffic. I'm not sure tea's going to settle my rattled nerves," Paige said.

"We can, if you want," said Addie, starting to rise in her chair. "Serena just mentioned she wanted to go to a traditional teahouse, and since we didn't make it to any in Leeds, I thought this one—"

"No, sit back down," said Paige. "This is just fine. Tea helps my nerves too. I should be alright in a minute or two."

"Are you sure?" asked Serena "We can go to the pub, if you'd rather. After all, we're not here on a sightseeing holiday. We are here to get Hailey out of jail so you"—she gestured to Addie—"can come home, where you belong." Serena sipped her tea, set it down, and looked from Addie to Paige. "But going to an authentic village pub after tea does sound good, so drink up, and we can go to the pub for a pint." She laughed at her attempted British accent.

"Even the sound of it—a pint—sounds like we're in one of those British murder-mystery television shows." Paige giggled.

"We are, if you remember correctly—with a dead body found on the moor and everything," Serena said.

"Yes," said Paige, "now it's only a matter of figuring out whodunit."

"Miss Marple would have had it figured out by now." Addie smiled at a gray-haired woman who appeared to be listening to their conversation intently from the next table.

"Just think," said Paige, scanning her soundings, "she lived in a village like this one. With a teahouse facing the village green, and all the shops running along—what did you call Crooked Lane—the high street of Moorscrag?"

"Yes." Addie glanced back over at the woman and lowered her voice. "So we have to start thinking like her too. What did you think about what Mrs. Fenton and Alice told us?"

"I guess the fact that Hailey really didn't do it seems more likely—"

"You doubted her innocence before?" Addie's voice rose, and the woman at the next table appeared to be amused by her outburst.

"No," said Serena quickly, "it's just clear now that, after hearing how the necklace made its way to Hailey and Tony, she doesn't seem like a probable suspect because Hailey is the last person Ivee would have wanted to see her wearing the necklace, right?"

"Exactly," added Paige. "If she stole it from Hailey, she's not going to say"—Paige hooked air quotes—"'hey, look at me, I stole your necklace right off your neck.'"

"That makes a lot of sense," said Addie. "If she had recognized Hailey in the party announcement in the newspaper as the person she stole the necklace from, she certainly wouldn't have been flaunting it in her face at the party."

"You're right," said Serena. "Hailey is the last person she would have wanted to see her wearing it."

"So," said Addie thoughtfully, "she must not have recognized Hailey from the night in the restaurant when she took back what she believed was lawfully hers, but she knew that someone else was going to be at the party, and that person was who Ivee wanted to see her wearing the necklace."

"Was there a guest list published in the paper?" asked Serena.

"Not that I know of. I can check with Tony," said Addie, tapping off a text.

A minute later, his reply came back.

No, a guest list wasn't published, and no date for the party was given. It only said in the newspaper announcement that a small celebration of love with family and friends would take place at Milton Manor, West Yorkshire.

"Now, that's interesting." Addie held up her phone for Serena and Paige to read.

"It's too bad dead people can't talk," said Paige. "Here I thought we might have a lead, but now nothing. How are we supposed to know who the person was?"

"Actually," said Addie, deep in thought, "we do have a lead with this. If a party date wasn't announced and there was no public guest list, Ivee knew the person who turned out to be her killer would be there."

"And was probably Mollie's killer too, right?" added Paige matter-of-factly.

"Right," said Addie, "since the necklace had been Mollie's, and Fern said she found it on the train."

"Fern probably knew who killed Mollie," added Paige, "which means Ivee may have too, and she wanted that person to know she knew."

"Do you think Fern and Ivee were blackmailing this person?" asked Serena.

"Maybe," said Addie thoughtfully, "and after Fern died, Ivee took over, and she wanted this person to know she still had the goods on them."

"That leaves us right back where we were before. Who would have been on the train with Mollie twenty years ago and also be at Hailey and Tony's engagement party?" said an exasperated Paige.

"Not exactly," said Addie. "It means there must be a paper trail somewhere. One thing we have now that we didn't have before is that Alice and Mrs. Fenton are in possession of Fern and Ivee's belongings."

"And you have me." The petite, gray-haired woman from the next table rose to her feet, clutching her handbag. "I'm Mildred Wallace and live out on 42 Crag Lane. I'll expect you tomorrow for elevenses." She brusquely nodded and set off down the road at a brisk pace before any of them could respond.

"Did that just happen?" asked Addie, taken aback as she watched the woman turn down the lane that led to the churchyard. "Did that woman just order us to be at her house tomorrow?"

Serena and Paige mutely nodded, and then Paige asked, "What in the world is elevenses?"

Addie shrugged. "I have never heard of it."

She spotted Olivia inside the tea shop by the doorway talking to a customer. She frantically waved, and when Olivia's face lit up in a smile, she started to head their way.

"If anyone knows, it will be Olivia," Addie said.

"Addie, I didn't see you come in. Sorry, I must

have been in the back. I hope Mandy has been taking care of you and your friends?" Olivia looked at Serena and Paige.

"Yes, she's been great. Olivia Green, this is my dear friend, Serena Ludlow. She's the one I told you about who runs a tea shop back in Greyborne Harbor, and this is Paige Stringer, my assistant manager slash manager of my bookstore for the past year."

"It's great to finally meet both of you. Addie talks about you all the time. I feel like I already know ya." Olivia said with a laugh. "Is there anything else I can get ya?"

"Ah, no, we're fine. I think we'll just finish up here and head to the pub for a bite of supper and a pint, but I do have a question for you."

"Sure, what's that?"

"What does elevenses mean?"

Olivia chuckled. "I take it you met Mildred Wallace?"

"Yes, how did you know?"

"Because she's the only person I can think of who still uses that term. It's an old way of saying having a coffee or tea break with biscuits or cakes, and it's usually taken around eleven or midday."

"Oh. Well, that makes sense," said Serena. "I like it, and think that's what I'll start calling my mid-morning rush back home and advertising it as"— she hooked air quotes—"'Join us for elevenses.' That should get people talking, shouldn't it?"

"I take it," said Olivia, "that she invited you round for morning tea tomorrow?"

"No, more precisely, she invited us for elevenses, and we had to have it translated," Paige said with a laugh.

"All I can say is to consider yourselves honored by the invitation. Mildred doesn't invite anyone besides the Reverend Hornsby and his parish office assistant, Mrs. Patterson, for tea these days. She is very particular about whom she invites into her home."

"That's odd. She didn't strike me as the shy or reclusive type," Addie said.

"She's not. She just doesn't like anyone in her home. She says it's because people are too snoopy, and they try to steal things from her. She wasn't always like that, but I hear it's getting worse as she ages." Olivia shrugged. "Be prepared, though. When you arrive tomorrow, she might not remember inviting you."

"That doesn't sound promising." Addie looked at Serena and Paige. "Since she seemed to be listening to our conversation and interrupted saying we had her as another lead. I thought we had found someone who was actually there and not going by second-hand information she got, like Ivee, from Fern."

"If it has anything to do with the goings-on with people in the village who worked at the manor back then, she is the person you want to talk to."

"She worked there?"

"Yeah, she was the nanny for Lord Bentley's son, Lewis. When he got too old for one, she had become such good friends with her ladyship, the first

Mrs. Bentley, that she stayed on as her assistant and companion until she passed away some twenty years ago."

"Well, I'll be." Addie sat back in her faux-wicker chair and stared off across the green. "I sure hope she remembers inviting us tomorrow, because I think this is exactly the lead we've been looking for."

Chapter 19

"It's not a far walk to Crag Lane from here. Do you want to walk, or do you want me to call Tony to see if we could have the car again?" Addie asked Serena and Paige as she finished fastening her hair in a messy top-bun.

"What do you think about one of us going up to the manor and talking to Mrs. Bannerman?" said Paige. "Since she seems to be everywhere all the time and no one ever sees her coming, she might have overheard or seen something that could point us in the right direction."

"I'd say you're braver than I am. Since she arrived from the States, I've worked like the dickens to avoid her."

"Worked like the dickens? Look at you, going all British on us." Serena laughed and continued playing tug-of-war with Pippi in the kitchen. "But

shouldn't someone stay here and look after this little girl?"

"Pippi will be just fine in my doggie tote."

"Yes, but if Mildred Wallace doesn't like people
visiting her home, I'm pretty sure she wouldn't be
too happy about a dog, even if she is the cutest
thing ever."

"You're right. I get so used to taking her most
everywhere with me, and England is such a dog-
friendly country, that I don't even think about it."

"I can stay with her. We've missed each other so
much, haven't we, girl?" Serena cooed and snatched
the rope toy away from Pippi and tossed it for her
to chase.

"Pippi is good on her own here for a few hours,
and I don't imagine our tea will take that long.
She'll be fine."

"Yeah, but I'm not feeling that great. My stomach's been acting up a bit, so it might be best I stay
here, then it would free you two up to go and talk
to Mrs. Bannerman after tea."

"So, Serena," said Paige, "are you volunteering
to stay here while Addie and I partake in elevenses
and then go and talk to the dragon lady who seems
to have eyes everywhere?"

"The way I'm feeling, I think it's for the best. Besides, you both have had past experiences with
Mrs. Bannerman at the estate in Pen Hollow, and
since I'll be here, I can look into a couple of things
I'm curious about surrounding Mollie's murder.
Like if any newspaper articles mention names of
people the police questioned back in the day.

Then we can see if they match anyone on the guest list from last Saturday night."

"Good thinking," said Addie, "and after we talk to Mildred Wallace, if she gives us anything that might help, I'll call you, and you can look it up online too."

"Sounds good, you guys go. Pippi and I will be fine."

"But if you start feeling any sicker," said Addie from the door, "you call me right away, and we'll come back, and I'll call the village doctor to come see you."

"I don't need a doctor," laughed Serena, as she darted this way and that way with the rope toy, cutting Pippi off at every turn in a game of doggie keep-away.

Addie closed the door behind her and paused on the front step, glancing sideways at Paige. "Did you find that very odd?"

"Which part, Serena not wanting to go on an adventure or her feeling sick?"

"Both."

"Yup," said Paige, "and it kind of reminded me of when she was first pregnant with the twins."

"Aye yai yai." Addie knew that, if this was the case, there would be no more putting off her return to Greyborne Harbor. Serena was going to need all the help she could get.

"I told you that, if we took a short cut across the east corner of the moor, it wasn't that far of a walk to Crag Lane from my cottage," said Addie, as she scooted over the ladder stile and down onto the lane.

Paige paused when she reached the top of the A-framed ladder. The wind played with her natural blond curls, and she pushed a dangling ringlet from her eyes, scanned the scenery, and drew in a deep breath. "I've never seen anything like it. The bright purple carpet of bell heather over the hills sure doesn't look like anything that Emily Brontë wrote about in *Wuthering Heights*, does it?"

With a tissue, Addie wiped off the dirt that had collected on her flats from crossing the moor. "Trust me, and take it from someone who just spent a winter here, the way the wind can whip up and bring in a blizzard blowing so hard that you can't tell the land from the sky is real and very much like the descriptions found in *Wuthering Heights*." She held out the tissue to Paige as she descended the stile. "Just remember, *wuthering* comes from the Old Norse term *hvithra*, meaning 'squall of wind.' In Old English, it generally means 'wild, and subject to persistent and blustery winds.' "

"Well, whatever. This time of year, though, it really is beautiful, all covered in the purple heather as far as the eye can see." Paige took the tissue, wiped the dust off the toes of her shoes, and glanced around. "I can see why you have been in no rush to come home, though."

"It is quite beautiful, isn't it, and so different from the States, but that's not the only reason."

"I know," said Paige with a nod of sympathy. "It's been a tough year on you, but"—she glanced back across the moor—"you have to admit that you've had the perfect place to heal and recuperate. Every direction you look is like a storybook." Paige pointed to the first cottage on the lane leading toward Moorscrag village proper. "Like that. I hope it's Mildred Wallace's. It looks so perfectly English, with its window flower boxes and white picket fence around the front garden," she cooed. "I'd love to see the inside of it."

As they approached the cottage, Addie checked the number on the postbox by the gate. "Sorry, this isn't it. Hers must be that one." Addie pointed next door to a whitewashed cottage that looked straight out of a fairy tale, complete with a garden filled with roses, lavender, and wildflowers, all in full bloom.

"Ooh-ooh, even better. Except what if she doesn't remember inviting us?" asked Paige, a trace of panic in her voice when Addie reached to press the antiquated door buzzer.

"I haven't thought that far ahead." Addie shrugged, "I guess we'll play it by ear." She pressed the buzzer, crossed her fingers, and put her hand behind her back.

When the door opened, Addie searched the face of the unknown, much younger woman at the door for a sign of acknowledgment of their visit being expected, but she was met with dull, expressionless brown eyes.

"Addie Greyborne and Paige Stringer for Mildred Wallace," she said hesitantly, tightening the lock of her crossed fingers behind her back.

"Is it my American visitors, Grace?" called a familiar voice.

The woman presumed to be Grace scanned Addie from head to toe. "Yes, I think so, ma'am."

"Then show them in."

Without a word, the woman stood back and let Addie and Paige into the ornately decorated foyer.

On the outside, the cottage looked small but cozy and well-kept, if the flower planters under the windows were any sort of testament to the care Mildred Wallace and Grace took in their surroundings. Inside, the cottage was just as quaint and well cared for. but larger than Addie would have imagined. The ceilings and exposed beams were low, which was usual for the period it would have been constructed in, giving visitors a warm welcome, unlike Grace, who eyed the guests as though she were having an alien encounter.

"Come along, Grace," Mildred Wallace's voice resonated through the lower floor. "Bring in the guests, and then you can fetch the tea tray."

"Yes, ma'am."

As Addie and Paige hurried down the hallway behind Grace, Addie couldn't help but notice that the cottage appeared to be well-loved, as it clearly had seen better days. Some of the paint was peeling, and the occasional floorboard creaked under her feet. All that vanished when they entered the drawing room, where walls lined with shelves filled with books, knickknacks, and ornately framed photographs gave the room a cozy, lived-in feeling.

"Good morning." Mildred Wallace rose to her feet from an antique overstuffed chair and motioned to a small sofa opposite her. "Please have a seat. Grace will bring our tea along shortly, won't you?" She glared at the woman standing bug-eyed in the doorway.

"Yes, ma'am." Grace backed out of the room and disappeared.

"You'll have to excuse my housekeeper. We don't get much company these days, so strangers at the door are something of an anomaly for her, it seems."

"You have a lovely home here," said Addie, taking a seat. Her gaze darted around the room as she tried to take it all in.

"Yes," added Paige. "It's just so . . . English."

Mildred Wallace raised a brow.

"I . . ." Paige's cheeks pinked to a rosy red. "I mean the cottage is everything I imagined a cottage like this to be."

"Yes, Jane and I have similar tastes, it seems."

Addie hesitantly looked at the woman. Was this the beginning of the confused state that Olivia mentioned?

"Jane? Is she someone we know?" Addie asked and then bit her tongue. She should have just played along and not asked for an explanation. That's what she'd read to do with people who had become confused, at least.

"Yes, you know her well too, or so I assumed when you were talking about her yesterday."

Addie looked at Paige, hoping she'd see a glimmer of recollection, but was disappointed when Paige looked as confused as Addie felt.

Mildred Wallace didn't say a word when Grace returned with a large silver tea tray and motioned for her to set it on the table beside her chair. A glimmer of amusement lit her eyes as she poured the tea. "Jane? Jane Marple? You were talking about her yesterday at Tea on the Green."

Addie shook her head and rebuked herself and Olivia. Clearly, Mildred Wallace wasn't as confused about things as everyone thought. "Yes, yes, of course," she said with a laugh as she took her cup and saucer from Mildred. "And I'm afraid it's going to take Jane Marple to figure this one out too."

"As I said yesterday, perhaps I can be of some help. You wanted information about the day Mollie Pressman disappeared off the train. Isn't that correct?" She handed a cup and saucer to Paige. "Please help yourselves to lemon or sugar. I do apologize that there is no milk. I can't abide the stuff in my tea, so I never keep any in the house. I suppose, though, since we were having guests, I should have bought some. If you like I can send Grace to the—"

"No, that's fine," Addie said, waving her off. "This is fine. I prefer mine black anyway."

"Me too," said Paige as she reached over and took a square of what appeared to be lemon cake from the cake plate. "Umm, this is delicious," said Paige, covering her mouth as she swallowed. "It's made with real lemons too."

"Do you not use real lemons in America?"

"Yes, I only meant . . . Never mind," said Paige. "These are delicious." She looked awkwardly at Addie as she stuffed the last crumbs into her mouth.

"Yes, we are hoping you might have some information that can tell us who was on the train with Mollie Pressman twenty years ago?" Addie took a sip of her tea.

"Oh yes. You see, I was her ladyship's—the first Lady Bentley's—companion, back in those days, and knew all the goings-on of the household."

"Our friend Olivia Green told us you also worked as Lewis's nanny when he was a child?" asked Addie.

"She's correct. I went to work for his lordship's household when Lewis was a wee babe, a position I remained in until he went off to university some eighteen years later. By that time, her ladyship had fallen ill and required constant nursing and companionship. The nurse his lordship had hired from London was not the most agreeable of persons as far as companionship was concerned. Mrs. Howard, the housekeeper, was no better; therefore, it was decided that since her ladyship and I had grown quite close over the years, I should stay on to keep her company, which I happily did." Mildred Wallace dropped her gaze and took a long sip of her tea. "She passed away some seven years later, so I suppose you could say I was employed by the family for well over twenty-five years."

"I don't imagine," said Addie, setting her cup and saucer on the coffee table, "there are still many of the staff there from back then, aside from Mrs. Howard, are there?"

"You'd be surprised." Mildred rose from her chair, went to the bookcase, and brought a silver-framed picture of a large group of people on the lawn in front of the manor house over to Addie.

"See, here, front and center in the first row is Mrs. Howard. Here's Mrs. Stewart, the cook. Beside her on the left is Jim Bradley, the head gardener. Here I am, on the end of the middle row, beside Fern Hargrave when she was working as one of the maids before the incident with the books."

"When was this picture taken?"

"About twenty-three years ago. Most in the photograph are long gone from the manor or the world of the living now, but some, including the ones I pointed out, are still there or, at least, like me, still in the area."

"And you say you know who was on the train that week before Christmas when Mollie came up from London?"

She waved her hand over the photograph. "We all were."

Chapter 20

"**D**id you just say you were all on the train?" Addie asked, not certain she had heard correctly.

"Yes." Mildred Wallace cradled the framed photograph in her arms as she returned to her chair.

"The people you pointed out or everyone in the picture?"

"Everyone, at least as best as I can recall." She glanced down at the photo, smoothed her hand sympathetically over the glass, and handed the photo across the coffee table to Paige, who was craning her neck to get a glimpse.

"You see, for the last few centuries, the Baron and Baroness have always given the household staff two days off the weekend before Christmas. In the old days, when staff lived in, they didn't see their families very often. They would use those days to go home and spend time with them before the manor's busy Christmas social season began. In more recent years, of course, very few staff live in, and most are from the village and live with their families or see them regularly. So it's become sort of a group shopping trip to Leeds or London. I believe the term people use is 'team building.' "

Addie nodded and studied the image of Fern over Paige's shoulder.

"We would all vote on Leeds or London for that year's excursion, and all the staff would draw names as to who our roommates for the two nights would be. Mrs. Howard, being the head house-keeper, would book us all into a reasonably rated hotel. When I worked there, his lordship, as a bit of a Christmas bonus, would pay for the train tickets, and off we'd all go for a weekend of Christmas shopping and sightseeing."

"And this was done every year?"

"Oh, yes. I know that, for the twenty-six years I was employed at the manor, it had been a high-light of the year, and everyone looked forward to our little pre-Christmas getaway. Before her lady-ship took ill, the days leading up to Christmas and the week following were always filled with house parties, so it was our last time to enjoy ourselves before the Christmas season took hold with all the parties and festivities his lordship and her ladyship would plan."

"Fern was working as a train cleaner the year Mollie was killed, right?"

"That's true. The poor girl had to move to Leeds after that horrible event. No one in the village or the surrounding area, even in Haworth or Hamilton, would hire her once word got out she had been accused of stealing from his lordship."

"Did you see her during that trip on the train?"

"I did. We even spoke, caught up, you know. I always did like the girl and never thought she was capable of what she had been accused of."

"Did she ever tell you who she thought was behind the book thefts?"

"She indicated she might have a theory or two, but she was pretty tight-lipped about it all. She told me she couldn't come forward without more proof, but"—Mildred leaned toward Addie and Paige—"she did say Mollie had actual proof. She had a copy of *Wuthering Heights* with her that day. Fern had seen it herself in Mollie's satchel, but when Fern asked her about it, Mollie just smiled and told her if she was right, it would prove Fern didn't steal the books because she had proof about who really did. Fern was beside herself with that bit of news is all I can say."

"I bet she was." *Wuthering Heights?* The skin on the back of Addie's neck prickled. It couldn't possibly be the same copy that Tony had found in a south London bookstore twenty years later, could it? What were the chances that it had turned up in London twice and had made its way back to the manor, only to disappear again and be found two decades later? "But she didn't tell you who Mollie was talking about?"

"No, I don't think she knew for sure. I was under the impression that Fern only suspected someone at that point. I think, from what I recall Fern telling me, she and Mollie planned to meet for a few minutes when the train got into Leeds so they could compare notes, but, to my knowledge, that meeting never occurred because, after that day, Fern was none the wiser about the identity of the real thief."

"Fern was supposed to meet with Mollie when they got into the station in Leeds?" asked Addie.

"That was my understanding, but when we arrived, the weather had turned, and in a very short time, heavy sheets of sleet came down, and with the wind"—she shivered—"some poor woman took a tumble on the platform, and Fern and other staff were racing around to help and call the paramedics. Then they announced overhead that the train to Haworth was leaving early on a different track. They wanted to get out before the weather made the rails impassible, which meant Mollie didn't have time to talk to Fern that day. After that, well, we all know what happened, don't we?"

"Did you see Mollie get on the train to Haworth?"

"I didn't myself, although a few of the others from the manor said they did. Then, when she was reported missing, and later after her body was found on the moor not far from Haworth, the police did track down a number of them to find out what they saw, but, well, to be honest, I'm not sure I saw Mollie get on the train. I know she was supposed to, that's what it said in the newspaper, but I didn't see her, and it's an hour-and-a-half train ride with lots of stops." Mildred shrugged. "Perhaps she got off somewhere and got a ride the rest of the way. I can't see how anyone could have killed her on the train, removed her body, and left it on the moor. I read that her father was at the station to pick her up, but she didn't get off. Surely, she couldn't have just disappeared into thin air, could she?"

"What about the necklace? Was Mollie wearing it when you saw her on the London train?"

"I don't know. It was a wintery day, and everyone was wearing jumpers and scarves and such. She might have been."

Addie reached for her teacup, took a sip, and played out what Mildred said. "So at the time of everyone being on the train, you think that Fern only suspected who the guilty person was, is that right?"

"Yes, more cake?" She offered the plate of lemon squares.

Addie shook her head. "No, thank you. Did you ever see Fern again after that trip?"

"Yes, every time I went to London."

"Did she ever say anything more about it? Who she suspected? Did she see anything out of the ordinary occur that day between Mollie and another passenger? Did she have any idea what happened to the book or the necklace?"

"No, but Fern did seem like the cat that ate the canary after that horrible day. It was like she knew a secret none of us knew, and she wasn't going to tell."

"I see, but she never came forward with a name, so clearly Mollie never shared it with her, and she didn't ever find the proof herself to clear her own name." Addie motioned to the framed picture Paige held. "Would it be possible for me to take a picture of this so I can show it to Tony Radcliff to see if anyone besides the current staff you mentioned happened to be at the party last Saturday?"

"I suppose so." Mildred fidgeted in her seat and rubbed her hands together. "But do you really think it's someone in that photograph who killed Mollie? I knew all those people, and there's not one of them that seemed like a murderer to me."

"It has been nearly twenty years since you worked with them. Time can change people," said Paige.

"I know, but that still means one of them committed murder all those years ago, and I just can't see it."

"It's the only thing that makes sense at this point, since both women were wearing the necklace and were found on the moor and the necklace was gone."

"Do you happen to have a picture of this necklace?" asked Mildred.

"Yes, here. Does it look familiar to you?"

She shook her head. "I've never seen it before. And that's the one you say Mollie was wearing the day she died too?"

"Yes, apparently it was a family heirloom passed down by her father to her mother, then when Mollie turned eighteen her stepfather, Mr. Pressman, gave it to her."

"Reginald Pressman is her stepfather? I never knew that. I always assumed he was her birth father. I knew her mother, Julianna, but not well. The others said she was such a sweet girl that when she just up and left one day without a word, it seemed odd. She'd been well-liked, but next I heard, she was married to the bookseller, and they had a beautiful baby girl. I used to chat with her when I went into the bookshop to purchase books for young Lewis."

She gazed off across the room and then looked at Addie. "As enjoyable as it's been to reminisce, may I inquire as to why you are looking into a murder that occurred twenty years ago? Do you really think it has something to do with that young woman who was found on the moor?"

Addie shifted uncomfortably in her seat and looked at Paige, then at Mildred. "I'm sorry, I thought you knew. That woman who was killed last week was Ivee, Fern Hargrave's daughter."

"I had no idea." Mildred sat back and stared at the tea tray, as though deep in thought. "Yes, yes, I can see why you think it's going to take Jane Marple to solve this one and why you had so many questions about Fern and Mollie." She locked her gaze with Addie's. "It's clear whoever killed Mollie felt threatened that their secret would be revealed by something Ivee had of her mother's or information she knew." A distant expression filled Mildred's eyes as she toyed with her cup and saucer on her lap. She clicked her tongue. "Yes, I would say you have your work cut out for you."

Chapter 21

Addie's thumbs flew across the small keypad on her phone. After rereading what she'd written, she shoved her phone into her handbag. "There, that should give Serena a few more names to research until we get back."

"I'm not sure about you," said Paige, as they climbed the ladder stile and headed back across the moor toward the manor house, "but I found her whole story fascinating. Especially the part about how all the barons and baronesses over the years gave the household staff the weekend before Christmas off so they could spend it with their families." Paige sighed. "It's like something right out of a Victorian novel or *Downton Abbey,* isn't it?"

"Yeah, until she got to the part about how, after times changed and the staff was more local and didn't live in, it became a 'team-building' event," Addie said, hooking air quotes.

"Yeah, but it still sounded like fun."

"It's all fun and games until someone gets murdered," Addie said, standing in the long driveway leading up to Milton Manor. "Okay, are you ready to talk to the dragon lady?"

"I can't believe she's been here a few weeks now, and you've managed to avoid her so far."

"I haven't, that's the problem. But every time I do encounter her, she still sends shivers through me. To be honest, I always thought her dislike of me came from the fact that she thought I was going to take over Tony's life in a romantic way. When that didn't happen and he and I only remained friends, I thought she would be more accepting of me. But the few times Simon and I—before my personal life imploded—visited Tony last year, when he'd have to make a quick trip back to the States, she made it very clear that she didn't accept me in any way, and I have no idea why."

"How is she with Hailey? If she's worried about another woman stealing her little boy from under her wing, she might treat her with disdain too."

"I have no idea, and Hailey has been in custody since the party." Addie shrugged as they entered the manor through the back kitchen entrance, smiled brightly at Mrs. Ramsay and Amy, and came to a halt. Paige plowed into Addie's backside. "Inspector, this is a surprise."

A very relaxed-looking DI Parker lounged against the large kitchen island, his ankles crossed, happily munching on something good, judging by the pleased look on his face.

"Ah, Miss Greyborne," he said, setting the bowl

down. "Are you in the habit of using the staff entrance?"

"Does it really matter which entrance I use? Or does me using the kitchen entrance have any bearing on why you're here today?"

"Not in the least." He stood upright, appearing thoroughly upper-crust British in his rigid stance, and met her gaze straight on. "I was only surprised by your unexpected appearance."

Addie blinked. If she didn't know better, she'd swear DI Noah Parker had an obvious tell. How had she missed it before? But there it was again when his gray eyes locked with hers. His upper lip twitched in an unmistakable example of a micro-expression. Could it be a nervous twitch, or was it like Marc's jaw twitch when he was hiding something?

"He's brought Miss Granger back!" cried Mrs. Ramsay, breaking the tension between Addie and the inspector as they stared unwaveringly at each other.

"You have! That's wonderful! Does that mean you've found the real murderer?"

"No, it only means"—his gaze shot upward for a few seconds and refocused back on her—"it only means she won't be staying in custody at this time."

"So, you're not going to even give me a hint about who you suspect to be the real killer."

He remained mute, but Addie didn't miss the ever-so-slight twitch of his upper lip. "Ah-ha! You don't have any other suspects yet, do you?"

"I'm afraid I'm not at liberty to discuss an on-going inquiry with you, Miss Greyborne."

"That's too bad," she said over her shoulder as she swept past him, heading out into the hall. She paused at the bottom of the staircase, "because I have managed to come up with a whole list of names of suspects that I thought by now you and your constables would be questioning." Addie stifled a laugh and started up the stairs, Paige close on her heels.

When they got to the top, Paige grabbed Addie's arm. "You'd better have a good reason for brushing off and being so rude to that gorgeous police inspector."

"Looks are only skin-deep, and he's not as easy on the ears as he is on the eyes, let me tell you."

"What are you talking about?" Paige puffed. She struggled to keep up with Addie as they crossed the grand foyer to the main staircase. "He has that dreamy accent that I, for one, could listen to all day."

"I'm not talking about his accent when I say he's not easy on the ears. I mean he's rude, arrogant, pigheaded, overconfident, condescending, conceited—"

"You've managed to list off a whole page in a thesaurus that all mean 'The lady doth protest too much.' " Paige gave Addie a playful poke in the side. "Why don't you just admit you like him?"

"I do not. Didn't you hear what I just said?"

"I did, and I don't believe you somehow. When you talk about him, you get that cute little flush on your cheeks, and you were clearly flirting with him down in the kitchen."

The main doors to the manor opened behind

them, and Hailey and Tony came into the foyer from the front garden.

"You, I'll deal with later." Addie half-laughed, half-growled at Paige under her breath and pasted a radiant smile on her face for the couple. "Hi, Hailey and Tony. We heard the good news and were just coming to find you."

"Hailey needed a walk and to get some fresh air, so we were just in the garden."

"I bet you did need to stretch your legs, you poor thing," said Addie, giving Hailey a hug. "I don't think you've met my friend, Paige Stringer. She's the manager of my bookshop back home in Greyborne Harbor. She came over with my other friend, Serena, whom you'll get to meet later. She's keeping Pippi company while we were out doing some sleuthing—"

"Did you get any leads?" asked Tony excitedly. "The faster we can get Hailey's name off the top of the prime suspects list, the better I'll sleep."

"Yes, they still think I had the strongest motive. There just isn't any direct evidence, so until something concrete turns up, I'm at least out of the cells."

"As a matter of fact"—Addie squeezed Hailey's hand—"we have had an interesting few days, and I do have lots to tell you."

"Then you have come up with some leads?" said Hailey.

"Yes, and just as I suspected, there seems to be a strong connection between Mollie Pressman's murder twenty years ago and Ivee Hargrave's recent one."

"The necklace, right?" asked Hailey. "That's what the police were focusing on when they were questioning me. They seem to think I killed her just to get the necklace back."

"I think now it might have had something to with that copy of *Wuthering Heights*."

"You're kidding," said Tony. "How did you find all this out?"

"Yes, Miss Greyborne. Please tell us how you found all this out," snapped DI Parker as he strode across the foyer. "Were you aware that withholding vital information in a murder inquiry is against the law here in the UK?" he said and pulled out his mobile phone, tapped in a text, and then opened a door off the foyer and poked his head inside. "This room is vacant. We can have a little chat in here. Miss Granger, Mr. Radcliff, I won't need anything else from you today. Miss Greyborne, please." DI Parker gestured for Addie to enter.

Paige started to follow Addie into the small sitting room. "Just Miss Greyborne for now, thank you," he said, waving Paige off and motioning to one of two wingback chairs in the foyer. "I'll ask you to have a seat over there. DS Davis will be along shortly to take your statement," he said, closing the door before Paige could respond.

"That was rude," said Addie, staring in disbelief at him. "You just closed the door in my friend's face. And what about that text you sent? Are you getting an arrest warrant because you think I'm withholding information?"

"No, but may I remind you, Miss Greyborne, I am in the middle of conducting a murder inquiry in the home of a British lord, whose prominent

London guests have let it be known, right through to the halls of Parliament and all the way up to the top levels of Scotland Yard, that they are not pleased about being held captive in the Yorkshire countryside while I conduct this inquiry."

"They've been complaining to Parliament, you say?" Addie's voice squeaked.

"Yes!" he said, his gaze steady as he peered down at her.

There was no way around it. Addie was rattled. Her arsenal of witty comebacks completely evaporated as soon as DI Parker's face came close enough to hers for her to take in the musky amber scent of his cologne.

Sunrays through the room's diamond-shaped, leaded windows reflected in his fog-gray eyes, which blinked back at her from under thick, dark lashes. His wavy, silver-streaked hair created a halo around his head. Her bearings spun, which didn't help to stop the fluttering sensation in her chest or the racing of her heart. He licked his lips, and when they parted, she held her breath, not able to escape the feeling that he was familiar to her. A hot flush rose from beneath her blouse and crept up across her cheeks. She swallowed hard to try to release the catch in her throat.

He cleared his throat, and her daydream bubble shattered.

"Now, if you would be so kind as to take a seat and tell me exactly what information you think you have uncovered that leads you to believe this murder is related to a twenty-year-old case." He gestured to a sofa under the window. "Please also elaborate on the part where you have been interfering in a police inquiry and why you think it isn't against the law to do so." He smugly sat down in a chair opposite her, pen poised over a notebook.

Now Addie knew why he had seemed so familiar, right down to the set of his jaw and the shadowy stubble on his chin. He was the British version of Marc Chandler. "Tell me, Inspector, do you have a rule book you follow?"

"I beg your pardon. Of course, there is an English rule of law that I am bound to follow as a police officer."

"I don't mean the actual laws of the country. I mean your own personal book of laws or rules you follow when investigating a case?"

"Would they not be one and the same?" His eyes reflected his confusion.

"Never mind, it's just that a friend of mine back in the States is a chief of police and has a rule book he follows that is separate from the actual laws of Massachusetts."

"That sounds like a Wild West movie to me."

"Yes," she said, a smile tugging at the corners of her lips. "I guess he is a bit of a cowboy."

He shook his head, mumbled something about Americans, and tapped his pen on the notebook, indicating he was waiting.

Addie stared at her hands clasped in her lap, shifted in her seat, and relayed to the inspector what she had learned over the past few days. "So, you see, Inspector, the necklace that Ivee Hargrave was wearing the night of the engagement party is the same necklace that Mollie Pressman's stepfather, Reginald Pressman, gave her. It had belonged to her mother and was a gift from Mollie's biological father, and she was in possession of it when she was murdered twenty years ago. All we have to do is compare the list of names of those who were on the train when Mollie was murdered with those who attended the party last Saturday, and we have our killer."

Noah Parker sat back in his chair and studied Addie. "And you just happened to find this out today from"—he glanced down at his notepad—"Mildred Wallace?"

"She filled in some of the blanks, but most of the information came from Mrs. Fenton and her daughter, Alice. They used to be Fern Hargrave's next-door neighbors and were very close to her and Ivee."

"Mrs. Fenton, the same neighbor I warned you not to bother?"

Addie shrugged. "What can I say? We dropped by to offer our condolences on the loss of her friend, and she just filled in some of the blanks about what happened back then."

"Does that mean you were already working on the premise of the two murders being connected?"

"You might say that."

"Would you care to explain to me how you came to that deduction?"

"Well, it all started when Mr. Pressman recognized the necklace in a photo I had from the party."

When Addie had finished explaining what Mr. Pressman had shared with her, she opened her mouth to add one more point, but quickly snapped it shut again. The fact that Mrs. Fenton and Alice were now in possession of Ivee's and possibly some of Fern's personal belongings was one card she was going to keep close to her chest. If she shared this information with him, he likely would take the boxes into evidence, and poor Alice would likely lose her last connection to her best friend, especially if the journals she mentioned were in those boxes. She might not ever see them again.

Addie sat back, satisfied in her decision. After all, she had updated him on everything else she'd learned. He wasn't stupid, and he would follow up on the leads she'd uncovered. The Fentons would tell him about the journals, and he could decide what to do about them. It would at least give Alice more time to spend with her friend before her last memories were snatched away and locked up in some dusty old evidence room, never to be seen by Alice again.

Chapter 22

Addie searched Inspector Parker's face as he silently read over his notes and couldn't help but agree with Meg Gimsby. The inspector was easy on the eyes. It was only too bad that when he spoke, his true nature was revealed, and he became the most disagreeable person she'd ever met.

She recalled reading an article a few years ago about body language, specifically the seven micro-expressions and how to spot them. The paper went on to explain that these expressions were unlike regular facial expressions, which lasted up to four seconds. Micro-expressions, on the other hand, were rapid-fire, unconscious facial movements related directly to the subject's emotions, regardless of what they were otherwise exhibiting or saying, and could last as briefly as a half second, so the observer had to be quick to see them, and she believed she had been.

Not that she had been studying his chiseled jaw line or noticed how, when his lips pulled back in a smile, it brought out a small dimple on each cheek. Nor had she noticed his habit of running a hand through his silver-streaked hair when he was deep in thought, as he was currently. No, this was purely scientific observation.

He was standing in her way of investigating all aspects of this murder as efficiently and quickly as possible so she could return home to Greyborne Harbor. She needed to hurry this investigation along and have Hailey's name dropped from the list of suspects, and in order to do that, she needed to know her roadblock, aka Inspector Noah Parker, and why he was so fastidious and incapable of trusting anyone else to do the job. And what did it have to do with his reasons for leaving the Met? Never had the saying "Keep your friends close but your enemies closer" applied so well. She'd have to get to know as much about this man as she could—beyond his gray eyes, which were even more strikingly captivating when they were illuminated by sunlight.

His lip twitched. Addie couldn't help but compare it to Marc's jaw twitch when he was fighting an internal battle of head over heart or when Addie had struck a nerve with him. In this case, it was something Inspector Parker had read in his notes. She was dying to ask him what it was but didn't want to give away what she had picked up on by watching him. He'd probably go out of his way to not let her see it, as Marc had once she'd pointed out his tell.

A thought struck her. Could it be that even the fact she was sitting here thinking—no, fantasizing—about him meant her past was finally behind her, and it was time for her to move forward? Not with him, of course. He was pompous and arrogant and emotionally stunted and—well, given time, she could have thought of a few more adjectives, but she was noticing things about him she hadn't noticed about any man in a long time.

Not only had she been emotionally unavailable for the past year, but men in the village were too old, too young, or already in a relationship. It didn't hurt that Noah Parker was new and easy on the eyes. She only had to wait, however, for him to open his mouth, and every nice thought she had about him would vanish.

She edged closer to the front of her chair. Was she finally over the pain and shock of what had happened with Simon? If so, did this also mean she was indeed ready to go home? Her lips parted, and a soft gasp escaped with the revelation. Yes, and that meant no more stalling. She needed to wrap this up and get Hailey off the suspect list as soon as possible. It was time to go home, this time for real.

Parker looked up at her from under a lowered brow, snapped his notebook shut, cradled his fingers over it, and studied her. "Are you in the habit of staring at people with your mouth half open, Miss Greyborne?"

Peripheral vision—perfect—check. Fighting the urge to squirm like a child being scolded, Addie met his steady gaze. "No, I'm not. I . . . I was only wondering what you think our next move should be?"

"Our next move?" He shifted and pinned her with an astonished gaze. "There is no *our* in this investigation. I will make inquiries, and you will—"

"Don't you dare say it." Addie leapt to her feet and stepped toward him. "I was the one who found the body and the one who brought you all that information and have supplied at least a dozen more names of suspects. Yes, it's your job to interview them to see where they all were at the time of the murder, but there is also the little matter of still trying to figure out the motive, which will take you forever without my help and the connections I have within the household."

"If your theory about both murders being linked is correct, Miss Greyborne—"

"Can we stop with all the formalities, please? My name is Addie, and that's what I prefer you to call me."

"Very well then, Addie, as I was saying, if your theory is correct, I believe we already have the motive, and that is the value of the necklace."

"I have a gut feeling it's more than that, though. The murders happened twenty years apart. That must mean something, right?"

"Yes, it means that, twenty years later, the value of the gold, diamonds, and large sapphire would have increased immensely, and since there is more than one jewel thief in the UK who might kill to get their hands on such a high-valued piece, we in the police world call that a motive."

"Yes, it is a motive, but from everything I've told you—about the book thefts and that Mollie was known to have had one of those stolen books in her possession when she was killed, and it, like the necklace, miraculously disappeared, only to show up again the same night the second woman was murdered, and the same necklace disappears once again—"

"Has the book"—he glanced down at his notes—"*Wuthering Heights* disappeared for the second time since Ivee Hargrave was murdered?"

"No, Lord Bentley has it locked away in his library, I believe."

"There you go. Proof that the monetary gain from selling this necklace is the only motive in these murders, and they may or may not be linked by anything other than the would-be thief in each case stealing the necklace to sell it at a substantial profit."

"So even though I have given you evidence showing the links—"

"Correction. You have not given me any evidence, only speculation. Besides, motive alone is not enough. We need evidence that will solve Ivee Hargrave's murder. If we get lucky and they are related, as you suspect, we might also solve Mollie Pressman's too. So far, we only have conjecture."

"The way I see it, Inspector, there aren't only two murders to solve. There is also the mystery of the book thefts and finding out who Mollie Pressman's biological father is, because my gut tells me these are all related and there is one killer in both cases."

"So, until we find out the answers to those questions, we really don't know what the motive is?"

"Yes, until you know the exact motive and you're

not speculating on it being the value of the necklace, how can you be sure what the evidence you come across is?"

"The evidence would be anything that leads to the murder and solving it."

"Yes!" Her voice warbled as her exasperation won out. "But without knowing the actual motive, you don't know if a clue is part of the evidence chain, right?"

"I suppose."

"Okay," said Addie, her head spinning. This was like another go-around with Marc back in the old days. "You keep looking for evidence, and I'll get you proof of the motive, show that they are connected, and that this is about something other than a thief's monetary gain. Then we can put it all together to see what fits into this puzzle." Addie shot DI Parker a pointed glare and stormed out the door into the foyer, where she found Paige waiting for her. "I need to find Mrs. Bannerman, now." She huffed. "Do you know what that . . . that—"

"Oh dear," said Paige, racing along beside Addie, trying to keep up. "If you want to talk to her, then I'm guessing things went really badly with the inspector."

"You might say that," Addie said, pausing at the top of the back stairs leading down to the kitchen. "He is the most stubborn, obstinate, mulish, disagreeable, pi—"

Paige's eyes widened. She pressed her finger against her lips and gestured with her head that someone was behind Addie.

"Please continue, Miss—I mean, Addie—as it

was not my intent to interrupt your most illuminating soliloquy of my attributes."

"I plead the Fifth."

"You're not in Kansas anymore, Dorothy." He chuckled as he swept past her and started down the stairs.

"What . . . what's that supposed to mean?"

"You're the book merchant. I thought you'd enjoy the classics reference."

"Yes, I know the *Wizard of Oz*, but how does it pertain to what I said?"

He stopped, his foot hovering over the next step, and looked over his shoulder at her. "Do you need to be reminded that you are in Great Britain now, and we do not hold to the Constitution of the United States of America, which I believe is what your pleading of the Fifth is a reference to, am I correct?"

She nodded.

He continued down the stairs, and although he was silent, she could feel him laughing at her.

Paige slapped a hand over her mouth, and sputters of laughter escaped her fingers.

"Not you too?"

"I think I just got a good idea of why that meeting in the parlor didn't seem to go well." A mischievous glint lit Paige's eyes. "Why, I declare, Addie Greyborne, I believe you have finally met your verbal sparring match."

Chapter 23

Addie's eyes flew wide. Horrified by her friend's words, she sucked in a sharp breath. Did Paige really know nothing about her after all this time? She opened her mouth to set her straight, but when DI Parker turned right at the bottom of the stairs and headed in the direction of Mrs. Howard's office, she grabbed Paige's hand. "Come on. If my guess is right, we might only have a few minutes to get to Mrs. Bannerman before Mrs. Howard calls all the staff together to speak with Parker."

Addie peered around the bottom of the banister and could hear muffled voices coming from the housekeeper's office two doors down. The only words she could make out concerned meeting with the staff in a room large enough to accommodate them all, and Mrs. Howard suggested the morning room, which would be empty of guests. Addie turned to Paige, placing her finger over her lips, and they tiptoed in the opposite direction, toward the large manor kitchen. Once inside, she quickly glanced back over her shoulder and scanned the room.

"Mrs. Bannerman, I'm so glad to have caught you."

The woman looked down her hawkish nose at Addie.

"I don't have a lot of time to explain, but a police detective is about to call a meeting to ask all the staff some questions—"

"That, Miss Greyborne, is old news. We have—"

"No, some new information has come to light, and that's what he's going to be asking about." Addie glanced toward the hallway, motioned for Mrs. Ramsay and Amy to come closer, and whispered. "It seems there is some proof that the person who killed Ivee Hargrave also killed another young woman twenty years ago, and some of the people who were in attendance the night of the recent murder were also on the train when the other woman was murdered."

"That means the killer is still a guest in the house," cried Mrs. Ramsay.

"Or someone on staff," added Paige. "That's what we need to find out."

"All very hush-hush, of course," said Addie. "If the killer finds out we're investigating, we won't learn anything of value, and we will put our lives in danger."

Amy put her hands over her ears and hummed. "I don't want to hear anything else. I'm a horrible liar and worse at playing detective. I could never even figure out Nancy Drew books when I was a kid. No, no, not for me." She went over to the sink and kept quietly humming.

Addie looked at Mrs. Ramsay and Mrs. Bannerman. "This is important. Hailey Granger is still the number-one suspect in the murder, and that's who the police are focusing their investigation on right now; they are only looking at evidence that will convict her. We must find evidence that points to someone else. Are you with us?"

"If it's to help get our Mr. Radcliff's fiancée off, then you can count me in," chimed in Mrs. Ramsay.

"I agree," added Mrs. Bannerman. "The poor man is beyond himself with stress these days." She paused and met Addie's hopeful gaze. "I'll do anything to help our Mr. Radcliff," she nodded firmly. "Yes, it should be easy enough for me to casually make inquiries to Mrs. Howard about her movements the night of the party. Didn't someone mention she seemed interested in Ivee?"

"Yes," said Addie, "but I heard she denied it later."

"Leave it to me to find out if she recognized the necklace from twenty years ago and where she was exactly when that first young woman, Mollie, was killed."

"According to our sources," Addie said, "she was on the train with her, as were about a dozen of the manor's current staff and some of the guests now."

Mrs. Bannerman's lips pulled back in a knowing smile. Addie waited for her to say something, but she didn't. Addie looked at Mrs. Ramsay to see if she knew what was going on.

Mrs. Ramsay gave Addie a conspiratorial wink

and returned to the pot she had simmering on the stove. "You just leave it to us. We'll find out what the staff know."

From the doorway, Mrs. Howard, her gray hair pulled back in a tight bun, crossed her massive arms over her chest and cleared her throat. "All on-duty kitchen staff are to be present in the kitchen in exactly fifteen minutes."

"That doesn't make sense," said Addie. "Why would Inspector Parker want to talk to the American staff here?"

Mrs. Howard scowled at Addie. "Please be aware that this is not optional. It is a mandatory staff meeting. All outsiders and guests are asked to leave." With that, she turned and shuffled back to her office.

"What's she on about?" Mrs. Ramsay took a quick scan of the kitchen and shrugged her shoulders. "As far as I know, we're the only staff on duty now, and like you said, Miss Greyborne, we are American and weren't here twenty years ago." She tossed a potato into the pot. "That is, of course, unless Mrs. Stewart is hiding in the pantry and we didn't know it?" Laughter punctuated her words.

Addie opened her mouth, but DI Parker held up his hand.

"But—"

Her interruption was met by a harsh glare.

"DI Parker—"

He let out an annoyed sigh. "Miss Greyborne, as far as I know, you are not nor have you ever been on the staff of Milton Manor, so your reason for being present at this inquiry baffles me. Please explain."

Addie swallowed hard. "I'm acting as their union rep?" she hesitantly squeaked.

"Their union representative?"

"Yes, just think of me as a fly on the wall is all." She made the gesture of zipping her lips and leaned back against the island, allowing him to continue to address the three members of the kitchen staff who were present.

"Interesting." He eyed her skeptically from under a creased brow.

DI Parker then reassured the staff that, if there was something they wanted to report but felt uncomfortable about doing so in front of the others, they could speak privately with him later. When he asked the three staff members present if they were employed at Milton Manor twenty years ago, Addie couldn't remain silent any longer.

"I'm sorry." She choked as she waved off his look of shock. "It's just that these are not Milton Manor staff. They are Tony's staff from his home in Massachusetts, only brought over to help with the party, and they have remained while the guests have been sequestered here."

"I was a baby twenty years ago," Amy piped in.

"Perhaps," snapped Mrs. Bannerman, "that's something Mrs. Howard should have made you aware of before you wasted your time and ours." She turned toward Mrs. Howard, who was standing cheekily in the doorway. "Now, if you'll excuse us, we have work to do, unlike other staff members, it appears." Head held high, back straight, she marched past the woman, brusquely dismissing her with a flip of her wrist.

"Yes, yes, you're quite right." He directed a piercing glance at Mrs. Howard. "I should have been made aware before I wasted everyone's time here." He snapped his notebook closed. "Now, please take me to the morning room, where I assume you have the staff I want to talk with assembled?" He gestured to an unperplexed-looking Mrs. Howard, who still had a slight smile on her pudgy face when she led the way up the stairs.

"What just happened?" asked Paige.

"I'd say Mrs. Howard was stalling for some reason," replied Addie, still gazing in the direction the two had gone.

"The question is why."

"You're right," said Addie. "I think we'd better get up there to see what's going down in that room and her reaction to having all her staff together, because something feels off."

"It makes you wonder if she's protecting someone or having someone hide evidence for her while she keeps the inspector busy elsewhere," said Paige.

"Yes, yes it does." Addie eyed the door, mulling over what had just happened.

"Like we talked about before," said Mrs. Ramsay, "we'll do our part as best we can. You two go and see what she's up to."

Addie nodded at the cook and scurried out into the back hall, Paige close behind her.

"You just get our Miss Granger off those charges and see to it that that horrible woman is charged with something, if not the murder itself," called Mrs. Ramsay.

When Addie burst through the door on the main floor from the back stairwell, she thumped directly into Lewis Bentley's chest, which sent her reeling back into Paige. He let out a sharp gasp and staggered backward, clutching at the air to stop from flailing backward.

"Lord Bentley!" Addie cried and grabbed his arm, steadying him. "I'm so sorry."

He patted his chest and looked at her wild-eyed. "My father is the current lord in residence. Please just call me Lewis." He exhaled and leaned against the doorframe.

"I am so sorry. I was hurrying to get to a meeting, and . . ." Addie bit her lip and winced. "I—"

He waved off her look of concern. "No harm done," he said, slowing his erratic breathing. "I was just coming in from my daily run"—he gestured to his red running shorts and white T-shirt—"and saw Mrs. Howard ushering the staff into the morning room. She said something about new evidence in the murder and then went in and shut the door." He took a long drink from his water bottle and wiped his mouth with his sleeve. "What's that all about, do you know?"

"It seems some new evidence has been uncovered, and the detective inspector wants to talk to any staff that might have worked here at the manor twenty years ago."

"Twenty years ago? What bearing would that have on the woman who was murdered last week?"

Addie looked past him for a sign of any prying

eyes or ears and whispered, "It seems some new evidence has come to light, and this recent murder might be connected to Mollie Pressman's murder twenty years ago."

Lewis looked at her with vacant eyes. "Mollie Pressman?"

"Yes, she was the young woman who stamped all your father's library books with the black-light ink and recorded them for insurance purposes."

"Did she?" His gaze flitted upward in thought, and his eyes lit up. "Oh, yes. I do recall someone working in the library from time to time round about then."

"So, you do remember her?"

"Vaguely. If it's the young woman I'm thinking of, she seemed pleasant enough. At least she was the few times I did come across her that summer when I was up from uni with my friends." Concern filled his eyes. "And you say this Mollie person was also murdered?"

"Yes, she was, and apparently she was in possession of the same necklace that the woman who was killed the night of the party was wearing."

"Oh my. That sounds like a plot right out of one of Tony's books, don't you think? As his publisher, I should know." He narrowed his gaze and leaned in toward Addie. "Is that the premise of his new novel? A cursed necklace and anyone who possesses it dies a grisly death?"

"It very well could be since both women were killed on the same moor, only ten miles apart, and both were found at the bottom of a rocky crag."

"Hmm . . ." He stroked the graying hair covering his chin. "That is good. If he doesn't write it, I do have another author I could mention the storyline to. Let me think about it." He started up the back stair to the second floor.

"No, this isn't a story idea. It's a true-life murder," said Addie, leaning on the bannister, "and Hailey is the prime suspect because she was the last owner of the necklace before the woman who was wearing it at the party was found dead."

"And Hailey is a suspect?" He stopped mid-step. "My, my, this necklace is truly cursed, isn't it?"

"It seems that way, and"—Addie glanced over at the closed morning-room door—"the detective inspector is in there now, trying to find out which staff members worked here twenty years ago."

"Well, I can't help with that, I'm afraid. I really don't pay much attention to the staff—"

"I did have the pleasure of meeting your old nanny. You must remember her?"

"Mrs. Wallace? Is she still around?"

"She's retired now, but she lives not far from here. You never visit her?"

"That was a long time ago, and when I went off to school, she stayed on as my mother's companion for a number of years. I had little to do with her. No, Mrs. Wallace is but a blurry memory from my youth, I'm afraid. The only servant I recall, because she's been here as long as I can remember, is Mrs. Howard."

"Do you ever remember hearing about a woman named Julianna?"

"Was she on staff here?"

"Yes, I suppose she was, although I'm not sure

what she did. I was hoping someone who's been around a while could tell me."

"You would have to speak to my father or Mrs. Howard, I'm afraid. As I said, I didn't pay much attention to the staff. Now, if you'll excuse me." He motioned up the staircase. "I need to get out of my running gear and head straight into the shower before Mrs. Howard tosses me out onto the street for the stench."

"Yes, of course. I'm sorry to have detained you."

Paige stepped up beside Addie. "We have to get back to your cottage right away. Serena called while you were talking to Tony's publisher, and . . ."

"Did she find something in her research?"

"No." She shook her head and swiped at the tears that slid down her flushed cheeks. "Her father's in the hospital, and she has to go back right away."

"Oh no! What happened?"

"I guess he was building a tree house for little Ollie and Addie in that big oak in Serena's yard, and he fell off the platform."

"What? He knew Marc was going to build it for them when they got older."

"I know, and Serena's not happy. When she stopped crying long enough, she said there's no fool like an old fool, and her dad is paying the price now. He's being rushed into surgery tonight, I guess."

"Tonight? Okay, I'll call Tony to get the car." Addie whipped out her mobile phone and tapped in the number. "I hope she can get a flight back late tonight or tomorrow at the latest."

"Me too, and I think if she's in the family situation that we think she might be in with her stomach troubles, I had better go with her to make sure she's okay."

"You're right, and I'll get things tied up here as soon as I can and get back."

Chapter 24

Addie waved a tearful goodbye to Serena and Paige as they drove away in the car that Tony had arranged to take them to the airport in London. She held her pinky and her thumb to her ear and mouthed "I'll call you." Serena vigorously nodded her agreement through the back window of the limousine, and Paige brought her hands together, forming a heart, and blew her a kiss before they disappeared out of view down the long driveway.

Addie cradled Pippi in her arms, fingering the soft fur at the back of her head. "It looks like we're heading home this coming weekend, Pippi, if this case is closed or not."

Pippi yipped and whined.

"I know poor Hailey is still a suspect, but you know that we have to be there for our best friend and help with the kids. She and her mom are going to have their hands full dealing with Wade after he has pelvic and hip surgery."

Pippi whimpered softly.

"Yeah, it's going to be a long recovery, I'm afraid." She nestled her cheek into Pippi's fur. "And they're going to need all the help they can get."

Pippi woofed.

"Yes, Hailey is a friend too." She kissed the back of Pippi's head. "But Serena is special, right?"

Woof.

"Okay, what should we do now?" Addie sighed and checked the time on her phone. "Well, I'm still on a day off from work." She glanced down at Pippi. "To be honest, I don't feel much like going into the bookshop for the rest of the day, anyway. I don't think I could focus enough to work after the past few hours. The stress of the day has really taken a toll." Pippi whimpered and licked Addie's cheek.

"Yes, I love you too." Addie giggled. "Tell you what, how about we head to the pub and have a visit with Lexi? We haven't talked to her much lately, and the pub should be fairly quiet this time of day, so let's go there, okay?"

Pippi perked her ears and barked.

"At least it will be nice and cool in there. This afternoon is turning into a scorcher."

Pippi woofed again.

Addie laughed, released the kickstand, and sailed down the long manor drive through the front gate and into Moorscrag village.

By the time Addie reached Crooked Lane Pub, she felt like she had just cycled the ten miles to Haworth, not the two miles to Moorscrag from the manor. Despite the air rushing past her as she peddled, her hair was damp and stringy. She wrapped it in a high messy bun, shoved stray strands in place, checked her reflection in the window glass, shrugged, grabbed Pippi, and headed inside.

Even though she couldn't see anything but black with occasional gray shadows, she could tell by the lack of conversation that the late-afternoon crowd of regulars hadn't started to filter in yet, and she was hopeful that she and Lexi could have a pint and a chat. She had so much to tell her friend about what had happened, she didn't know where to begin. It also helped that Lexi had a head for puzzles, and Addie kept her fingers crossed that she could lend some insight into this one.

When her vision had adjusted to the muted light, it didn't take her long to spot Lexi standing beside a table. Her choppy, bright-blue-tipped hair framed her porcelain complexion, making her vivid blue eyes sparkle. It was clear from Lexi's coy expressions that she was enjoying the conversation she was having with a patron. As Addie made her way farther into the pub, she realized her friend wasn't just enjoying a conversation with an unseen patron. She was quite openly flirting with someone. *Cheeky girl*, Addie chuckled, dying to get a look at who in this village had managed to turn her friend's head, because, judging by the flush on her cheeks, she was utterly smitten.

A central wooden support beam in the old Tudor pub blocked Addie's view of the man who, from the laughter and smiles his words were inducing in her friend, must be quite a catch. Addie zigzagged around the beam and an adjacent table to get a view of the man who had turned her friend into a femme fatale, but when she came around the beam, she stopped. "Traitor!" She gasped and backed up a step. She took a quick look over her shoulder at the door to make sure she could make a clean exit.

"Addie, 'ello, luv!" Archie Craven, the balding owner and Lexi's dad, called from behind the bar. "Ya in for a pint, or is it wine today?"

"Ah, shoot," Addie murmured and headed for the bar. "Hi, Archie, I just came in to talk to Lexi, but she seems to be busy right now. So . . ." Heat crept across Addie's cheek.

"I'd say, judging by the flush on yer face, it must be hotter than Hades out there, so a pint it is then." He set a glass in front of her.

"Yeah, the heat outside, that must be it." Addie glanced over at Lexi. She knew there was a shortage of eligible men in the village, but really? Lexi really could do so much better than DI Parker. Addie shook her head, smiled at Archie over the top of her glass, and took a big gulp. "Thanks. I needed this. It is very hot today and going to get hotter, I think." She took another gulp and set her glass down. "Any chance I could get a bowl of water for Pippi?"

"Aye, of course, ya can. Here, bring her around the end of the bar, and she can have some down here by Bertie's dish."

"That would be perfect, thanks," Addie said, setting Pippi on the floor. "Pippi likes Bertie. I just don't think that big old ginger cat of yours likes Pippi half as much, though."

"Bertie likes Pippi just fine. She likes to play hard to get, that's all."

Addie glanced at Lexi again and shook her head in disbelief. "Something that other members of your family should learn, I think."

"What was that?" asked Archie, pulling another pint from the tap.

"Nothing, just mumbling about the weather." Addie gulped down her beer and started rising from her stool.

"Naw, you can't leave yet," he said, plunking another glass down in front of Addie. "Me girl's going to wanna have a good chin-wag. Been too long since the two of you got to visit. What with all the goings-on up there at the manor and all."

"Yeah, it has been a crazy time, but"—Addie looked at Lexi, who was now seated at the table with DI Parker—"I think she's going to be busy for a while, so I'll call her later, okay?"

"Drink yer other pint before ya go, lass. You'll need it for the ride back to yer cottage."

Addie wavered on her feet, looked down at Pippi curled up on the cool, stone-slab floor, and sat back down. "Okay, just this one. Then I really will be off."

"That's me girl." Archie grinned as he pulled two more pints and set them on the bar for a customer.

Addie took a sip from her glass and jerked when a waft of warm air breezed by her cheek. "Your hair looks lovely, by the way," DI Parker whispered and flashed Addie a nonchalant smile before making his way out of the pub.

Addie turned to look at the table where he'd been sitting. A jolt of shock surged through her. Of all the windows she'd picked to use as a mirror before she came in, why did it have to be the one he was sitting in front of? If only the floor would have opened up and swallowed her. She wouldn't have complained and would have sunk away quietly without kicking and screaming.

"That was a total waste of time," moaned Lexi, dropping onto the barstool beside Addie. "One new face in the village who just happens to look like that *Witcher* actor, Henry Cavill, and he couldn't care less about my best 'I'm single and available' performance. Didn't even ask me what time I got off work. Gimme a pint, will ya, Dad?" She gestured to Archie. "I think I've lost me touch." She groaned and leaned into Addie. "Can ya believe he didn't even check out these." She gestured to her chest.

Addie paused mid-sip of her beer and eyed Lexi from under a creased brow. "Just because you think some guy is good-looking, you shouldn't be okay with him ogling you like that." She set the glass down. "By the way, good-looking or not, that is the detective inspector in charge of the murder case, who is trying to railroad Hailey so he can get a quick conviction."

"I'd take a copper as a son-in-law over the likes of old Mickey there at the end of the bar any day," said Archie, setting a pint in front of Lexi. "'Cause I'm afraid if ya wait much longer, lass, he might be your only option for ya to be wed."

"Not that copper. You wouldn't want him as part of the family," Addie said, shaking her head. "He's the most arrogant, pigheaded, self-important, conceited—"

"Ya fancy him, don't ya?" Lexi cried, jumping to her feet, laughing. "Here I'm thinking he didn't fancy me, but when he leaves, I see him whisper something to you, so he fancies you too, hey? Are ya trying to keep it on the hush-n-hush, is that it?" She slapped her hand on the bar top. "See, Dad, I haven't lost it yet, so don't go picking out yer wedding togs with old Mickey just yet. I just couldn't compete with the likes of this exotic American here." She jabbed her thumb toward Addie. "Good going, girl. Ya snagged yerself a good one, and don't worry. Yer secret's safe with us, right, Dad?" She leaned into Addie and held up her hand in a high-five gesture.

Addie pushed her friend's hand down. "There is no secret to be kept because this 'exotic American' does not fancy the likes of Inspector Noah Parker, and if you are as smart as I think you are, Lexi Craven, you wouldn't be moaning over the fact you couldn't make his heart go pitter-patter, because he doesn't have a heart to begin with."

Lexi crossed her arms over her chest, pursed her lips, looked knowingly from her dad to Addie, and grinned. "What's the matter? Did he turn ya down 'cause yer not his type, if ya know what I mean? Or did ya find out he's married? Because I can't believe a fine man like him is single."

"I'm not his type, and I don't mean that the way you said it. He's just so . . . so insufferable. Now, can we change the subject? I haven't talked to you in weeks, and I have to go back to the States on Sunday, so please let's just have a nice visit."

Lexi's normal porcelain complexion turned a sickly ashen color, and she dropped back down onto the stool. "What do you mean yer going back to the States on Sunday?"

Addie tightened her tooth-hold on her bottom lip and looked apologetically at Lexi. "You know I was booked to go home after the engagement party, right?"

"Ya, but when ya didn't, I figured ya'd changed yer mind and decided to stay, just like all them other times?"

"I know." Addie hung her head and studied a nonexistent stain on her tea-green summer dress. "It's just that this time, I really was going back. I'm ready to face whatever the future there holds for me, and—"

Lexi turned her body away from Addie. "Then why didn't ya go?"

Addie cringed at the bite in her friend's voice and struggled not to respond in kind. She took a deep breath and whispered, "Because a friend was in trouble, and she needed me to try to help her, which is the same reason I have to leave this Sunday. My old friend, Serena, is in trouble back home, and she needs me."

"What about me? Did ya ever think I need ya too?" Her voice cracked, and tears formed in her baby-blue eyes. "Never had a best friend before. I was the pub-owner's daughter and must be a wild one, they said. Decent girls weren't allowed to hang out with me, and that never changed through the years. Heck, Olivia and Emily used to cross the road to avoid me. Then you came along, didn't judge, and my world changed, and so did they." Lexi sniffled.

"I'm sorry, but nothing has changed since we had this same conversation the last time I was supposed to leave. This isn't the end of our friendship, and it won't be the end of your friendship with them either. You guys have become too close now for that to happen, and I will be back to visit. I promise. You'll come to visit me, right?"

"Ya, not on my wages." She waved at Archie chatting with a couple and motioned for another pint.

"Look, as bad as I feel about leaving you and Emily and Olivia and Mr. Pressman—because I know he's got his hands full with Jasper—I feel sick to my stomach that I also have to leave while Hailey is still the prime suspect."

"I thought they'd let Hailey out of the nick?" said Archie, setting two pints on the counter.

"They did, but not because they have evidence leading to someone else, only because they have no hard evidence leading to her."

"What are the coppers saying?" He folded his arms and leaned on the bar.

"They're not saying much to me. I came up with a number of leads, and to be honest, I think Inspector Parker is too pigheaded and egotistical to follow up on any of them because they came from me and he didn't discover them."

"Ah, so that's what's got under your skin?" Lexi said with a knowing wink. "I get it now."

"No, you don't get it. That's not what's bothering me about him. It's just that I came across some valuable information that led to several other suspects, but he still thinks Hailey is the guilty one. He hasn't even questioned any of the people I suggested or followed any of the leads I gave him, which doesn't make sense because they were solid leads from credible sources. I thought he'd be thrilled to get some help from the public on this, but it seems I was wrong."

"Hmm, tell me"—Lexi grinned—"were any of the leads you gave in Leeds?"

"Yes, how did you know?"

"Because when he left, he told me he had to go to Leeds to follow up on something."

"Really? Hmm, imagine that."

"Maybe he did listen to you, but was only too stubborn to let you know he was. He kind of sounds like someone else I know, hey?" Lexi playfully jabbed Addie in the ribs with her elbow.

"Yes, but that's only one lead. There were other things I told him he should investigate."

"Like what?" Archie pulled a pint and took a swig.

"I told him I didn't think there were only the two murders to solve. There's the mystery of the book thefts from Lord Bentley's private library twenty years ago and the mystery of who Mollie Pressman's biological father was. My gut tells me it's all related, and there is one killer involved in this recent murder, and it's the same person who was responsible for Mollie Pressman's death all those years ago."

"Mollie's biological father isn't much of a mystery to those of us who were around back then."

"You know who it was?"

"Not a hundred percent, but"—Archie finished his pint and set his glass down with a plunk—"it's his lordship himself. I'd bet me pub on it."

Chapter 25

"Really?" said Addie. "You think Lord Bentley was Mollie Pressman's biological father?"

"Aye, I do." A hazy glimmer of recall veiled his faded-blue eyes as he stared off in the distance. "Her mother, Julianna, was the most beautiful woman in the entire village. Men from all over the county vied for a smile from her sweet lips, and all were mesmerized by the swaying of them full round hips when she walked. Most dreamt of having that long, ginger-blond hair of hers cascade over their—"

"Dad!" cried Lexi. She turned to Addie. "Now ya see why I was considered too common for the other girls in the village, with stuff like that coming out of his gob."

"Sorry." Archie looked sheepishly from his daughter to Addie. "I was young and just as besotted by her beauty as every other lad in the village—to no avail, I might add. We got the smiles, but . . ." He shook his head, and a somber look washed over his face. "She had her sights set elsewhere, I'd say."

"And you really think she and Lord Bentley were involved, and he was her baby's father? Wasn't he married and had a baby with his first wife then?"

"Aye, but if ya ever saw a picture of Julianna, ya'd know the bewitching effect she had on a man. Even Lord Bentley wouldn't have been immune. He was no different than the rest of us, except, well, he was posh and all." He glanced at Lexi. "This was, of course, long before I met yer mum." The top of his balding head turned as red as his cheeks, and he quickly began mopping the bar top with a sopping rag from the sink.

Addie pedalled back to her cottage, not certain if what Archie had said was gossip or the truth. It wasn't abnormal for people to gossip about celebrities or public figures such as Lord Bentley. Add to the mix a beautiful woman like Julianna, who also just happened to work at the manor, and the end result was the stuff of romance novels: the beautiful servant girl and the lord of the manor falling in love.

However, if what Archie said was true, it did sound as though Julianna may have rebuffed the attentions of most of the village men. To save face, they might have thought it was because she and his lordship were involved in a scandalous affair and not the fact that she just didn't fancy them. Egos were fragile and may have been the reason for an innocent's loss of reputation and ruin.

Even Mr. Pressman, the lucky man who eventually did win over Julianna's heart, apparently didn't know the identity of Mollie's father, or so he said. So how would the likes of Archie Craven, an ordinary pub-owner's young son back then, know for certain? But what if the rumors were true? If the two murders were connected and Mollie's biological father was the key, that meant Lord Bentley was the murderer.

"Impossible," Addie muttered.

Addie leaned her bike against the dry-stone wall at the foot of her garden, set Pippi down to do her business, and headed inside. She collected all the scraps of wrapping paper she and Tony and Serena and Paige had written clues on, laid them across her table, and started to piece them together.

Somewhere in all this was the answer, and if she was going to confront Lord Bentley about fathering a child out of wedlock, she'd better make sure she had proof.

As she placed the scraps of paper, she viewed them as a jigsaw puzzle and sorted each piece to fit with the previous one. A knock on the door interrupted her just as she thought she might have a breakthrough.

Pippi twirled in her prancy dance, something she only did when she recognized the scent of a friend.

"Meg!" Addie cried when she opened the door and glanced over her friend's shoulder. "Or should I say PC Gimsby? How nice to see you."

"Meg is fine. I've lost me shadow for the day. His dad, the chief superintendent, needed him home for a family function." She rolled her eyes as she stepped inside. "Must be nice. I wish me Dad could call in and say I had to get home because me Gran was visiting."

"Yes," Addie said, leading the way into the kitchen, "but now you can breathe easy, knowing your little shadow won't report your every move."

"That's true." Meg glanced at the table. "What are ya doing here?"

"Just trying to get a handle on what happened at the engagement party before I have to leave Sunday morning." She grabbed the kettle from the stove and filled it. "I'm going to have some tea. Will you join me?"

"You're leaving for real this time, are you?" asked Meg, her voice distant as she continued to scan the scraps of paper on the table. "What's this one about a woman named Mollie Pressman and a missing necklace?"

While Addie prepared the tea, she gave Meg a quick rundown on everything she had learned about Mollie Pressman and her murder and how the necklace appeared to be a link between the two women's deaths. "I believe somehow the necklace is what connects the two murders, and my gut tells me that Mollie Pressman's biological father has something to do with it."

"But you're still not sure who her father was?"

"No, there are rumors in the village that it was Lord Bentley—"

"You know how rumors spread in a village like this. If he is the connection, you do know he can't be the murderer, right?" She pulled out her police notebook and flipped back pages. "I have your statement saying you and Tony were with his lordship at the time of the murder and well past that, so . . ." She shrugged her shoulders, snapped her book closed, and shoved it back inside her uniform pocket.

"I know, and that's what's got me thinking either I was completely off base or he's not Mollie's father."

"Then who?"

Addie snatched a piece of wrapping paper and showed it to Meg. "Mildred Wallace, Lewis Bentley's old nanny and his mother's companion, said that all the staff was on the same train from London the day Mollie was also coming back to the village for Christmas. Her biological father could have been one of the other staff on the train too."

"Why would her natural father kill her?"

"I don't know. That's just one of the theories I'm looking at, and it could have had something to do with the necklace or the stolen copy Mollie had of *Wuthering Heights.*"

"Did she steal it?"

"No, Mollie had been hired at the manor that previous summer to mark and catalog books in Lord Bentley's library in the hopes of stopping a thief who had already stolen a few rare and expensive books. When she completed that task, his lordship got her a job with a bookbinder in London."

"Wasn't her dad, Mr. Pressman, teaching her?"

"Yes, but this was a fantastic opportunity. The bindery is one of the best in England, probably Europe, and the plan was for her to work in London a few years, then come back and work alongside her dad. When he was ready to retire, she would take over Second Chance Books."

"Does Mr. Pressman have any other children?"

"No, she was all he had. Anyway, before she came home, Mollie came across a copy of *Wuthering Heights* in a used bookstore in London; it bore the same seal she had stamped Lord Bentley's books with just the past summer. She got a description of the man who had brought it into the bookshop and was bringing the book back to Lord Bentley, along with the man's description, of course."

"You have this on good authority?"

"Yes, Mr. Pressman."

"And you think this person she got the description of might have been her natural father and the actual book thief?"

"I don't know. Mr. Pressman said Mollie only told him on the phone, before she made the trip home for Christmas, that she had a description of the man who sold the stolen book."

"But she didn't tell Mr. Pressman what he looked like?"

"No, she said she'd tell him when she got home because he wasn't going to believe who it was, and she wanted to see the expression on his face when she told him."

"So she knew who the book thief really was?"

"She must have based it on the description the clerk at the bookshop had given her. There was never any proof that the housekeeper, Fern Hargrave, was the thief when she was fired and sent packing. Perhaps the real thief didn't steal just the books from Lord Bentley's library, but also some jewelry. Maybe when he saw Mollie wearing the necklace and carrying the book on the train, he was afraid he was going to be found out."

"If your theory is right, that would mean the heirloom necklace Mollie's father supposedly gave her mother was, in fact, stolen when he gave it to Julianna and he told her it was *his* family heirloom?"

"It's the only thing that makes sense right now, doesn't it? I mean, if he worked at the manor and wanted to impress Julianna, what better way than to give her a sapphire-and-diamond necklace and tell her some far-fetched story about his family's legacy?"

"But if he worked there and was on staff, as this Julianna was, why was she forced to leave and go to Leeds to have her baby in the first place?"

"Maybe he was already married to someone else?"

Meg frowned and examined a piece of paper on the table. "I think the romantic in you is raising its head." She softly chuckled. "It's probably something far less complicated. Like someone who worked at the manor saw Mollie with the book on the train, and they knew it had been stolen, and she was wearing a necklace they had seen in pictures at the manor and thought she was the thief. There was a struggle. Mollie was killed, and the killer panicked and dumped her body on the moor after they got to Haworth."

"And that's why you're going to ace your detective's exam when you take it. That makes so much more sense than my fantastical theory."

"But we know from what Mr. Pressman told you that Mollie didn't steal the books or the necklace. We're following three lines of inquiry here. One is the theory that Mollie's father would be found out as a thief, so he killed her to keep his identity unknown. Or someone mistook Mollie as the thief, knowing the book and the necklace had been stolen from the manor and accidentally killed her, and thirdly"—Meg stared down at the piece of paper—"that person was also at the engagement party and saw Ivee Hargrave wearing the necklace that was lost on the train and thought they would be found out and charged with Mollie's death twenty years ago."

"Yes, it could be any of those theories, and proving any of them is going to be tough, especially because your DI Parker thinks it was all coincidence and that someone saw the necklace on Ivee, guessed its value, and killed her for it to sell it. He's not going to allocate any police resources to that investigation."

"But I have an advantage DI Parker doesn't have."

"What's that?"

"I've known you longer than he has, and I know you're always the highest scorer on our Saturday night murder-mystery games because your gut feelings usually aren't wrong—"

"They have been on occasion," she said, recalling her wedding ceremony almost a year ago to the day.

"I'm inclined to go with you on this one, but—"

"Thanks for the vote of confidence, but either way, we have to find out who worked at the manor roughly forty-five years ago and could have stolen the necklace back then, and look at everyone who worked at the manor the same time as Mollie had twenty years ago and compare names of staff who attended the engagement party, right?"

Addie sorted through the scraps of puzzle pieces strewn across the table and continued to feed Meg some of the information about each piece as they went through the list of names Mildred Wallace had given Addie of the staff who were working at the manor twenty years ago and cross-referenced it with who was at the engagement party.

"Now to figure out who would have been working there when Julianna did and recognized the necklace and thought they knew where it came from and how." Addie scanned the short list.

"Yes, but that also means they would be between sixty-one and eighty years old now." Meg looked at Addie. "Do you really think a senior citizen followed Ivee Hargrave out onto the moor between eleven and midnight and pushed her off the top of the crag?"

Addie shook her head. "Then my theory is completely wrong. See, you shouldn't have followed me down that rabbit hole. There isn't anyone on staff now, to my recollection, who would fall into that age range."

"Your theory is solid. The numbers just don't add up, but let me make some inquiries about some of this," said Meg, rising to her feet and grabbing her police cap from the table. "However, I think you'd better be very careful before you go accusing Lord Bentley or any of his staff of murder. Everyone I talked to has a solid alibi for the time in question."

"Everyone?"

"Yes, well, except a couple of Lewis Bentley's London friends, old mates of his from his Cambridge days, I understand, but they said they were only out on the garden smoking, and some of the other guests did see a group of them out there, so . . ." She shrugged. "But I best be off. I'll try to find out if DI Parker followed up with that mother and daughter—"

"Mrs. Fenton and her daughter, Alice."

"Right, I'll see if anything came of that, and I'll let ya know, okay?"

"I'd appreciate that, since I doubt DI Parker will share any information with me."

"I shouldn't be doing so either. It would be me job if he found out."

"I swear." Addie pulled her finger across her lips in a zipper motion.

"Good," said Meg, giving Pippi's head a scratch and left.

Addie examined the clues she and Tony had written down, compared them to what she and Serena and Paige had added, and then thought about what Meg had pointed out. How could they have gotten it all so wrong? Perhaps DI Parker was correct: The necklace didn't mean anything, wasn't a link to the two murder cases, and was only worth a lot of money to any of the thieves in Britain willing to kill for something so rare and precious.

Chapter 26

Addie rifled through the box of books Mr. Pressman had shipped from London after his last buying trip and searched for any the bookseller might have missed, appraising it at a higher value than the sales receipts indicated. "No," she said, collapsing on a bench beside the box, gesturing to the inventory list in her hand. "I think you paid exactly what you should have. I don't see any hidden gems in there that are going to help put the shop's accounts in the black."

"What about that book I gave you that I thought might have belonged to your grandmother, Anita?"

"No," Addie said. "I forgot all about it, with everything that's been going on. With my friends visiting and trying to get Hailey out of jail before I left and—" She looked at the frail, sallow-faced man and the look of defeat that had overtaken his countenance. "You can have it back. I'm guessing if you did some restoration work on it, you could sell it for far more than what you paid for it. It is a first edition," she said, trying to keep a hopeful lilt to her voice.

"Nah, me dear, that book is yers. If I'm right, it was yer gran's, and ye should have it. I just wanted to know if ye ever asked Lord Bentley about it."

Of course, the book! She could have kissed Mr. Pressman for reminding her about it. After talking to Meg yesterday, Addie had been wracking her brain, trying to figure out an excuse to talk to Lord Bentley about Mollie and Julianna. Not so much because she still thought he was the murderer. Even if Archie was right and Lord Bentley was Mollie Pressman's biological father, Addie was his alibi for the time that Ivee was murdered. She couldn't, however, shake the niggling feeling at the back of her mind that the necklace had belonged to his lordship's family and that it was the key to the two murders on the moor. She just had to figure out how.

"I'd sure hate to leave Sunday without finding out if it is inscribed to Anita by Lord Bentley's father," she said, wistfully containing her excitement over the plan she was hatching.

"Then ye best be off, lass. I overheard Mrs. Howard at the post office this morning telling Ginny the whole kit and caboodle of them Londoners are off tomorrow. That inspector fella is finished with 'em, I guess."

"They're leaving tomorrow?" Addie looked at the wall clock. There was still over an hour until the six o'clock closing, but maybe, if she hurried home right after, she could catch Lord Bentley before he dressed and went down for dinner. After that would be a waste of time, since he'd be busy entertaining his guests, especially since it was their last evening in the country. Her face must have telegraphed her impatience, because Mr. Pressman told her to go and said he'd make sure Jasper stayed and locked up the shop.

When Addie grabbed her backpack, picked up a startled Pippi from her bed, and bolted for the door, Jasper didn't appear to comprehend what Mr. Pressman told him. "But I'm supposed to be off at five, and I've made plans to meet me mates."

"Aye, and our girl there is solving a family mystery. Yer mates can wait."

That was all Addie could hear before the door closed and a delivery van rattled past. "He's right, Pippi. I might not have time to figure out who the murderer is before I go home, but I sure as heck can find out if this book belonged to my grandmother."

Addie stopped off at her cottage. She fed Pippi, gave her a quick belly rub, told her she'd be back soon, and raced along the forest path to the rear garden door. She waved a quick hello to Mrs. Ramsay and Amy as she flew through the manor kitchen and up the back staircase to the main floor, where she paused, contemplating taking the main staircase to the next floor. She promptly dismissed the notion. Dashing up the back stairs like a maniac was one thing, but the main staircase was another. She shuddered at the looks she'd receive from Mrs. Howard and Mrs. Bannerman if were to be spotted and stayed where she was until she reached the second floor—the first floor, as the British called it—where his lordship and her ladyship's suites were located over in the west wing.

When she left the stairwell alcove and came out into the portrait gallery hallway, her book clasped to her chest, a thought struck her. On the few occasions she'd actually been upstairs in the manor, it had been to speak with Tony, and her mind had always been on something else. She had never given the wall of portraits of past barons and baronesses much more than a cursory glance. What if she could find a painting with one or more of Lord Bentley's ancestors wearing the necklace?

It would be perfect, as she wouldn't have to ask him about Julianna, a topic that was none of her business and one that might open up old wounds he'd rather not speak of, especially to a stranger. If she could find the necklace in one of the paintings, she could reference it by telling him how beautiful it was and ask him if the necklace was still in his family.

If he said it was stolen, along with the books, she'd at least have one of her answers. The tricky part was going to be finding a murderer between sixty-something and eighty-plus years old who not only had the opportunity but the ability to hike out onto the moor at night, throw Ivee Hargrave off the crag to her death, and return to the party without raising suspicion. Although, regardless of age, self-preservation was a strong motivator, and if the killer felt threatened, it wouldn't have been such a Herculean task. She had to stop thinking of age versus ability and start thinking of who had the most to lose if the necklace were to resurface twenty years after Mollie's murder.

But that was only one of the theories she was working on. Addie stood on her tiptoes and scanned the closest portrait of a woman. Maybe following it would lead her in the right direction, because she really wasn't certain where she was headed as she glanced at the brass plate beneath a portrait that read LADY WINIFRED, MILTON MANOR, 1762.

There was no other reference to which baron was the woman's husband or if she herself was a baroness. Although by the looks of the dour, plainly dressed woman, Addie didn't think fashion adornments, let alone a sapphire-and-diamond necklace, had been the lady's style. Addie shivered at the cold, haunted look in her eyes. They reminded her too much of Mrs. Bannerman, and she wondered if perhaps she was a long-lost relative.

She giggled as she moved to the next portrait of a woman, but her thoughts were interrupted by someone clearing their throat. She slowly turned and came face-to-face with a real-life version of the glowering eyes in the painting as she locked her gaze on Mrs. Bannerman's.

"Hi," Addie meekly said, clasping the book closer to her chest.

"Can I help you find something, Miss Greyborne?"

"Ah, no, not really. I was on my way to Lord Bentley's suite, and something in one of the portraits caught my eye, that's all."

"I see." She glanced up at the portrait of Lady

Winifred. "However, Lord Bentley is in the study with his son, Lewis, in a business meeting, I assume. I was on my way to speak with his lordship's valet, Hubert, about the request for formal dinner attire this evening and to set out Master Lewis's formal wear, at his request, of course."

"I'm surprised Lewis doesn't have his own valet, or are you it?"

There was that look again, the one that could pierce a person's soul. Unexpectedly, Mrs. Bannerman's face softened, and her eyes took on a mischievous glint. "Shhh." She held her finger to her lips, glanced over her shoulder, stepped closer to Addie, and whispered, "I offered to lay out his dinner clothes tonight because over the last two days I have noticed some questionable exchanges between him and one of his university friends, and I want to check out something in his suite."

"Lewis's suite? Like what?" Addie asked, excitement bubbling up inside her.

"All I can say at this point is they both seemed quite interested in something Master Lewis was jotting down in a notebook, and they went to great lengths to keep it a secret. When I know for certain what it relates to, I will tell you." Mrs. Bannerman straightened and gave Addie her usual disapproving glower. "Now if you'll excuse me, Miss Greyborne"—she tapped the side of her nose and winked—"it's time for me to go to work." She clicked her heels and marched down the corridor.

"Okay then. You go get 'em, Miss Marple." Addie chuckled to herself and looked back up at a portrait of a seated, mutton-chopped, gray-haired gentleman and a prudish-looking woman wearing a dress with a high neckline standing beside him. No necklace was visible.

As Addie moved down the gallery of portraits, she realized that, after the painting of Lady Winifred in 1762, none of the ladies of Milton Manor wore much jewelry at all. Had they taken their cue of restraint in fashion and embellishments from Lady Winifred? If so, it was no wonder the current Lady Elizabeth turned and fled back to London three years ago after she and Lord Bentley were married. These portraits probably scared the bejesus out of her, and she may have seen them as a window into her future.

When she reached the end of the gallery wall, she was still in the dark about the necklace being a family heirloom, and Lord Bentley hadn't passed her on his way upstairs to change for dinner. Mrs. Bannerman also hadn't passed on her way back downstairs, which meant she must still be in Lewis Bentley's suite, setting out his dinner clothes or searching for the mysterious notebook.

If she checked in on the housekeeper, Mrs. Bannerman would think Addie was checking up on her, and she certainly wouldn't be happy about Addie poking her nose in her business. Addie shrugged, gripped her book tighter, and walked down the central staircase to the main floor. She wanted to get her conversation with Lord Bentley over with, and to make sure she didn't miss him, she planted herself in the hallway outside his study. Hopefully, she'd catch him before he went upstairs to change.

Soon after Addie had sat down in one of the two eighteenth-century French Aubusson tapestry chairs, the study door flew open.

"Both of us running this company is not working, Father. It's high time you retired, as you said you were going to five years ago!" cried Lewis, slamming the study door, cutting off his father's words. Lewis's long strides took him out the front door, banging it closed behind him.

Lord Bentley rushed into the hallway, and Addie wished she could disappear. His fingers interlocked behind his neck, he paced back and forth in front of the door. Then he stopped, drew in a deep breath, dropped his arms to his sides, and turned toward the door, his eyes coming to rest on Addie.

"Well, what is it, girl?" he snapped.

"I wanted to ask you about something."

"Can it wait?"

"Perhaps after dinner would be a better time?" Addie smiled uneasily, her fingers playing over the cover of the book she clutched on her lap.

"What's that you have in your hand?"

"It's a book I wanted to ask you about."

"Is it another one of mine? One of the ones that were stolen from my library?"

"No, I don't think so, but I do believe it did belong to your family at one time. Or, at least, that's what I'm hoping to find out."

He curiously eyed the book and gestured to the study. "Perhaps you'd better come in and explain what you mean by that."

Chapter 27

Addie skirted past Lord Bentley. "Thank you." She smiled when she entered the study. The dark wood, offsetting the walls lined with bookshelves, and the antique globe that sat beside the window gave the room a sense of warmth, instead of the stuffiness so many other rooms in the manor exuded. "It's beautiful," she murmured.

"Thank you. So, you say this book belonged to my family at one time?" he asked, slipping the copy of Agatha Christie's *Death on the Nile* from her hand.

"I believe so. Do you recall going on a trip with your parents to Egypt when you were a young boy?"

"Yes, Egypt, Saudi Arabia, Turkey—that was the excursion my mother fondly referred to as our desert tour. My father was a member of the Society of Antiquaries of London. He had discovered he had a passion for not only studying but also seeking out and exploring ancient ruins, and came to fancy himself a bit of an amateur archeologist, I suppose. On that trip, he was bound and determined to seek out and explore every ancient site in the Middle East, I'm sure."

"Do you recall meeting a young woman on this trip, perhaps someone who also shared an interest in amateur archeology?"

"Hum, I vaguely recall we did meet someone"—his eyes narrowed in thought—"and she and my parents got on well together. Why do you ask?"

"Was this young woman's name Anita, Anita Greyborne, by any chance?"

"Anita?" He stared at the Persian rug at his feet and stroked his gray goatee. "I don't recall what her name was. I was only about six. It was so many years ago." He looked at Addie. "I just vaguely remember how the three of them laughed a lot at dinner. Oh, and the woman was nice to me. She used to buy me sweets in the markets, and she ruffled my hair a lot." His eyes lit up, and a soft smile came to his lips. "I remember now how she and my mother would go shopping in the bazaars, my father following along behind, carrying their bags like a pack mule." His gaze drew distant. "Yes, that was a wonderful trip." The smile touching the corners of his lips grew wider.

"Well, Mr. Pressman, the owner of—"

"Yes, yes, I'm well acquainted with Reggie Pressman."

Addie took a breath. "Mr. Pressman came across this book in a shop in London, and the inscription on the title page made him wonder if this person was my grandmother, Anita Greyborne, whom he also knew."

She took the book from his hand and flipped to the title page. "He said she often visited your parents during the years she lived in England, and whenever she was in the village, she would stop at Second Chance Books and, well, I was wondering if this could possibly have been a gift to her from your parents?" She steadied herself against the large, ornately carved walnut desk behind her and read the inscription aloud.

Our dearest Anita, here is a simple reminder of our first shared adventures, save the murder, thankfully. Her Ladyship, my young son, and I shall always cherish the time we spent together under the Egyptian skies. We are forever hopeful this was only the beginning of a lifelong friendship and the first of many adventures we four rapscallions might share.

Fondly, Lord and Lady Bentley and Master Robert

Tears formed in his soft blue eyes and rolled down his craggy cheeks. "Yes," he whispered, "I recall Anita clearly now." He went over to a side cupboard, withdrew a large leather album, flipped it open, scanned through a couple of pages, and brought it over to Addie. "Is this your grandmother?"

Addie gazed down at the photograph of a young Anita Greyborne standing alongside a couple and a small boy in front of a pyramid.

"Yes, that's her."

A dreamy smile filled his eyes and graced his lips. "I think until I started at Cambridge, I believed the woman we met in Egypt was going to be my wife." He laughed. "It was so long ago that it all seems like a dream now, and sadly, I never saw her again after our desert tour. On our return, I was sent off to Eton for boarding school and only came home for holidays. However, I understood from Mother that the nice lady from the pyramids often came up from London to visit. I recall being angry that I hadn't been there and had missed all the fun with the lady who gave me sweets."

"Mr. Pressman said she was a regular visitor to the bookshop when she came up, and well . . ." Addie's cheeks grew warm. "He said he had a bit of a crush on her, but I think he's a few years older than you, isn't he?"

"I think every man she ever met fell in love with the woman from the pyramids. She and my mother had become great friends too. To be honest, I think it was my father who encouraged the visits because he was a little in love with her, just like young Reggie would have been. As a matter of fact, I recall now that, when I was away at school, the three of them would often go off on weekend adventures over to Ireland or up to the Highlands, investigating old stone rings and Celtic ruins."

"Yes, according to my grandmother's journals, she did have a strong interest in historical sites."

"I'd say they all fancied themselves as amateur archeologists back then." He laughed and gazed fondly at the photograph. "According to my nanny, your grandmother was a godsend because she brought life into their stuffy British aristocratic marriage of convenience." He looked at Addie. "The latter are my words, not Nanny's, based on my observations of their marriage as I got older and began to make comparisons to my first."

Addie sensed a shift in his nostalgic mood and that he might lose his focus, so she gestured at a photograph on a side cupboard. "Is that a picture of your parents?" She hoped it was and that it would keep him talking. She still needed to find a way to bring up the necklace.

"Yes." He snapped out of whatever trance he had drifted into. "Actually, that photo was taken on their first anniversary and soon after I was born."

Addie gazed down at the photograph of a man who was unmistakably Lord Bentley's father. The family resemblance was uncanny, and not something she saw when she looked at his lordship and Lewis, who were so dissimilar to each other. "Your mother was very beautiful." Her breath caught. There was no doubt about it. Poking out over the top of her 1950s sweetheart neckline dress was the sapphire-and-diamond necklace.

Addie's heart pounded erratically, and she fixed a smile on her face in response to the questioning look Lord Bentley gave her.

"This necklace your mother is wearing is truly breathtaking and appears to be very old. Is it a family heirloom?" she asked, fighting to keep her voice even.

His face lit up in a broad smile, and he gently took the photograph and gazed down at it. "Yes, one of my mother's ten times great-grandfathers back in Germany had the piece commissioned as a gift for his wife when their first child was born. Since then, the necklace has been handed down to the mother of the firstborn daughter in each generation's family. It didn't matter if there was an older sibling. Whoever produced the first girl received the necklace." He chuckled softly.

"It truly is spectacular. One of a kind, I'd say, and no doubt worth a fortune by today's standards."

"Yes," he said quietly, admiring the photograph. "I imagine it would be." Tears formed in his eyes, and he set the photograph back on the side cupboard and looked at Addie. "Sadly, my family is no longer in possession of the necklace."

Quick, Addie, think, or you're going to lose your opening. "That's too bad. Was it . . . was it stolen?"

"To be honest, I have no idea what became of it."

"Is . . ." Addie sucked in a bracing breath. *Go for it. You have nothing to lose.* "Is that because you gave it to a woman named Julianna?"

His usually ruddy complexion drained of color, and his mouth opened and closed, but no words came out.

"Is the reason . . ." Addie stepped forward, laid her hand on his arm, and lowered her voice. "Is the reason you don't know where it is now that it was later given to her daughter, Mollie, and was stolen when Mollie was killed on the moor by Haworth twenty years ago?"

"How . . ." His voice cracked with a sob. "How did you know?"

"Mr. Press—"

"Ah, Reggie." He nodded knowingly. "Yes, I

should have known. With the death of that other poor girl out on the moor the night of Tony's engagement party, the secret I've carried for over forty-five years was bound to come to light. The similarities between the two cases, as I understand from Detective Inspector Parker, are far too uncanny."

The similarities told to him by the inspector? Did that mean DI Parker did actually entertain her thoughts about how the two murders might be connected and that the necklace was the link? "Detective Inspector Parker told you this?"

"Yes, yes. I sit on the board as a community representative for the Metropolitan Police Commission in London. He and I go back to the days when he was a detective chief inspector. A fine officer and leader. It's only too bad, isn't it, how his career took such a sidetrack after his wife was murdered, and he ended up in Yorkshire? I thought he would rise in the ranks of the Met, but I guess others didn't see it the same way."

"His wife was murdered, and he was railroaded out of the Met?"

"They weren't exactly without cause at the time, but still, given the circumstances, I think leniency would have been called for, don't you?"

"Circumstances?"

He met her inquiring gaze. "Forgive me, I've seen the two of you talking, and just now you seemed to know more about his situation than you clearly do. I will say nothing more of the matter. It's best you have any future discussions with DI Parker himself."

"Yes, of course, nasty business back in London,

but I am not prone to gossip either, so you're quite right. It's not our place." She glanced back at the photograph of Lord Bentley's parents. "That is still an exquisite necklace. It is too bad it was lost."

If Lord Bentley was fazed by the sudden change in topic, he didn't show it. As a matter of fact, he seemed relieved by it. That really made her wonder how much worse DI Parker's personal tale was than the death of two women who had worn this necklace?

"I think that necklace was cursed and it was me that brought it on. Perhaps our dear friend, Tony Radcliff, should write his next novel about it. Truth is stranger than fiction, after all," he scoffed.

Chapter 28

"Lord Bentley, why would you think the necklace was cursed?" asked Addie. "It must have been in your mother's family for hundreds of years. Or was there a history of deaths around the women who possessed it?"

"Not that I have heard," replied Lord Bentley, "but it appears that Reggie Pressman has made you aware that I gave the necklace to Julianna and not my first wife, Lady Gwendolyn." Lord Bentley's shoulders took on a less-hunched appearance as he met Addie's gaze.

"He never revealed who gave Julianna the necklace, only that it was given to her by her child's father and that it was a family heirloom. He told me he didn't know who Mollie's father was."

"He always knew. I don't think she told him, and Reggie was too much of a gentleman to ever say anything to anyone, but he knew. I could tell by the way he looked at me whenever I dropped into the shop." He forced a faltering smile. "I have a photograph of Julianna. Perhaps then you'll see what I'm talking about, and why I—as well as every other man in the county—was completely enchanted by her."

"I'd love to see it."

Lord Bentley strode over to a landscape painting on the wall behind his desk and flipped it aside on a hinge, revealing a wall safe behind it. He retrieved a silver-framed photograph and lovingly gazed down at the image. His finger stroked the outline of something in the picture. He drew in a deep breath and handed the photograph to Addie.

On the top of a crag, a stunning young woman smiled and gazed at bundles of heather in her arms. To judge by the long, ginger-blond hair flowing behind her and the green skirt fluttering around her legs, the wind must have been toying and teasing that day.

"I took that picture of Julianna. I'll never forget that day." His hoarse voice cracked. "It . . . it was the day we first . . ." His gaze drifted to the windows that perfectly framed a view of the moors; the crag where Julianna had been standing in the photo was visible off in the distance. "It was the day I professed my love to her and her to me." Tears rolled down his age-lined cheeks.

He sniffed and dabbed at his nose with a handkerchief. "In that moment, nothing else in the world existed. I had never felt a love like that, so pure, so real, so right, so special, until . . ." His voice drifted off to a barely audible murmur. "A few months later," his gaze went to the window, and he softly smiled. "Julianna informed me she was expecting our child. I was over the moon." He glanced at Addie, his eyes reflecting the smile he still had on his lips. "I loved her so much and thought at the time that I would do anything for her. That I'd even do what someone in my position should never consider doing, and that was to leave my very well-to-do wife from a powerful political family."

He expelled a heavy sigh and hung his head. "Julianna and I planned to move to America so we could raise our child," he said wistfully and turned his now tear-filled gaze to Addie's. "But before I could finish making all the arrangements, my wife announced she was also pregnant with our first child, Lewis."

He cleared his hoarsening throat and raked his hand through his thick gray hair. "It was horrible. The love of my life and my wife of a loveless marriage based purely on social rank and esteem, both pregnant, and I was forced to choose between them and ultimately between the children. It was then I realized I was a coward." A deep sob of sorrow ripped from his chest. "I loved Julianna, I really did." He choked out. "And the baby, my daughter, Mollie . . . but"—he straightened his back and met Addie's gaze—"I was a lord, a baron, and that comes with certain expectations, duties, and obligations. I was forced to do the very thing that literally tore my soul in two, and I told Julianna she had to leave my house and my life forever."

He gazed back out the window toward the crag, and a single tear slipped down his cheek. "I have never loved anyone the way I loved Julianna, and the day I watched her walk down the drive, knowing I could never be with her again, was the worst day of my life. It shattered me when I heard she'd moved to Leeds," he said, his voice a gravelly whisper. "But," he looked at Addie, "when she moved back to Moorscrag and had married Reginald Pressman, I was absolutely giddy. I didn't even care that she was married to someone else. My Julianna was coming home, and I was trapped in a soulless marriage with a woman I had nothing in common with; we couldn't even stand to be in the same room as each other. I thought all my prayers had been answered."

"Did you . . ." Addie thought of Mr. Pressman and his reaction to learning Lord Bentley was returning to the manor. "Did you and she pick up where—"

"No!" He emphatically shook his head. "She made it clear the first day I saw her after she returned that I could never be with her. I had to learn to live with the fact that I could never hold her again in my arms or smell the scent of heather in her hair, and it broke my heart. Then I realized that at least I could see her. All I had to do was go into the bookshop, and she'd be there, along with my little girl playing in the back room, and no one would be the wiser as to her parentage or the forbidden love her mother and I had once shared."

"Except Reginald Pressman."

"Yes, Reggie." He huffed out a sorrow-filled breath. "He hated me for it, but I also knew he loved her and my child with all his heart, so I could deal with his hatred. Even though I ached for Julianna with every part of my being, I had made my choice, and she had made it clear she loved Reggie and all he offered to her and Mollie. She would never do anything to jeopardize what they had as a family." He sighed. "Eventually, I learned to become content with the small talk when I dropped into the bookshop and the glimpses I got of Mollie as she grew up." He held the photograph close to his heart, and tears silently rolled down his cheeks.

"And when Mollie was older, you gave her a job at the manor?" Addie whispered.

He nodded.

"Did she ever know you were her biological father?"

He shook his head. "Unless Reggie told her, but I doubt it. She never said anything or asked about it."

"Then when she was killed and the necklace disappeared, your secret disappeared with it, right?"

"What are you saying?" His eyes flashed with unexpected fury. "Are you accusing me of murdering my daughter, the last reminder I had of the only woman I ever truly loved?"

"That's not what I meant. I'm sorry, that came out wrong. It's just that you said the necklace seemed to be cursed, and I was only—"

"Yes." He slammed his fist on his desk. "And I was the one who cursed it."

Addie took a step back as rage wracked Lord Bentley's body.

"Don't you see?" His voice grew to a fevered pitch. "The necklace should have gone to my wife with the birth of Lewis. Not to my lover, who was forced to leave Milton Manor in shame. I brought dishonor to my mother's ancestors with what I did. I might as well have spat on their graves, because if

I hadn't done what I did, Mollie might not have been killed. Can't you see? I cursed my daughter by my careless, selfish actions."

"Who knew you had given the necklace to Julianna and not Gwendolyn?"

"No one."

"Are you sure? This person might be responsible not only for Mollie's murder but also the murder of Ivee Hargrave."

"Which I can't figure out, because I have no idea who this Ivee Hargrave is—was—and what she would have to do with the necklace."

"She was the daughter of the housekeeper you fired for stealing books from your library twenty-odd years ago."

"Really? Ivee was what's-her-name's . . ." He snapped his fingers.

"Fern Hargrave."

"Yes. That was it. She was Fern's daughter?" He frowned. "How did she come to have the necklace?"

"Her mother worked on the trains as a cleaner, and the day after Mollie disappeared, Fern apparently found it wedged between the seat and the window of the train car where Mollie had been sitting. A few days later, Mollie's body was discovered by hikers out on the moors by Haworth."

"So she just kept it and never told the police or anyone. They might have been able to fingerprint it or something and find out who killed my daughter!" he shouted. Tears of anger replaced tears of sorrow.

"It seems a number of your household staff were also on the same train as Mollie, returning from their pre-Christmas holiday weekend in London. So, I'll ask you again, who knew how the necklace was passed down in the family?"

"No one. I'm positive. I told my wife the necklace had been accidentally buried with my mother. When Lewis was a little older and asked about the necklace his grandmother always wore in photographs, and wanted to know if his wife would get it when he was married and had a child, I told him the same thing I had told his mother."

"He knew the story about the necklace being passed down to the mother of the firstborn child in the family?"

"Yes, apparently, Mrs. Howard was told the history of the necklace by her predecessor, my mother and father's housekeeper." He shook his head. "I don't recall her name, though, and Mrs. Howard told Lewis about it. Of course, neither knew I hadn't given it to my wife when she was pregnant with him but had given it to my lover, who actually did give birth to my firstborn child."

Something about his words resonated with Addie, and goose bumps raced down her arms. "Mrs. Howard, you say." A piece of the puzzle on her kitchen table snapped into place.

"You're not thinking Mrs. Howard had anything to do with Mollie's murder on the train that day or is connected to the death of that young woman at the party, do you? She's been in my employment for over forty-five years."

"No, it's just interesting, that's all." She shrugged and pasted the sincerest smile she could muster on her face. "Thank you for this chat, Lord Bentley." Addie looked down at the copy of *Death on the*

Nile she still clutched in her hand, excited to tell Mr. Pressman that he indeed had found a real gem in that secondhand bookshop in London. "Having you verify that this book was a gift for my grandmother helps me put more of the puzzle pieces of her life together. I can't thank you enough for telling me those stories about her and your trip. It makes me feel a little closer to a woman I never really knew, except through her journals."

She checked the time on her phone. She'd better hurry if she was to catch Meg before she was finished with her shift. "I really must run now. Thanks again."

He stared at her, his face blank, as though her words weren't computing. She hated to leave him in the state he was in. Clearly, their conversation had opened old wounds that were probably best left as distant memories. She paused at the study door, dashed back, and hugged him. She gave him a quick kiss on the cheek. "Thank you. It meant a lot to me." She gestured to the book in her hand, then hurried out the door, closing it quietly behind her.

Addie leaned against the wall, shaking. Could it be true? Mrs. Howard was the only one who knew the history and legend of the necklace, which meant when she saw Ivee wearing it at the party, she was following her.

"Miss Greyborne," a hushed, raspy voice called.

Addie started and glanced around.

"Miss Greyborne."

"Who's there?" she asked, trying to see where the disembodied voice was coming from.

Mrs. Bannerman stepped out of the shadows of the back staircase alcove. "I have something you should see," she whispered hoarsely and waved Addie toward her.

Addie quickly scanned the hallway and hurried over to the alcove. Talk about a cloak-and-dagger meeting. She would have laughed had the expression on Mrs. Bannerman's face not been ominous. "What is it?" Addie whispered.

After looking down the hall and over her shoulder down the stairs, Mrs. Bannerman pulled out her mobile phone. "This is all I managed to photograph. I was too afraid Master Lewis would return and catch me rummaging through his suite. I wouldn't make a very good spy, I'm afraid."

Au contraire. Addie knew firsthand Mrs. Bannerman's superpower of having the ability to skulk in the shadows and see everything without herself being seen. A gift that she had no doubt honed over the years.

"These are pictures of the pages from the notebook I saw him writing in when he was with his Cambridge friend, that Stewart fellow, and they didn't know I was watching them."

Addie took the phone from her hand and scrolled through the notebook images. "Do you know what these are?" asked Addie. "Was there a title or heading on the page?"

"No, but I've looked after household accounts long enough to know it is an accounting sales journal of sorts." She pointed to a line on the image. "This appears to be an inventory list of some of the antiques in the manor house, if I'm not mistaken.

Perhaps the first column of numbers is their appraised value, and the next column is—"

"What they actually sold for, since in most cases it's a higher number?" Addie squinted, enlarged the image, and reread the page. "Or like this one, for a portrait of a huntsman, 1768, by George Stubbs; the second column is blank. That could mean he hasn't stolen it yet, because I know this painting is still in Lord Bentley's library. I saw it the night I was in there with him and Tony."

Was Lewis stealing antiques from his own family home and selling them to prearranged buyers? Was that why there was a blank beside the Stubbs painting? Addie's breath caught. "Of course, if this is what we think it is, Mrs. Bannerman, Lewis Bentley was most likely the book thief twenty years ago. When he discovered his father had Mollie mark all the books in his collection with the invisible ink, he had to start taking other items that he could sell without the risk of being caught. After all, who would ever suspect Lord Bentley's son of stealing from his family estate?"

"But why? All this"—Mrs. Bannerman waved her hand toward the main foyer—"would be his one day anyway."

"Tony mentioned his publisher has a gambling problem, and he thinks that's why Lord Bentley hasn't completely stepped down yet and turned over the company to his son."

"I have overheard a few of the longer-serving staff say that the younger Bentley does spend a lot of time in Monte Carlo. Perhaps his father is afraid he'll lose the company on the tables?"

"That's a possibility. I have to show this to Meg, and I'll tell her what we're thinking it means, so she can follow up. I'll let you know what she says."

Addie waited with bated breath as she sent the images from Mrs. Bannerman's phone to hers. After a quick goodbye, she ran back through the forest to her cottage, her mind swirling with the random pieces of information she had learned. She just needed to fit it together with the pieces of the puzzle she already had. It all had to fit. She just needed to take a step back and look at it through fresh eyes. Fresh eyes, that was it! She needed Serena.

Once they had figured it out, she'd call Meg and fill her in. Addie fished her phone out of her skirt pocket, and her heart sank. Serena's dad's surgeon was meeting with the family today to talk about Wade Chandler's care plan following his emergency surgery. She looked at Pippi. "We'll call later to see what the doctors said. Okay?" She checked the time. It was nearly six in Moorscrag, so with the five-hour difference . . . *Paige, you're a great puzzle-solver too, and with any luck, you're taking your lunch break right about now.* She punched in Paige's mobile number and waited for her to answer.

The call went to voicemail, so she punched in the main number for Beyond the Page Books and Curios, and her call went immediately to voicemail too. "Hum, Pippi," she said looking down at her tail-wagging friend. "The store must be busy. I'll call Auntie Paige later. In the meantime, maybe you can help me sort through all this?" she said with a short laugh and gestured to the table.

Pippi yipped, then perked her ears, yapped louder, and darted for the door, just as it resonated with a loud knock.

"Who needs a doorbell with you around, hey?" she said with a laugh and gasped when she opened the door. "DI Parker, can I help you?"

Chapter 29

The look in DI Parker's eyes had her stomach whirling with a mixture of fear, dread, and bliss. She wanted to hate that confounded twinkle in his eye and those endearing dimples in his cheeks. Was that a nervous twitch she just saw at the corners of his lips? His ears, just below his silver-streaked, dark hair reddened when their gaze met. Yes, it was, and for that split second, there was no denying it. Addie was no better than Archie or Lord Bentley or apparently half the village in their ogling of Julianna based on her appearance.

Despite the feeling of superficiality, it did tell Addie something important about herself because it had been a long time since she had looked at someone the way she found herself checking out DI Parker while she poured his tea. Perhaps her heart was finally healed, and she was ready to move forward not only with her life but also with her emotions.

Not your type anyway, she mentally chanted, but then pursed her lips. Wait a minute, after what had happened last year, and then everything she had learned about her family, she barely knew who the real Addie was any longer, so did she really know her type?

She did know it definitely wasn't any man who could marry someone else sixteen years previously and never say a word about it. Not that a previous marriage disqualified a man, but Simon had hidden it from her, leading to disastrous repercussions that imploded her life before her eyes. *Whoa.* She took a deep breath and pushed back the resentment rising in her gut. *All life lessons lead you to who and where you are now.*

She also knew from experience that, deep down, Marc Chandler wasn't her type, or he was too much her type perhaps. He was very much like David and had made a perfect replacement for him, and that wasn't fair to Marc. He would have always been a reminder to Addie of the man she had deeply loved in her past, a man who had been forever snatched away from her, not because they had fallen out of love but because he had been murdered.

Tall, dark, short, blond? Did she even have a type anymore? One thing for sure was that the restless feeling in the pit of her stomach—or was it a fluttering in her chest—was something she hadn't felt in a long time. "Would you like a biscuit to go with your tea?" She smiled as she offered him a plate of biscuits.

What was she doing? This man was insufferable,

but when he had stood at her doorway, hat in hand, a deer-in-the-headlights look in his eyes, asking for her help, she hadn't slammed the door in his face like she had been wanting to do. Stunned that the dismissive, typically emotionally distant British police inspector had asked her opinion on something, Addie had welcomed him with open arms—not exactly, but with an offer of tea, at least.

Well, girl, she decided as she took a seat at her kitchen table, *it seems any kind word from a man with a pulse appears to be your type these days, doesn't it?* She wanted to laugh at herself for being so juvenile, but bit the inside of her cheek to keep her erratic emotions in check. "As far as I am aware, any efforts to remove the invisible-ink stamps inside Lord Bentley's books would cause either damage to the paper or leave discolored markings that would be visible to the naked eye."

"That's what I came up with too in my inquires," DI Parker said, taking a biscuit from the plate. "I thought perhaps, since you worked at the British Museum at one time, you might be aware of a method that has eluded my sources."

"Wait," she said and stopped mid-motion taking a biscuit. "You looked me up?"

He shifted in his chair.

"And here I didn't think you wanted anything to do with me or my opinions."

"Don't flatter yourself. I did it because I figured there must be something in your background that could tell me why you're the most incorrigible person I have ever met."

"That's hilarious. Someone else I know used to say that exact same thing about me," she said with a laugh when an image of Marc popped into her head. "I hope you saw the part where my records said I worked at the British Museum a long time ago, and I was only there as part of a six-month work exchange program."

"I did read that in my background check." His cheeks turned as red as the roses on his teacup. "Along with some other interesting references."

"Ooh, do tell." She drew her knee up and got comfortable on her chair as she popped a piece of biscuit into her mouth.

"I was rather surprised to see that this is not the first time you have interfered in a police investi—"

"*Interfered* is a harsh word. It was more like 'assisted the police in bringing the guilty party to justice.'"

"That's the way you see it, is it?"

"Yes, and the district attorney for Essex County, Massachusetts, even made me an official consultant on a few cases."

"I read that too, particularly cases that involved rare books, which seems to be your specialty and the thing that brings me here."

"Really, and here I thought it was my magnetic personality, and you couldn't help but be drawn to me." The fluttering in her chest since his arrival dropped like a rock to her stomach. Had she just said that out loud?

His eyes held a smidgen of a twinkle, and a tiny smile touched the corners of his lips as he cleared his throat. "I thought since you'd researched and cataloged old and rare books, removing security markings might be a process you were familiar with."

"When I worked there I was basically a grunt—"

"A what? That's an American job title I'm not familiar with."

"Now you're teasing," she coyly smiled. "You know full well it's not a job title. It's the description of the work I performed there. I worked my way through crates of pieces the museum had collected that had been boxed up and left to collect dust in the warehouse until someone had the time to appraise them. I was the grunt that got the job no one else wanted to do."

He sat back, eyeing her across the table. "And during your time as a grunt, did you ever come across a book or an item that had been marked with invisible ink and that you could prove had been stolen?"

"Sure, well, not so much the invisible-ink thing, but I came across lots of objects, from paintings to books to artifacts, that had worked their way through the black market before coming to the museum."

She looked at him over the rim of her cup, knowing she should say something about the photographs she had of the notebook on her phone. What if she was wrong? It would be horrible to send the police after Tony's publisher if she was. She needed Serena or Paige first. This was too big for her on her own. The fact that she was having biscuits and tea with the most pompous, insufferable man she had ever met and was enjoying his company was proof enough she couldn't trust her instincts anymore. "May I ask why all the questions about the ink and stolen property?"

He glanced uneasily away from Addie's inquisitive gaze. "I followed up with Fern Hargrave's old neighbors."

Addie fought the urge to smile, knowing that, if she wanted any information out of him, she was going to have to play it cool and not gloat. "How lovely. How are Mrs. Fenton and Alice doing after hearing the news about Ivee?"

"They're dealing with it, although Alice is struggling. She informed me that she's still in possession of Ivee Hargrave's effects because there was a court order declaring they must remain where they are until the investigation is closed."

So much for trying not to let him know they had Ivee's personal belongings. "Couldn't the police impound everything so Alice and her mother could have some closure and move on?" she asked.

"It wasn't my decision to leave the items with them. Ivee wasn't a suspect. She was the victim. The district commissioner decided her personal effects didn't need to be locked up at the expense of the taxpayers." He took a sip of his tea, and his ears pinked up to match the fading color on his cheeks as he stared at an unseen spot on the table.

Did this man really have a heart after all? He appeared to feel bad for Alice and shared in her grief. "Another biscuit?" Addie held out the plate.

He shook his head and cleared his throat. "When I went to see them, Alice reluctantly showed me a diary she'd come across in Ivee's belongings."

Darn it! She guessed one might be there the day Alice had brought the boxes in, and she wished she'd stayed to help sort through them or gone back to check if Alice and her mom had come across anything. What she wouldn't have given to get her hands on that diary before DI Parker.

"From what I read, Ivee appears to have made notes based on stories she recalled her mother Fern telling her as she grew up, and there were some interesting notations in it about Lewis Bentley."

"Really, what did it say?" Addie's mind immediately went to the photos on her phone.

"It said her mother, Fern, was working on the train the day Mollie Pressman was returning from London for the holidays, and she saw Mollie and Lewis having a verbal altercation of sorts."

"I wonder," said Addie, "if he saw her with the copy of *Wuthering Heights* and questioned her about it?"

"The passage I read went on to say that a few of the other staff members from Milton Manor asked Fern if she knew what they were arguing about, but she told them she didn't."

"Was there any mention of the book?"

"Not in the diary." He stretched out his long legs and toyed with the handle of his teacup. "That was something I found rather interesting, since none of the police reports from that time mention an altercation, which means the police did not question the staff or Fern Hargrave. As a matter of fact, police reports do not mention Fern or other members of the manor staff being on the same train as Mollie. Most curious, since it was a murder inquiry, don't you think?"

"Could it have been not reported because it involved Lord Bentley's son?"

"That was my thought too, but there were a number of mentions of the other manor staff being on the train. However, I couldn't find anything in the old reports about them having been questioned."

Addie glanced over at the stack of notes she'd quickly cleaned off the table when Inspector Parker came in and made himself at home. "Yes, the Milton Manor staff were returning from a team-building weekend in London, but I never got the impression that no one was questioned after the reported argument between Lewis and Mollie."

DI Parker's eyes widened. "What do you mean you never got the impression that no one had been questioned? Have you been talking to and questioning the staff about this?"

Addie shifted uncomfortably in her chair. *Shoot!* This was exactly the kind of reaction from him she had been hoping to avoid, and just when things were going along so well between them too.

She opened her mouth then snapped it closed. *Tread carefully.* She took a breath and tried again. "Yes, well, you didn't seem too interested in a cold case and told me you didn't think it was related to Ivee Hargrave's death anyway, so . . ." Her eyes lit up. "I did tell PC Gimsby what others told me. She said she would follow up, and if she came across anything, she would let you know."

"I see." He drummed his fingers on the table. "I'll follow up with PC Gimsby, then."

"Yes, you should do that." Addie sat back in her chair, confused by the abrupt change in Inspector Parker tonight. Until now, he hadn't been willing to give her the time of day. Suddenly, he appeared interested in what she had been trying to tell him all along? Besides what he told her before, was there something else that he'd found in his background search on her?

Perhaps it was the fact that her father had been an NYPD detective, and he felt some sort of kinship? Then she recalled what Lord Bentley had said. *It's only too bad how his career took such a sidetrack after his wife was murdered.* She pressed her lips firmly together. He must have read about David. Kinship was right. The two of them belonged to a very select club. She shook it off and refocused. "I'm sorry, what did you say?"

"I said, it seems, from Ivee's recounting of her mother's stories, that Lewis Bentley was a spoiled, smooth-talking playboy, who had his eye on Mollie Pressman as they were riding in the same car. Apparently, this infuriated Fern, because at one time when she worked at the manor, she and Lewis had had a relationship—"

"You're kidding? Lewis Bentley and Fern Hargrave were involved with each other?"

"According to what Ivee wrote in her diary, yes. Why is that so shocking? Is it because he was a member of the aristocracy, and she was a servant and beneath him?"

"No, because she was accused of stealing the books from Lord Bentley's library. But what if she didn't . . ." Addie leaned forward and pinned her gaze on DI Parker. "What if he was the thief and used Fern's position somehow to his advantage?"

"That's exactly what it says in Ivee's diary."

"You're kidding?"

"I assure you, Miss Greyborne, I would never kid

about something as serious as theft on this level."
He took a long sip of tea and an equally long
pause before he set his empty cup on the table.

It was as though he was going out of his way to
taunt her with the suspense of what he was going
to say, and she hated to admit it, but it was working, because he had her full attention as she waited
for him to continue.

"It seems," he finally said, with a glimmer of a
smile in his eyes, "that over the years, Fern had
told her daughter, Ivee, or insinuated that Lewis
convinced Fern to help him steal his father's
books by promising to marry her and take her to
France to live off the money they collected by selling the books. He had convinced her to help him
by telling her it was a victimless crime and that it
wasn't really theft, as his father could make an insurance claim now that they were cataloged and
he'd be reimbursed for their value. Selling the
books would give him and Fern the money they
needed to get away."

"She believed him?" said Addie. "But then she
got caught and lost her job, and he got off scot-
free."

"Exactly, and when Lewis was the one who
pointed the finger at Fern and she lost her job, her
desire for revenge grew. Grew exponentially too
as, for years, he let everyone go on thinking she
was a thief."

"I bet her desire to get revenge did grow. She
had Ivee to raise, and no one in the village would
hire her. That's why she had to move to Leeds."

"It seems, in the meantime, that Lewis was covering his own tracks, from what Fern heard through the manor grapevine, which was why they could never find any concrete evidence against anyone and only had speculation about Fern's involvement. As the son of a well- respected lord, he was the last person anyone suspected as being the book thief. It said in the diary that, as long as Ivee could remember, her mother had vowed to get revenge on Lewis Bentley and the way he'd used her."

Addie jumped up and shuffled through her stack of notes. "Yes, look at this," she cried, clearing off a space on the table and slapping pieces of paper down.

"What's all this about the faulty clasp and Ivee coming across the necklace in London?"

Addie explained what Alice had told her and how Ivee had come into possession of the same necklace her mother had found on the train and had kept for years to give to Ivee as her inheritance, but then that their landlord sold off Fern's belongings after she died to pay Fern's back rent.

He tapped his finger on a piece of paper. "And this one here about Mrs. Howard seeing Ivee Hargrave at the party." He looked questioningly at Addie.

Addie explained that scene as it was told to her and showed him a picture of Mrs. Howard's face when she was in pursuit of Ivee at the party.

"Mrs. Wallace, Lewis's nanny?" He picked up the piece of paper the name was written on. "How does she fit into this?"

Addie filled DI Parker in on what she had

learned about some of the other staff, including Mrs. Howard, the day they went to her cottage for tea. When she finished and got the papers into a sequence that made sense, she looked at DI Parker, who finished scanning the clues at the same time as she moved the last scrap of paper into place.

"Lewis Bentley," she said confidently.

"Mrs. Howard!" He jabbed his finger over the woman's name at the same time as Addie's revelation.

"Mrs. Howard?"

"Lewis Bentley?" he retorted.

"Both do make sound suspects."

"Yes, they do," he said, studying the clues. "It only takes one warrant of the manor house to catch either bird. It's the one thing that makes sense and links the two murders." He looked up at Addie, the corner of his lip tugging at a half smile. "That is, if we follow your hunch that they are related."

Addie pointed to a scrap that had *LB on train with Mollie, seen arguing* written on it. "Yes, and there are photographs from the party showing Ivee Hargrave standing close to Lewis."

"If he saw her wearing the necklace, he most likely recognized it, and—"

"It must have come as a real shock to him to see his family necklace around a stranger's neck," said DI Parker. "Especially since his father had already identified the book Mollie Pressman had with her the night she was killed; it had disappeared after her death, but then it also showed up the night of the party, thanks to your friend, Tony Radcliff."

His eyes narrowed. "I have a hunch myself." He pointed to the clue she had written about Mrs. Howard. "I think she knows more than she's letting on."

"I agree. She's always reminded me of a British Mrs. Bannerman."

He looked curiously at Addie.

"Never mind," she said, waving him off. "I think that's why she held that bizarre meeting the other night in the kitchen with the American staff. It felt contrived, like she was buying someone time to do something."

"I think you may be right."

"Especially since I ran into Lewis upstairs soon after that weird meeting. He had just come in from his regular run and appeared nervous about the fact that you were there talking to the staff, and he was suddenly in a hurry to get upstairs to his suite."

DI Parker picked up his hat from a nearby chair. "I'm going to contact my chief inspector and see about obtaining a magistrate's search warrant for the manor. I have a feeling the proof we need to solve at least one of these murders and the book thefts is in that house somewhere."

"Are warrants easy to get here in England?"

He put his hat on and steadied his gray eyes on her. "They are unless you're getting one to search the country home of a baron." He turned and left, closing the door behind him.

"Did you hear that, Pippi? We have to do something—and quickly. Lewis will be returning to London tomorrow, and he will probably take all the evidence with him. If he has the necklace, it will be sold and long gone by the time Parker can get his warrant."

She picked up Pippi and gave her a cuddle and a scratch behind the ear. "Well, he might need a warrant, but I don't, so wish me luck." She set Pippi on the floor, gave her another head scratch, and headed up the path to the manor.

Chapter 30

The deeper Addie got into the woods, the more she found herself stumbling over the uneven ground and protruding roots. She'd walked the path hundreds of times over the past year, but today there was something sinister about the light, or lack thereof, due to the thick overhead tree canopy. Shivers snaked across her shoulders.

It didn't help that, a few minutes ago, she was sharing clues to a murder that took place not far from where she was, and she couldn't shake the irrational sense that she wasn't alone in the woods. A noise off to her left pierced the quiet of the dense forest, and goose bumps rippled up her arms.

She stopped, cocked her head, and listened. A distinct scraping sound was coming from the other side of a berry-bramble thicket off to her left. Shivers turned to a burning prickle across her neck.

She knew full well there were no bears or panthers in England any longer, but the sound was loud enough to tell her the source wasn't a rabbit or a squirrel.

She took a series of gulps of air to try to calm her erratically pounding heart, slowly turned, and quietly wheezed out her last breath when a blur of a red and white appeared through the bushes. She recoiled with the thought that whatever she was seeing was far bigger than a rabbit and not colors found in nature. Since it appeared to be moving in and out of her view, it had to be alive.

She kept her gaze fixed in the direction of the form and cautiously stepped forward. The gut feeling she'd had earlier, about not being alone in the woods, shifted from her gut and nestled at the base of her skull.

Friend or foe, she didn't care. She'd let her imagination run away with her. She needed to get out of the forest and out into the open, just to breathe again. Addie judged that, by where she was on the path, the clearing into the manor gardens should be not too far ahead. Only a few more steps and she'd be past the thicket and the mysterious figure, and she could safely make a run for it.

Addie kept her eyes pinned on the obscured image she could just make out through the bushes while she continued to creep along the pathway. *Breathe deep and step slowly. You're almost past the thicket. Get ready to—Lewis?* She gasped with the clear view of what the brushwood had been screening. Her adrenaline-induced flight response retreated, and she took an easy breath. Yes, it was Lewis. There was no mistaking the blur of his red-and-white spandex running shorts and the white shirt he usually wore when he ran.

Excitement bubbled up in her chest. This was perfect. If Lewis was out in the woods, if she hurried, she might be able to search his room to see if she could find anything that linked him to Ivee or Mollie's murder, like the missing necklace.

Her gazed remained steadfast on the red-and-white images, and she carefully edged along the path. When she got past the blackberry bushes, she stopped and squinted, trying to make out why he was hunched over beside a fallen tree. Perhaps he had injured himself running. Since he hadn't moved from that spot, maybe he needed help getting back to the house. She veered off the path and took a step toward him to get a better look. He wasn't hunched over because he was hurt and in pain. He was digging in the dirt.

Addie ducked behind a tree and peered around the trunk. The sun was sinking closer to the horizon. The shadows from the faint light peeking through the overhead branches played tricks on her eyes, and she couldn't figure out exactly what he was doing. He pulled something from the hole. She took a step closer to try to make out what he held in his hand, and a branch snapped beneath her foot. His head pivoted toward her, and his eyes locked on her.

"Addie?" He wheezed out a breath, rose to his feet, and clutched something in his dirt-covered hand.

"Hi. I . . ." Her voice wavered when the expression in his eyes flickered from initial surprise to outrage, reigniting her adrenaline-induced burning skin prickles. "I'm . . . I was just on my way to see Tony and saw you." She edged toward the foot-path. "Are you hurt?" She motioned with her head to his dirt-covered hands. "Did you fall? I could send someone back to help you."

Lewis looked down at his hands. He clutched a gardening trowel in one hand and a small black bag in the other.

"No," he said and slowly stepped forward. "I'm not hurt."

The robotic inflection in his voice, combined with the glazed-over look in his eyes, caused an acrid lump to form in the back of her throat. *Keep him talking and keep walking,* but words refused to form. The urge to run overwhelmed her, but as her mouth filled with cotton, her legs filled with lead.

Addie drew in an uneven breath, squared her shoulders, and met his piercing gaze with one of her own. She slid her hand into her skirt pocket, fingers fishing for her phone. Empty. Her chest tightened. She recalled how quickly she'd run out of her cottage to search for evidence that might disappear with Lewis's return to London, and her gaze flitted to the bag he clutched in his hand.

Keep him talking. "Did you lose something?" Her gaze darted again to the bag, then back up, where it was met by a sinister sneer. No matter how much she willed her feet to move, it was to no avail. She was as rooted to the path as the trees were rooted in the forest surrounding her. "Or were you dig-ging something up?" She stood as tall as she could manage and thrust her chin out defiantly. "Like perhaps the necklace you tore off Ivee Hargrave's neck before you pushed her off the crag?"

As her words tumbled out, she bit her tongue. *Great! Show your hand while you're stuck in the forest with a killer, you idiot!* Well, she'd done it now, and not being one who could ever drop the bear-poking-stick act once she'd picked it up, Addie decided she might as well go ahead and give the bear another poke to see what happened.

"It must have shocked you that night of the party when you saw her wearing it after it was lost so many years ago." She didn't miss the twitch in his cheek. "I've struck a nerve, haven't I?"

Lewis continued to draw closer, an unmistakable glint of pure devilry in his eyes. His lips twisted into a sardonic smile, and he took another step toward her. The fine hairs on her arms quivered, and she braced her trembling knees.

"Is that what happened? You saw Ivee wearing what you thought was your mother's necklace, and you tried to get it back?" Addie stiffened her spine, inhaled two quick breaths. She hoped that, with the recovery of her voice, her legs would also get the fight-or-flight message, and right about now she was opting for flight.

She thrust her upper body in the direction of the manor gardens, willing her feet to follow. They did, and she did it again, managing to put a bit more distance between her and Lewis, all the while keeping her gaze fixed on him as he inched his way around a thorn-covered branch and closer to her and the footpath.

"You think you've got it all figured out, don't you?"

"What happened?" she jeered, mentally calculating how many steps it was back to the path. "Did you panic when you saw it, knowing the last time you'd done so was twenty years ago and it was around Mollie Pressman's neck? Were you afraid Ivee Hargrave knew your secret about Mollie and she was going to turn you in?"

"My secret about Mollie? If you only knew."

"I think I do."

"Then you know that tart was in possession of a book that belonged to my father and a necklace that had belonged to my mother. So she deserved what she got." His voice hummed with rage.

Addie flinched. Was that a confession? *Dang it!* Where was her phone when she really needed it?

"Why are you sticking your nose where it doesn't belong, anyway?"

"Because a dear friend of mine is the prime suspect in Ivee Hargrave's murder, and we both know she didn't do it," she said, while she continued to work her way back to the path.

"I hear the police have built a solid case against your dear Miss Hailey Granger." He pushed an overhead branch from his face as he stalked closer to her.

"Not quite solid enough, and I'd say it's clear that you aren't aware that the tart, as you called her, was in fact your half sister. Is that why you killed her? Because she was actually the person in line to inherit all this?" Addie waved her arm in the direction of the manor. "Is that why you stole from your own family estate? Had you learned of your father's infidelity to your mother? Were you worried there was another heir hiding in the wings? When you saw Ivee with the necklace, did you think she might question your inheritance claim? After all, she would have been the right age to be your older sister's daughter, which would have made Ivee your niece and the rightful heir."

His eyes blazed, and the veins in his neck bulged and pulsated.

Addie glanced up the path.

His gaze flashed to where she'd looked. "You really shouldn't have telegraphed your next move," he sneered and lunged the last few steps, putting himself between her and the path.

She darted behind a tree. "Is that why you killed Ivee?"

"It's not my fault that she fell off the crag and broke her neck."

"So it had nothing to do with you struggling with her to get the necklace off her. I mean, you couldn't make the same mistake you had made with Mollie, could you?"

"What mistake?" He crept toward her like a wild animal stalking its prey.

"The mistake you made on the train when you ripped the necklace off her and it fell between the seat and the window. You'd killed her for nothing, didn't you? You still didn't have the necklace."

"No I didn't but I couldn't just walk away from what was rightfully mine. I did go back the next day, sat in the same seat, and searched for it, but . . ."

"But the same woman you tricked into helping you steal from your father found it before you could get back to it. She robbed you of the satisfaction of possessing what you thought was yours, and you knew then you had killed Mollie for nothing."

"For nothing?" His head jerked, and he let out a jeer. "I got rid of what stood between me and a multi-billion-pound inheritance, so I wouldn't say it was all for nothing."

"Something's been puzzling me. How did you manage to get Mollie's body off the Haworth train without being seen?"

"That just goes to show how little you know." His breath was coming short and fast as he continued to tramp toward her, forcing her back even father into the dense shrubbery. "I never take the train from Leeds to Haworth. It is much faster to take the motorway, so I keep a car in a garage near the station."

"So she never got on the train to Haworth?" Addie's mind flashed to what Mildred Wallace had said about not recalling having seen Mollie on the train, even though she should have been. Perhaps the crowds of holiday shoppers and commuters made it hard to keep track of people, especially when the woman fell on the platform and everyone was scurrying around in different directions.

Addie's eyes widened. "That's how you got Mollie to go with you, isn't it? When a woman fell on the platform, you saw her and suggested she go back to Moorscrag with you because the train was going to be delayed, and you knew she was in a hurry to get back to her dad."

He laughed and toyed with the trowel in his hand. "I couldn't believe she agreed. Not at first, mind you. I had to apologize for our little misunderstanding on the train earlier, tell her that when I saw her wearing the necklace, I had assumed she had stolen it when she worked for my father the previous summer. I swore it was a simple misunderstanding and knew now that it wasn't the same necklace, but one that had been given to her by her father."

"Since it's unlikely you killed her right there on the platform, I'm taking it that she agreed." *Keep him talking—distract, distract, distract.* She eyed the distance from where she was backed against the bramble bushes to the path and her way out.

"Not at first." The corner of his lip turned up in a sneer, but his eyes glimmered with a glint of satisfaction. "As the platform became more chaotic with the arrival of the police and paramedics, and with a little nudge from Mrs. Howard, who was going to be accompanying us, she did." He turned the trowel over in his hand.

"Mrs. Howard?"

"Don't look so shocked, Miss Greyborne. Surely you must know that dear old woman is like a mother to me. More than mine ever was or that simpleton Mildred Wallace, who never cared a hoot about me but only in pleasing my distant mother."

"It was Mrs. Howard who told you Mollie was the daughter of your father's lover, wasn't it? She just didn't tell you the story about the necklace being passed down in the family. She also knew about your father and his love affair with Julianna. So when he told you the necklace was lost, you knew he was lying, right?"

"No, when I repeated to Mrs. Howard what my father had said about the necklace being lost, she told me what she knew had occurred and named the woman he gave the necklace to instead of my mother, his legal wife. Wasn't even someone of nobility or social stature but a mere servant in his household."

"That might be true, but that servant still gave birth to your older sister, making her the rightful heir to the Bentley estate." She continued to circle the tree, keeping distance between them. "You finally have your hands on the priceless piece of jewelry that you think should have come to you, and now you're afraid it's going to slip through your fingers again, like it did twenty years ago, right?"

"You know nothing!" He lunged forward. His shorts caught on a thorny branch, and he staggered as thorns ripped at his skin.

"Really?" She forced the rising bile from the sight of blood dripping down his leg back down her throat and sucked in a steadying breath. *Breathe, just keep breathing. You have to breathe to think.* Reassured by the continued rise and fall of her chest, she concentrated on the clues and theories flashing through her mind.

The hatred burning in his eyes reflected on his face as he untangled himself from a branch.

"I'm surprised that when you took the necklace off Ivee's body and pushed her—"

Confusion flashed across his perspiration-beaded face.

"Or did she fall to her death? Either way, I'm surprised you didn't take the time to hide her body in the rocks. It would have given you more time after the party, and no one would have been the wiser to her having been there."

"What are you talking about?"

"The fact that no one knew who she was at first or that she had been at Tony's party. If you had taken the time to hide the body—it was in the middle of the night and no one was around—you could have covered it with rocks or stuffed it in a crevasse, and it would have been years until someone came across it. You might have gotten away with her murder."

"I should have." His cheek twitched. "It might have stopped you from sniffing around so much," he spat, glaring at her as he moved closer.

"Then you don't know me very well, do you?" She forced a laugh, but something was off in his expression. He appeared confused by her accusation.

She envisioned her makeshift crime board, and a puzzle piece slipped into place.

"You didn't kill Ivee, did you?" She gasped with the realization. DI Parker's words rang through her mind. *Mrs. Howard knows more than she's saying.* "You're covering for Mrs. Howard, just like she covered for you twenty years ago and helped you dump Mollie's body!"

A slow grin spread across his lips. Addie's chest twisted. She inched backward. A humorless laugh ripped out of him, but the mocking glint in his eyes grated on every nerve ending in her body.

She bolted toward the path, but like a cat after a mouse, he sprang at her over the outer edge of the prickly bush patch and grabbed the hem of her skirt, yanking her back toward him. She twisted and fell onto her back, her legs wrapping in the material, and she met his menacing eyes above her.

She wasn't going to die tonight. Not here like this.

She swallowed hard, managing to get her knee up, and kicked with a power she didn't know she possessed. He gasped and doubled over. He dropped the black bag and grabbed his groin. She kicked again, aiming for his face as he stooped over. There was a sickening popping sound when her foot contacted his jaw. He wheezed and reeled backward.

Before he could regain his footing, she flipped onto her hands and knees, scrambling crab-like until she got her feet under her, and raced up the path until she burst out onto the manicured lawn of Milton Manor, taking evening strollers off guard. She glanced over her shoulder just as Lewis staggered out into the clearing, still cradling his groin.

"Tony!" she yelled when she spotted him and Hailey sitting on the bench by the front fountain. "Stop Lewis. He's one of the murderers. Hailey, call the police." Addie paused beside them and managed to pant. "Mrs. Howard is the other one. Is she in the house?"

"Yes," Tony yelled, as he leapt to his feet and took off after Lewis.

Addie raced toward the manor when a movement in a second-floor window caught her eye. She dashed through the main door and scanned the top of the staircase as the blur of a dark shape moved across the second-floor landing. She hiked her skirt up, took the steps two at a time, and raced down the hallway in the direction of Lewis's suites. She threw the door open just in time to see Mrs. Howard stuffing a notebook into the ample bodice of her housekeeping dress.

"Not only did you murder to protect Lewis, but it also appears you're an accomplice in his little theft ring."

"I have no idea what you're talking about." The cool, flat tone of Mrs. Howard's voice sent quivers up Addie's spine. Yes, this woman was more than capable of pushing someone off a cliff, and twenty years ago, she would have had no trouble helping to dispose of a body at the bottom of another stone crag on the moor.

"I'm afraid I'm going to have to ask you to leave. Master Lewis will be coming in shortly to change for dinner, and—"

"No, he won't be." Addie eyed the book poking out from under Mrs. Howard's dress. "As a matter of fact, right about now, I'd say, he's rather busy with the police, just as I suspect you will be in a moment or two."

"I beg your pardon?"

"I think they're going to want to discuss Ivee Hargrave's murder, and I'm also certain they will be most interested in your connection to a grand larceny case." Addie held out her hand and crooked her fingers. "The notebook, please."

Chapter 31

"Can I take the blindfold off now, Mr. Pressman?" Addie asked.

"Not just yet, lassie. That's it, just keep walking, and when I say, take a step down, okay?"

The crunch of gravel under her feet and the screech of metal on metal were like nails on a chalkboard and confused her senses. These weren't sounds she was familiar with on a daily basis. Where in the world was he taking her?

"That's it," said Mr. Pressman encouragingly. "I'm gonna turn ye around, and you'll sit straight down, okay?"

She nodded.

When he'd first blindfolded her and ushered her out of Second Chance Books and Bindery, the sun had warmed her skin, and the sounds and smells of the street had filled her senses. She had been certain he was leading her to the pub for the surprise party she'd caught brief murmurs of over the last couple of days. However, after he guided her this way and that and spun her around, she was confused and disorientated. A wild guess was out of the question, and clouds must have veiled the sun, so she couldn't use its warmth as a gauge to what direction she was headed.

It was a lot like the sensation she'd had when she was young and her father had steered her on her tricycle. He never would say where they were going, but when they got there, it was always a wonderful new adventure, so she remained hopeful that this was all an elaborate way of getting her to her goodbye party. "Pippi is safe, right?"

"Aye, she is that. Don't ye worry, lass. Ye just sit here and relax. It'll all become clear to ye in a moment."

It crossed Addie's mind that this might be another variation on their Saturday-night pub game. They had simply taken the game to the next level. After all, it had morphed into a team sport already. Why not one that deprived its players of sight and confused their spatial awareness too? She was failing miserably, however, if they had intended her to be the guinea pig to see if the new game would work. With the last turn and the unfamiliar sounds and smells, she was lost.

She sniffed the air, like she'd seen Pippi do thousands of times, but it was no use. The surrounding aromas didn't give her a single clue. There were just too many odors mingled together. She sniffed again, and her nose twitched. She sneezed. The wind must have shifted, because there was a distinct odor of rotting food that hadn't been there earlier. She sniffed again, but it was no use. Not one thing stood out and gave her insight as to where she was, and unless she was sitting in the middle of the town dump, which, even as a joke, her friends wouldn't do to her, especially on her last evening in Moorscrag, she was lost.

She cocked her head and strained to hear whatever sounds she could, but all she could make out was the sound of Mr. Pressman's breaths close by. "Can I take it off now?"

"Not yet, lass. Soon, though."

Her surroundings went eerily quiet, and the sound of his breathing disappeared. A wave of panic surged up from her stomach. Was this a joke her friends were playing on her? Had they stuck her in a room somewhere to lock her in so she couldn't leave tomorrow? She whipped the blindfold off, and even though her eyes were blurred from being covered, she could make out that she was in the garden area of Tea on the Green, Olivia's teahouse, and on either side of her on the grass was a bucket of composting food. Weirdest of all, however, was she was completely on her own. Not one smiling face greeted her. Not even Mr. Pressman, the only person she was certain would be present when she took the blindfold off. He seemed to have vanished into thin air.

"Whoever said the English didn't know how to party couldn't have been more wrong, could they?" she said, with an edge of sarcasm. "You guys really know how to throw a girl one heck of a goodbye get-together. The buckets of garbage were a nice touch to throw me off," she chuckled as she scanned the garden.

Birdsongs were the only sounds she heard.

"This is fun," she called out, rising to her feet, "but since I still have packing to do, I think I'll just pass on all this celebrating tonight and head on home." She paused, waiting for someone to appear or something to happen.

Still nothing.

She shrugged and looked at the back gate and understood her confusion about the gravel and metal-on-metal screeching sounds. She had never entered from the back lane before. She cocked her head and strained to listen for any sounds outside the teahouse garden. Silence. There were no sounds coming from inside the teahouse either.

A chill raced across her shoulders, and it had nothing to do with the sun being obscured by the overhead threatening clouds. She poked her head inside the door. The room was dark, but not so dark that she couldn't see that it was empty, thanks to the dim light coming through the front windows. The situation turned from weird to spooky, and the sensation of icy fingers snaked up her spine.

She shivered and stepped inside. She had learned this past year that the English did have a different sense of humor from their American cousins, but this was just plain odd. They had to be here somewhere, ready to pop out and at her anytime time now, right? She peeked behind the sales counter. No one. She walked over to the table at the back beside the kitchen door, where she envisioned all her friends were huddled, ready to jump out at her. She took a deep breath, kicked the swinging door open, and jumped through. "Ah-ha! Got you!" she yelled to a dark, empty room.

Her heart sank. She was, in fact, completely alone, and for the life of her, she couldn't comprehend a reason why her friends would have gone to these lengths to make it so. What was the end game? Or was this it? She'd said her goodbyes so many times before that they were probably tired of hearing them, and this was their way of letting her know. Either they didn't believe she would really leave this time and decided to not waste their time and money on a going-away party, or they really hadn't become the dear friends she thought they were to begin with, and this was their way of saying goodbye to someone who would always be an outsider.

She thrust her head high and marched toward the tea shop's front door. The evening might be a bust, but her year in England had not been. It had allowed her the time she needed to lick her wounds and to face the fact that her whole life was a lie. The people she had loved the most, like her grandmother Hattie, her father, and Simon had all lied to her and were not who she had thought they were. Those had been hard pills to swallow, but after fighting and gagging them down, she had come to face the fact that her life had been built on a foundation of lies. She had learned how to move forward and not only live with it but also make the best of it.

She was ready to face the facts of what life might be like for the new her when she went back to Greyborne Harbor. She'd not only purged herself of ghosts from her past but had also managed to put some space between the old her and the new her. Going home to all the changes in her little town was going to be, going to be . . . what? Whatever it was going to be, she'd be ready for it. She held her head high, pushed the door open, and stepped out into the street.

"Police. Put your hands in the air! You are under arrest for burglary," called PC Poole from beside a police car in front of the tea shop.

Addie took a step back and tried to comprehend what was happening when another police car pulled up, and DS Davis and PC Gimsby got out and headed toward her.

"Arms out." Meg Gimsby removed her handcuffs from her police belt as she marched toward Addie. "Miss Addie Greyborne, you are under arrest for suspicion of burglary. You do not have to say anything, but it may harm your defense if you do not mention, when questioned, something which you later rely on in court. Anything you do say may be given in evidence. Is that clear?" She clipped the metal cuffs closed.

Addie couldn't wipe the grin off her face. "Okay, I get it now, another version of our game. Yes, officer, I plead guilty to the crime you are accusing me of. I unlawfully entered Tea on the Green, so lock me up."

Meg eyed her curiously. "I assure you, Miss Greyborne, this is no joke. We received a call from a concerned member of the public reporting suspicious activity at this location, and you were discovered by PC Poole to be coming out of a closed business which you do not have legal right of access to after business hours." She opened the car door and pressed Addie's head down as she steered her into the back seat.

"You guys are good. This is one way to get me to the party, isn't it, even though it's a bit contrived and obvious now? Although, I will admit you had me going when I removed the blindfold and discovered I was completely alone in the tea shop, with only buckets of trash to keep me company. Tell me, whose idea was this?"

Meg got into the driver's seat as DS Davis came out of the shop and got into the passenger's seat. "We can add malicious damage to the charges, PC Gimsby," he said. "The suspect here placed rotting food in a public food-service area as bait for mice and rats, I assume. The DI might want to add that to the charges too."

Chapter 32

"I did not set bait for mice and rats," cried Addie indignantly. "And don't you both think you've taken this far enough?" She glared at the back of DS Davis and PC Gimsby's heads. "Yes, you got me. I fell for the 'there is no party for you' trick, and now you can take the cuffs off, and we can go to wherever everyone else is gathered and have some fun."

"You have to admit, though, that when you took the blindfold off and realized you were alone in the tea shop, it was pretty funny," said DS Davis with a chuckle.

"You British have a warped sense of what's funny, don't you?"

"Ah, come on, Addie. We wanted you to try to solve where you were before you took the blindfold off, but I guess the compost bin was a step too far. Ya can blame Jasper for that one. He thought it would be a hoot. Then when ya got freaked out, we couldn't get here fast enough before you took it all the wrong way and not as a joke until you saw us outside. By then . . ." DS Davis shrugged.

"Wait. I was alone in there. How did you know when I freaked out?"

"Umm . . ." Meg glanced at DS Davis and winced. "We were watching a live stream through the tea-house's security cameras at the pub."

Addie shook her head. "So I'm the laughing-stock of Moorscrag now?"

"Not at all," said Meg. "If anything, it showed us how cool you can remain under pressure . . . well, until you can't." She giggled.

"I guess since every Saturday night you put my amateur sleuthing skills to the test, I should have known you'd plan something big for my last night here."

"Speaking of testing your sleuthing abilities, you were right when you told me you thought there might be clues in Ivee Hargrave's belongings and you couldn't believe that the regional commissioner didn't take everything into custody until it could be searched." Meg pulled up in front of Crooked Lane Pub.

"Why, what did you find?"

"After Alice Fenton called DI Parker and told him about the diary, he confiscated everything else of Ivee's that wasn't clothing and sorted through it."

"And . . . ?" asked Addie.

"He found another book, and it said right there in black and white why Ivee wore the necklace to the party that night."

"What did it say?" Addie leaned against the back of Meg's seat.

"It said her mother knew Mollie was Lord Bentley's illegitimate child and had even hatched a blackmail plan to get back at Lord Bentley after he sacked her."

"She was blackmailing him?"

Meg shook her head. "Nah, she never went through with it. She decided it would be worth more to her if she sold it one day or kept it to give to Ivee than she'd ever get blackmailing his lordship, especially if she ever got caught and thrown in the nick, which she couldn't chance on account of little Ivee and all."

"Mrs. Fenton told us how, after Fern got so sick and couldn't work to pay her rent, her landlord sold all her belongings when she died to collect the back rent, so she lost it anyway," said Addie.

"That's what it said." Meg nodded. "Ivee was devastated too, by the sound of it. She'd been counting on the sale of the necklace to help get her through after her mum died. But the landlord basically stole it and everything else Fern had, and Ivee's dream disappeared along with the necklace."

"Until that night Hailey and Tony went into the restaurant in London, right?"

"Yes, at least, that's what she had written."

"What did she say about it?"

"She said she saw Hailey wearing it at the restaurant in London. As a hostess, part of Ivee's job was to help customers take their coats off or help put them on. It seems Ivee knew about the broken clasp because of when Lewis and Mollie had their argument on the train years before and he had torn it off her. It damaged the clasp or something. Because of that, Ivee knew how easy it would be to slip off Hailey's neck as she helped her put her coat on."

"That's why, when they got to Hailey's flat, she noticed it was gone," said Addie. "She just thought it had fallen off due to a faulty clasp, and not because someone had made use of that little tidbit of prior knowledge."

"I guess, and then there was a diary note about seeing the notice about the engagement party in the newspaper, and Ivee decided she was going to do what her mother never did. With everything her mother had told her over the years, she knew she had dirt for a blackmail scheme and was going to the party to make her intentions known."

"To Lewis or Lord Bentley?"

"To Lewis. She knew from her mother that he was the last person to see Mollie alive, because she saw Mollie leave with him."

"I wonder if Mrs. Howard knew Ivee was there to blackmail Lewis."

"As far as she's admitted so far, she was only trying to get the necklace back for him, in case Ivee was there to set herself up as a lawful heir to the Bentley estate."

"Wow," said Addie, getting out of the car. "I am so glad it's all over, and Lewis and Mrs. Howard are exactly where they should be, with enough evidence to keep them both locked up for a very long time."

"Me too," said Meg, coming to her side at the pub door. "The only problem is, now that the real killers are apprehended, you're leaving, and I, for one, know how much I'm going to miss you. You're my only friend who really gets what I do and actually encourages it."

"Hey, what about me?" DS Davis joined them. "I have your back, Gimsby."

"I know you do, Sergeant, but"—tears formed in her eyes, and she sniffled—"Addie's the best mate I've ever had." She gave Addie a bear hug that reminded Addie of the ones Serena and Paige gave her, and she smiled as she gave Meg a big hug in return.

The pub was filled to capacity. Addie was certain everyone she'd ever dealt with in Moorscrag had turned out to wish her well. As the evening wore on, her cheeks ached from smiling, and her arms were sore from being hugged by everyone who passed by. She needed a break and thought it was a good time to take Pippi outdoors for a few minutes' reprieve, especially since some of her well-wishers were on their second and third round of hugs now. She looked under the table and then checked between her feet for her wayward friend.

"Have you seen Pippi?" she called to Archie, who was caught up in a game of darts at the back.

"Check behind the bar," he replied as he let a dart fly, hitting the bull's-eye.

She stepped behind the bar, and the tightness in her chest eased when she spied Pippi curled up contentedly alongside Bertie, the big ginger pub cat, on her bed in the corner.

She grabbed a glass, filled it with ice and water, and took a long drink. As much as she occasionally enjoyed a pint of English beer, it did dry out her mouth, and nothing could remove that cotton feeling like a tall, cool glass of water.

"Are you working here now too?"

Addie swung around and came face-to-face with DI Parker as he took a seat on a barstool.

"I didn't expect to see you behind the bar, but since you are, I'll have a pint, thanks."

"Ah, I don't think I'm qualified to make anything besides ice water. Can I get you one while I'm back here?"

"No thanks," he said with a short laugh. "I think I'll have something a bit stronger, if you wouldn't mind pulling a pint of your best ale for me."

"Then you'll have to wait for Archie." She pointed to the balding man at the dart board.

"I see." He looked in the direction Addie gestured to. "Does he usually leave someone who's unqualified behind the bar, especially when it's so busy in here?"

"It's not usually this busy. I guess it is tonight, though, because it's a bit of a celebration." Addie glanced over at Archie, heavily involved in his game, looked at the various kinds of beer on tap and the pint glasses on the shelf overhead, and shrugged. It couldn't be that hard, could it? "I hope this is okay. I've never done this before," she said, setting a glass down in front of him.

"It's funny," he eyed his glass filled with foam, "that you're working in a pub and don't know how to pour a proper pint."

"I don't work here. I was getting a glass of ice water." She gestured to the drink in her hand.

"My mistake," he said, hanging his head and staring into his glass of beer foam. "I guess that explains this."

"You insisted on having one," she said with a short laugh.

"It does appear to be busy tonight," he said, scanning the room. "But I imagine there'll be a lot of celebrations going on in the village, with the murder being solved and a local hero like Anthony Radcliff and his fiancée, Hailey Granger, being cleared of all charges." He struggled to take a sip past the foam in his glass, set it down, and wiped the suds from his upper lip. "So this is where you and your friends come every Saturday night?"

"Actually, we come every day after work for a pint, but Saturday night is the night we stay and kick up our heels, as they say."

"I can see a lot of that going on here now." He raised his voice as the din in the room increased.

"You'll have to join them, my friends I mean, some Saturday. It's a lot of fun," Addie yelled over the background noise. "They play a whodunit murder-mystery game. You might enjoy that and, of course, darts." She gestured toward the dartboard. "It would be a good way for you to get to know some of the villagers since your police station covers this area now."

"And who would you recommend that I get to know first in this sea of faces?"

"Well, you already know DS Davis and PC Gimsby."

"I do. Are they regulars?"

"When they're off shift, they sometimes can be.

DS Davis is dating my friend Emily. She's the brunette sitting against the wall beside him. She owns the bakery at the top of Crooked Lane."

"Now I understand why he's gained a few stone," he said with a chuckle. "And everyone around that table is your friend?"

She nodded.

"But I thought you hadn't been in England very long."

"I've been here a year, and it's been long enough to make friends. Ginny and Nate Goulding run the village shop and post office. That tall brunette standing with her back to the dartboard, talking to Emily, is Olivia Green, and she owns Tea on the Green." Addie stood on tiptoes. "The colorfully haired one, Lexi, you've met already, and her dad, Archie Craven, who owns this pub. Oh, and, of course, there's Mr. Pressman and the bookshop assistant, Jasper, over there by the dartboard. They're a great bunch." She met his inquisitive gaze. "I'm sure they'd love to have you join them. You might even end up being the best DI in their murder games," she said lightheartedly and laughed.

"As long as the murders are make-believe, and you're there to show me how it's played, I'm sure I will. After all, we do make a great team."

"Yeah . . ." Her breathing hitched in her throat. Had she just heard him right—they made a good team? "It's too bad I'm leaving." She took a quick glance in the mirror behind the bar to see if her face had actually turned the fifty shades of red she felt with the searing heat radiating up from her collar.

"You're leaving?" He pushed his glass away. "I

can give you a lift home. It is after dark, and I know you ride a bicycle—"

"No, I'm not leaving now. This is my goodbye party."

"Your goodbye party?"

"Yes, I'm flying home to the States tomorrow."

He looked around the pub and back at Addie. "I'm sorry. I had no idea." He rose to his feet.

"I see me girl's taken care of ye, Inspector, while I showed them who was king of the darts around here." Archie took his place behind the bar and clapped a hand on Addie's shoulder. "Is there anything else I can get ye?"

"Nothing. Thank you." DI Parker glanced at Addie and gave her an awkward smile that captured the growing dimness in his usual glimmering-gray eyes. "I'm sorry I kept you from your friends. I had no idea," he said, backing away.

"Wait," she said, grasping his upper arm. "Why don't you come and join us? They'd love to meet you."

A tiny smile touched his lips, and she lost herself for a moment when their eyes met.

His fingers lingered on her hand as he eased it from his arm. He shook his head, as he continued to back toward the door. "Sorry again. I didn't mean to—never mind. It was nice to have met you, Addie Greyborne." He pushed the door open, letting it bang closed behind him.

"What was all that about?" asked Archie, pulling a pint for a customer.

"I have no idea." Her voice faltered as she stared at the closed door.

Mickey slid down from the end of the bar and

stared wobbly-eyed at Addie. "The bloke was trying to ask ye out, lass. He's head over heels fir ye."

"What? No." She glanced through the front window, and from the light from the corner streetlamp, she could barely make out Parker's hunched shoulders as he walked to his car. Could Mickey be right? Was Noah Parker, in his roundabout way, trying to ask her out?

"Come on, Addie, you're up for darts next," called Olivia. "Ya gotta give me one last chance to show a Yank how the game's really played."

Addie looked over at her friends and then glanced wistfully to where Noah Parker had been on the street and drew in a deep breath. For a moment, she savored the image she recalled of them sitting at her table discussing the case, just like she and Marc used to do. The sudden pang in her chest wasn't for any unresolved feelings she had for Marc, or any she may have developed for Inspector Parker, but for the unexpected sensations that came over her.

She was heading back to an unknown future in Greyborne Harbor, but this place, these people— she glanced over at her friends, cheering on Olivia as she hit the bull's-eye with her last dart throw— came with a sense of belonging. She released the breath that pressed heavily on her chest and headed to the table, where her friends were gathered to celebrate and give her a send-off she would no doubt remember forever, as she glanced regretfully out the window at the taillights of a gray Vauxhall Corsa disappearing up Crooked Lane.